*Dance the Rocks Ashore*

Lesley Choyce

Other books by LESLEY CHOYCE

ADULT STORIES
*Eastern Sure* (1980)
*Billy Botzweiler's Last Dance* (1984)
*Conventional Emotions* (1985)
*The Dream Auditor* (1986)
*Coming Up for Air* (1988)
*Margin of Error* (1992)

ADULT NOVELS
*Downwind* (1984)
*The Second Season of Jonas MacPherson* (1989)
*Magnificent Obsessions* (1991)
*Ecstasy Conspiracy* (1992)
*The Republic of Nothing* (1994)
*Trap Door to Heaven* (1996)

POETRY
*Reinventing the Wheel* (1980)
*Fast Living* (1982)
*The End of Ice* (1985)
*The Top of the Heart* (1986)
*The Man Who Borrowed the Bay of Fundy* (1988)
*The Coastline of Forgetting* (1995)

NON-FICTION
*Edible Wild Plants of Nova Scotia* (1977)
*An Avalanche of Ocean* (1987)
*December Six: The Halifax Solution* (1988)
*Transcendental Anarchy* (1993)
*Nova Scotia: Shaped by the Sea* (1996)

LESLEY CHOYCE

# Dance the Rocks Ashore

GOOSE LANE

Published by Goose Lane Editions with the assistance of the Canada Council, the Department of Canadian Heritage, and the New Brunswick Department of Municipalities, Culture and Housing, 1997.

Edited by Laurel Boone.
Cover illustration after Jacques Henri Lartigue.
Book design by Julie Scriver.
Author photo by George Georgakakos.
Printed in Canada by Gagné Printing.
10   9   8   7   6   5   4   3   2


Canadian Cataloguing in Publication Data

Choyce, Lesley, 1951-

        Dance the rocks ashore
        ISBN 0-86492-218-3

I. Title.

PS8555.H668D36 1997        C813'.54        C97-950041-9
PR9199.3.C497D36. 1997


Goose Lane Editions
469 King Street
Fredericton New Brunswick
CANADA  E3B 1E5

*For the memory of Alden Nowlan*

*There are no facts, only interpretations.*
— Friedrich Nietzsche

# CONTENTS

## The Shore

## The Road

**The Town**

# The Shore

# THE THIRD OR FOURTH
# HAPPIEST MAN IN NOVA SCOTIA

The first time I saw Ray Doucette he was climbing up a thirty-foot spruce tree out by the mouth of the inlet. The top of the tree had been sheared right off by the lightning, and just below the damage was a giant nest. Ray was climbing up to that nest, his boots slipping on the wet branches and his hands clutching each new hold like vice-grips. He was carrying something in a red handkerchief pouch that dangled from his mouth. Inside the pouch was some frightened creature that was screeching like a banshee.

I was afraid to say a word. Finally, Ray looped one arm over a lightning-splintered branch and lowered his head until his package sat snugly back in the nest. Then, just as the screeching subsided from one source, it rose again tenfold from out of the sky. Ray lost his footing and hung by one armpit as his feet kicked the empty air.

The mother eagle made a lunge for Ray and knocked his hat off. Then it flew upward, hovered, tucked its wings, and dove straight for Ray's face. Ray didn't flinch. I just closed my eyes and heard one god-awful shriek. Then nothing.

When I looked up, the mother eagle was sitting perfectly still on her young one returned to the nest. Ray was smiling eyeball to eyeball with the giant bird, and his one free hand was petting it on the neck. I could just barely make out that he was singing something. "Rock-a-bye baby."

Ray Doucette lived with his wife, Adele, in an old crooked house near the head of Tom Lurcher Inlet. He had a tumble-down wharf, and every day of the year when the seas allowed, he went out fishing in his boat.

It was such a deceptive little inlet, with jutting rocks and an incorrigible channel, that more respectable fishermen had given up on the place long ago. I once asked Ray about the problems with negotiating the inlet. He said, "Well, the channel's just like a snake that's got its back broke in maybe twenty-five places. And, when you get to the mouth, if you don't plant the boat dead between the gull rock and the Cannonballs, you'll run aground." The Cannonballs, he explained, was a hidden shoal of perfectly round rocks that shifted around with the storms and the seasons.

"Did you ever think of moving to another inlet?" I asked.

He looked at me like I just told him that he should try eating arsenic for breakfast. "This is one of the deepest, cleanest, most interesting channels on the Eastern Shore," he told me.

Altogether, twelve families had lived in the ramshackle houses on either side of Ray in years past. But the families were all gone. The men had taken city jobs or moved off to fish inlets less interesting than Tom Lurcher.

It was around the time of the exodus that Ray had married Adele. She had grown up in the house next door. Adele, so the story goes, just moved in with Ray when everyone else moved away. Ray said that it was Adele who had made him the third or fourth happiest man in Nova Scotia. All you had to do was look into her blue, summer-sea eyes and feel better about living. Adele entered Ray's life with a rooster and a hen.

Aside from Adele moving in with him, I don't think Ray paid much attention to all the other families moving out. He always paid more heed to wind direction than neighbours, anyway. He hauled in his fish, checked the oil in his engine and went about his life as usual.

Then the rooster got sick. "I hadn't thought that much about living things up till that. I guess he was mean the way roosters are, and he was always underfoot. But I couldn't stand to see him die." So

Ray nursed the rooster back to health by feeding him fish oil and corn flour. After the rooster recovered, Ray sometimes took the bird out to sea with him on calm days. The rooster recovered so well that Ray had thirty other chickens by the end of that first year. They gave the chickens the Slaunwhite house to live in and the chickens seemed to like it fine.

By the time I met Ray, the rooster was gone, dead, but his descendants roamed freely up and down Tom Lurcher Inlet. It was impossible to walk across Ray's yard without stepping on eggs. Adele could never keep up with which ones were fresh and which ones were old, so most of the eggs got fed to the gulls.

The first sea gull came into Ray's life when a hunter arrived at the inlet from the city. The hunter couldn't see any ducks, so he started shooting at a couple of Ray's chickens. The chickens were too quick for the hunter and took cover in the mossy rocks. But the gulls weren't as wily. Pretty soon the hunter had shot the wing off one herring gull. Ray was just snaking his boat back in from the sea when he saw it fall out of the sky. He steered toward the wounded gull, knowing full well he might tear the bottom out of his boat.

Sure enough, Ray's boat plowed into something and she started to leak. But he fished the gull out of the sea and got his boat back to his wharf before it sank and settled on the bottom. The gull, of course, was big and mean as only three-year-old herring gulls can be, and it tore into Ray's wrist like a chainsaw into softwood.

The hunter saw Ray at his wharf in the sinking boat and came over to see what was going on. There was Ray dripping blood from the wrist, standing waist-deep in the cold water that had sucked up the deck of his boat. The hunter asked Ray what happened. When Ray explained that he had saved the seagull, the hunter just laughed, called him a fool and then drove off.

Adele had to stitch up Ray's wrist with twenty-pound test fishing line, and Ray had never been prouder of his wife. The one-winged gull lived, and, once Ray got his boat seaworthy again, it fed happily every day on cod heads and mackerel guts.

News seemed to have leaked out to the gull community up and

down the shore because injured birds kept turning up. One gull had swallowed a fishing hook, another had lost a leg. Some had broken wings that could be set with splints and tape. Others arrived with no outward signs of injury but stayed on nonetheless. Many of the creatures that arrived could live outside, but some seemed to want housing, so the empty village was turned into a rest home for injured animals.

By the time I met Ray, he had maybe twenty-five sea birds. His arrival home from sea each day was heralded with raucous, enthusiastic approval. Ray loved it. He had also taken to hiking the shoreline with Adele looking for creatures that needed help. Together they adopted a porcupine without teeth, an anorexic heron, a blind otter, wild rabbits that were missing body parts from snares, and an assortment of small birds crippled in various ways by the cruelty of men and nature.

When Adele died, the doctor told Ray, "It was something she was born with. There was nothing you or I could have done about it."

Ray said, "But that's not right."

The doctor just shook his head. "Sometimes it happens that way."

Ray told me that he just sat at the kitchen table with a cold cup of tea in his hand and didn't move for four days. "I'd of sat there like that, too," he said, "except that the gulls began to swarm all over the roof. And the heron kept staring at me through the window. And when I opened the door, the yard was a sea of hungry chickens."

Then, one day, a planner from the government drove the rutted lane down to Ray's house. He'd never seen so many one-winged gulls and maimed creatures in his life. When Ray walked over, the planner rolled down his window and tried to explain something. But the words just went in one ear and out the other. Whatever it was the man was talking about, Ray decided to pay no attention.

When I read about the harbour development program in the

paper, I knew Ray was in for big trouble. Somebody had determined that Tom Lurcher Inlet had one of the deepest, cleanest, most interesting channels on the whole shore. The channel would just have to be dredged and straightened, the article said, and they'd blast the Cannonball Shoal to smithereens if they had to.

Ray was heaving fish heads to his gulls on the morning I told him the news. He didn't believe me. "What do they want this place for?"

"They want to put in a new wharf and bring more boats back."

"But nobody lives here."

"They will," I explained.

Ray received notices in the mail, but he refused to read them. Then the planner drove up again, this time with a Mountie.

The man pointed to Ray's house. "We're willing to make an offer . . ." But Ray didn't listen to the rest.

He got in his boat and headed to sea. The tide was wrong and he barely squeaked past the Cannonballs without ripping the engine out of her. I hired Bill Mannette to take me to sea to look for Ray. We saw Ray's boat beached at Riley's Island. When we came in close, I jumped out and ran up and down the beach, finally finding Ray sitting alone on a drift log.

"This one's not right, either," Ray said. "But I'll keep looking." Ray pulled a wad of two-dollar bills out of his pants and shoved it into my hand. "Feed my creatures. I'll be back in a while." I tried to talk him into coming back now, but he'd have none of it.

I kept an eye on Ray's creatures, but I couldn't get any of them to eat. I was sitting on Ray's back step looking to sea when his boat appeared. The chickens and gulls exploded into life. I held my ears and covered my head. The gulls that could fly made a beeline toward the boat. Ray pulled up tight to the dock, cut the motor.

"I found it," he said.

He'd say nothing more. He fed his creatures from a boatload of fresh cod and over the next week built a barge out of wood from Adele's first house. I offered to help, but he wouldn't let me lift a finger.

Ray took his time about what he was doing. I checked in every day, but he had little to say to me. It was about a week later that I heard the bulldozer thundering down the lane to Tom Lurcher Inlet. I ran down the path to Ray's wharf, but I was too late.

Ray's boat, towing his barge full of animals, was on a slow, zigzag path to sea. A whirlpool of sea gulls swirled above the boat in the bright blue sky. I waved, but I don't think he noticed me. I wanted to see his face, but he was too far away. I wanted to know if he was smiling, but I'll never know. The boat and the barge passed by the Cannonballs and on beyond the lightning-splintered tree at the mouth of the inlet. Ray turned neither east nor west but went straight south until he was lost in the squint of the sun and the swell of the sea.

From *The Second Season of Jonas MacPherson*

## LOSING GROUND

When I was thirteen, my best friend was John Kincaid. In late spring the lifeblood of the planet began to run free, and the gaspereau were making their way up inside the land. John was a hard knot of a kid, with chipped bones from falling off back steps and close-cropped hair over a skull that suited the Reaper himself. He was always unhappy, dissatisfied with everything, primed with so much anger it shot out his arm like electricity. He threw things — rocks, wood, fists — because his father had hit him so often, pounded fear and hate into him in the evenings so that he would come out into the world and throw it around at everything. He always wanted to teach me how to kill things, and I hated him for that, for his private unbent cosmology of crippling living things and siding with the blatant burning death wish of all things that moved. But there was a kind of love between us, although I could never have called it that. The emotional economics of our ageing had dismantled what little love we had and sent it off to scrapyards where we would have to go looking one day for the rusted remains, so that we might rehabilitate the engines of childhood and translate love into sex and sex into love and believe again in girls and women. It would not be impossible, but for now the corrosion was effective, and we were all but lost.

So John Kincaid and I were by the brook where it swept soft curves of cold water light up into the sky and sped unsalted freshness into the sea forever. This tiny stream went miles inland to find

*17*

its source at a stagnant, weed-choked pond that grew mosquitoes in summer and hatched dragonflies the size of toy airplanes and spawned frogs free and restless for Kincaid killings. But here at the edge of salt, the last instant of fresh water about to salt down its blood for good, we sat on a rare sunlit afternoon waiting for gaspereau to come flapping up the shallow brook so that we could do what? Catch them to eat? We had tried that once. "Better to eat razors," John had said. "Better to sit down to a plate of hot sewing needles and chew hard, better to swallow fried radio tubes and wire." The gaspereau were hopeless fish to us. Somebody's mother (it was reported at school) cooked the fish for three days straight until all the bones were dissolved and a cord of softwood consumed, and then you could sit down to a plateful of mush which almost still tasted of fish, while you could be assured your house would stink of gaspereau until Christmas. No, I don't think we had hope of catching them to eat.

I didn't even care to catch one. It was too easy, too pointless. To Kincaid, it was as if they hovered offshore all winter waiting for a chance to slap themselves out of the deep into the thinning waters of an unnamed brook, looking for his stones to club them to death. Each year I hoped Kincaid would be different, that the death lunatic in him would die out so that he could go on with life, but I always expected too much of him.

Then they appeared. I always felt my own blood race to my head to see a still and shining surface go mad with an avalanche of life, a vast churning orgasm of fish splashing about in a fevered dance to snake themselves up the stream, to swim between rocks and trade up salt for fresh. They were there on this late afternoon in May. It was so beautiful that I almost forgot to see the damn boulder that blasted John was holding over his head ready to go, ready to get in the first bash at the first flawed creature who found his way inside the rock's shadow. But as I turned and saw him ready to pound, I decided this was the year he had to change.

So I tackled him, and the rock came down hard on my back as we poured down into the wet moss. He let go a flock of curses learned from a professional, his father, a man with the devil's own dictionary under his skull. I could feel the weight of the pain drive down my spine from John's ancient weapon, but I didn't care. He tried to grab a dead branch to skewer me, and, had I not known him, I would have run for my life, figuring he would kill me instead of fish, death having its warrant out and willing to settle for spilled blood, cold or hot. But I kept him busy. I knew his spirit and knew he could fight, but so could I for different reasons. We were so equally powered that there could never be a winner. John had an easy temper to strike, but his hate could only drive him so far. I simply had a stupid sort of stubbornness that wanted me to finish whatever I started. So we both fought till we bled enough to satisfy our pride. Then we quit. The fish were gone, the first wave of the year safely upstream in deeper pools for the coming night. And Kincaid didn't care then. A fight was as good as a bucket of bloodied fish, and we were friends as usual. John said he'd kill me next time, and I said, "Try."

Later that spring a man from Halifax came out with a pickup truck and a pair of pitchforks. Kincaid and I were walking up the road to the railroad bridge, and this guy pulled over and asked us if we wanted to make a few cents shovelling fish. We both said sure and got in the truck, where we had to sit on bare springs that had torn free of the seat. The radio was on, but there was nothing but static. Mr. Otto Bollivar, the man said his name was, and that we could call him Mr. Bo-liver, but we didn't call him anything. And then he asked where he could find a good gaspereau run, and I knew enough to shut up.

But John spoke up sharp, ready to give out time-honoured secrets that sent us straight to the spot. Mr. Bollivar was pleased and started coughing like maybe he would die or something if he didn't quick light a cigarette that he had to roll first. That seemed to stop the coughing. He threw me a pitchfork that would have gone through my boot if I hadn't moved quick. He told John, "Here. Use this net. It'll do."

From *The Second Season of Jonas MacPherson*

"I ain't helping you with the fish," I said. Mr. Bo-liver looked at me like I said I was born on Jupiter.

"I'm paying you, ain't I?" He hadn't said how much.

"How much?" John wanted to know.

"Twenty cents apiece. Now shut up and let's get to work." I could already see that the stream was wrestling with itself the way that it does when the gaspereau are running.

"Look, you can't eat the damn things anyway," I shouted at him. He was a townie, a stupid city-slicker who probably didn't know. Instead of thanking me for saving him the work, he dropped his pitchfork, bit down on his cigarette and angled over to me.

"You know that. And I know that. But them stupid buggers in Halifax don't know cod tongue from coffin hinges. They'll buy it if it's the right price. And it'll be the right price." He coughed up something and spit a wad of yellow, awful phlegm on the ground.

"Forget it," I told him, "twenty cents or no twenty cents," and I walked on home. I knew Kincaid would stay, and he did. Later, he told me that he got the full forty cents, which was a lie because he only got a dime, if he got that.


A couple of years after that, John Kincaid and I had our own boat. It was a boy's boat because no man would ever have set foot in it, at least not in the condition that it was in. It wasn't what you'd call a skiff and it wasn't a dory, and, as far as we could figure, it wasn't anything that anybody had a fixed name for.

We found her right side up in the wide marsh at the foot of Rigger's Lake in the winter. When the lake froze over, you could go walking out there and feel the arctic wind bear down until it made you feel good, all cold and clean inside like someone had just taken lye powder to your soul, and you wanted to just suck in that cold frozen air, let it paralyze your nose hairs, then knife down into your chest. It felt that good. Kincaid and I didn't have ice skates, but we liked to slide our feet out across the glazed wilderness. No one ever felt as free as we did then, and it didn't catch up to us until the north wind drove white teeth marks into us with frostbite. Then we'd have to run back home and sit in front of the cookstove, where our faces bloomed beet-juice red, and our legs, Lord, how they'd itch, but we knew for sure we were alive.

I think it was hunters who had lost the boat or simply left the damn thing. It was half-rotten, poorly made to begin with, and filled with brown tide frozen up to the oar locks. Ironically, it was me who was the first to pick up a rock and want to bash in the sides just for the hell of it. But Kincaid, God, the light of Jesus took over his eyes because he had before him a boat, a rotten, dull and worthless thing, but a boat, a miracle, a frozen revelation from on high, the possibilities of life-ever-after and the means he had been looking for. He stopped my hand and let the rock fall at our feet, sending out a giant crack in the ice that shot northward halfway to Truro. "We've found a frigging boat," was all he said. Water seeped up from the crack, and I worried that we had split the whole bloody planet in two, that it would turn inside out and the devil would present himself out of the depths and thank us for setting him free for good. He would have ice for a beard and icicles for hair and white blinding stones for eyes, for we knew that the Bible had gone through a number of translations and was all wrong. Hell was a cold, frozen place, damp and bone-numbing like a winter fog.

But nothing happened, save the setting free of one devilish spirit. The boat. I had never seen John so dedicated and so gentle. First we used dead limbs cracked off marsh spruce, then we tried chipping away the ice like Indians with sharp stones, and finally Kincaid ran off all the way to Baylor McNulty's chopping block to confiscate Baylor's double-bit axe for the rescue, while I stood guard as if there were hordes of other half-wits out wandering the frigid wasteland wanting to salvage the carcass of this pathetically contrived duck-hunting boat, fragile as an eggshell and rotten as the politics in Halifax.

But Kincaid made good with the axe and chipped away like a sculptor until it was free and all the worse for it. Then he let out a long, maniac yelp in triumph. "We got our boat, Joney boy," he repeated three times over, and I knew what it meant to him, and I wanted it to mean as much to me. I knew it would always be Kincaid's, but we'd have to do it together, whatever was to be done with that ice devil. So we dragged it home across two miles of frozen grass and paper-ice shelving left high and dry by a retreating tide. The blasted thing was heavy as lead over the rough little hillocks of chumped-up ice that had corrugated in the shallows. She was still weighted down with the freight of her own brown ice, and Kincaid wouldn't let me touch the inside, fearing I'd split the gunwale and destroy whatever mysterious vortex of spiritual energy held the boat together. There we were, human flesh hauling dead, brown frozen water two miles over a pitiless lake in a gale come down special delivery from Hudson Bay. So of course we made it. All the way to Kincaid's back step, and sure he wanted to haul the thing inside to thaw, only we would have had to remove the door frame, then chase out his father, propped up like a mannequin with a bottle in the kitchen listening to a near-shot radio playing opera.

You have to understand that John's father had lost the boat he owned to the bank and the government, he wasn't sure which, but the boat was gone. Not a boat like ours, but a real Cape Islander with a German engine of some kind and a couple of sails. It was just about the biggest boat that anybody had seen on this shore for one man to own and to fish with, and you wanted to see that pile of cod it would deliver. Only something was frigged with the way the world worked because one day the people wanted to eat cod, the next day, so the buyer said, you couldn't give it away with pitchforks for a penny, and what do you do with a boat with an engine yet and a hungry bank and a government that has made promises for you? Inevitably, the boat was lost, sent to Halifax and set up in dry-dock, where it would rot until the economy improved or until folks got their tastebuds back for cod or mackerel but none too soon at that.

George Kincaid galvanized himself with illegal rum and swore to God Almighty that he should have become a runner of rums himself like his father had suggested and used that German engine for some good business and let the fish go to hell. But he had been stupid. Here he already owed Lance Inkpen more money for his booze, what with nothing coming in. And what could you do but sit around in your own venom and get good and angry at everybody and nobody and forget about ever being the man you once were? John's mother had become a ghost. She was there but she wasn't. She always made the meals, and then it was like she slipped into a trance and waited for George to cancel himself out for the day. Late at night, John said, she waltzed around the kitchen alone with the radio on and hummed. This didn't make a damn bit of sense to him. He thought she was cracked. But he believed in his old man.

John couldn't wait for spring to loose the chains on the boat of his, so he set to carving out the ice with a hand axe ever so slow and painstakingly, and once I tempted him to pour hot water on her, but he shot the idea down, fearing it would crack the moulded ribs and the boat itself would melt into the soil. Maybe it would just drain away in the spring rain or simply self-destruct, evaporate or dissolve.

Finally, a tense winter sun in late February began to burn holes through the snow piled on the roof, and Johnny hauled out some old framed windows to set over the boat. By the end of the afternoon, she was dry and sound. Sound and solid as cork. You could have put your fingernail through her just about anywhere, but this didn't bother John at all, and what the hell, I was getting excited. "She'll take a little paint. That's all she needs," I said for no good reason. Good God, then I had to turn away, because John Kincaid was about to cry, and for once I realized I loved him. I didn't know up until that time that you could love a friend. But I let it be at that. I couldn't say a word, knowing that it was the same sort of love John felt toward me for saying something so foolish in his favour and believing that this pitiful gathering of planed spruce was more than a memory gone sour.

\* \* \*

From *The Second Season of Jonas MacPherson*

23

Sopping spring again. Cold, damp and angry with life there just beneath the surface, ready to break the locks and sweat itself into summer. The ground cracked finally one day and was about to swallow up the cars and the horses and pull man back to mud at last. The boat had been glazed to lightning gloss with stolen green paint, so that when the sun broke like warm champagne on our navy she sang bright chords of sea shanties locked up in her rotten wood. We had to carry her half a mile to Rigger's Lake, then farther down the shore to where the ice had given up and salt water lapped fresh. The gulls still sat on the ice in favour of winter, and they watched as we slid our hopes out into the blue-green water. Kincaid was in a trance, a spiritual ecstasy, a man of water at last. To hell with land, such a sad substitute for the floating world. A man arrived, a child acquitted, a soul saved.

"Sit down before we both drown," I told him as he danced about lightly as a sandpiper and crazy to boot. He sat. We were floating, oarless, the obvious tools forgotten, left on the shores. What did we know of reason? Left to himself, John would have let the current slip him out to sea as soon as it was able. He didn't care. I did.

"Dig, damn it!" I chastised him, meaning to use his hands. We had to quick paddle back to shore, retrieve the ends to our means. It was like pulling Lucifer out of heaven. But I made the lunatic dig.

Each leaning over a side, we plied the water up to our elbows, in slow painful strokes. God Himself had performed a dirty miracle and allowed this body of water to stay liquid well below the freezing point. It was like dipping your arms full-length into a barrel of razor blades and stirring them up. The cold was magnificent, absolute and horrendous. John howled from the pain. My arm cramped up and I had to switch. It was maddening and wonderful. The logic of boats, of currents, was not with us, and we lost ground, only to be saved by a sunken trunk that nabbed the boat just as we were about to slip into the channel itself and make ready for the sea, where the waves were cracking like fireworks over the rocks at the shallow mouth of Rocky Run. I jumped for shore and landed on a wafer-thin shelf of ice left from another tide, then danced through sheets of glass and jeweller's mud until I was on the bank with the rope.

"Good work, Joney, good work," Kincaid rattled, not shaken a bit. Death and life were all the same to him now he had the boat. Either way he was saved.

In the summer that followed the salvation of the boat, we were at it. Fishing. Making real money. Not much, but our own. Cod, hake, haddock, mackerel. Sold to women for half its worth and only the best fish. Independence. John, a changed creature. Self-respect, pride, the ability to endure the world forever. In August the sun turned benevolent and peeled our shirts off, then painted our skin red. Even the water warmed against its better judgement. By our own tiny wharf, we gutted and scraped and heaved heads to gulls and pretended it would go on like this forever — blue sky, mica-mirrored fish scales electric with light; it was like some wonderful balloon was bursting in my chest. There was nothing to do but wait till Kincaid had put down his knife for an instant to wipe snot, and I launched at him and we arced off the wharf through a cloud of herring gulls and into the inlet, slapping down on the afternoon chop like tandem divers. Ten feet of water, hardly more. Green-blue, with seaweed at the bottom and crabs in miniature armies shuttling away from the invasion.

The miracle of ignorance is always a wonder to behold. John's ignorance in not being able to swim a stroke and my own at never once realizing the obvious fact. Kincaid held on around my throat with a wrestling hold and tried to pull me down to where it seemed he wanted to writhe upon the rocky bottom. I understood his curses even below air and feared for us both. I had often noticed my in-ability to remain civilized when deprived of oxygen, and John obviously shared that affliction. Kicking him in the gut to free the elbow bent around my Adam's apple, I pushed away and shot up for air, only to be hauled back down by a lead anchor around my feet. John, somehow refusing to even flap his way up to kiss air, preferred

From *The Second Season of Jonas MacPherson*

death for us all, but a man without legs is not without arms to whip about and fight for lung privileges. So I, too, cursed and hauled and hoped that, in fact, Kincaid held on, which he did, knowing nothing else below the waterline but my socks and the kick of my shoes in his face. And even after I had regained shore, it was like he didn't want to give up in the shallows till I crawled up across the stones and busted glass, at least one us of still human. John finally heaved himself up on a stump and coughed and vomited and let go of the blue in his skin. It wasn't a pretty picture.

"You can't swim, you bastard," I swiped.

"In a boat you don't need to swim."

"In our boat you do. You could kill us both."

"Seemed like you were the one out for killing."

"The hell I was. Look, you stupid fisherman, if you want to fish, you bloody well better learn to swim."

"My father don't swim and neither does any man on this shore who fishes."

"Stupid, God Almighty. I'll teach you to swim."

"Never in a million years."

I didn't have that much time, but I knew damn well Kincaid was going to do nothing but fish for the rest of his days, and if he couldn't swim he might be getting a sad discount on his career.

"I'm not going back in that damn boat with you until you can tread water."

"Go to hell with you."

I left fifty pounds of fresh cod on the cutting table to rot and walked home.

I stewed over it for three weeks, until the first hurricane cut loose from Barbados and made unwholesome threats outside my windows on an evil, dark night. I wondered how many days John would wait for the swell to die off before he would try to run the inlet. He seemed to have no fear of waves and was masterful at rowing our frail little craft right out through ten-foot breakers, then on our way home skate us down the face of a wave nearly into the railroad bridge. I couldn't let him continue alone. Besides, I missed the boat myself, so I joined him the next day, and we tempted eternity once on the way out and once on the way in with a haul of fish that should have sunk a boat twice our size. John was cocky and corrupted by his victory, his ability to cheat fate, and the fact that I had given in.

Only I hadn't. I waited until the first of November, knowing that we'd have to quit soon anyway. The water temperature was still less than cauterizing. On a dead calm sea, just beyond the shallows of the run, I waited for John to start untangling a hand-line, then quickly hauled the hand axe out of my pack and, with a single swift blow, chopped a hole through the bottom of the boat that sent the axe diving toward a mussel bed. It was only a matter of seconds before the boat was swamped, and I made a dive for it over the side, away from my panicked partner.

Maybe some boats don't sink, but ours was not one of them. The sea was greedy, and I knew soon it would want Kincaid, but it wouldn't be today. I let him curse and let him flounder and stayed close enough so he would fight hell itself to get his hands around my neck, but good God, he swam. He swam like a dragon breathing fire, a runaway water-wheel, a venomous roiling inhuman thing, but he swam.

We landed ashore on fresh clean sand, white and fine as snow, Kincaid out of breath and boiling in the blood. He thought I had gone mad but wanted to kill me before I had a chance for a cure. He found a rock the size of a marker buoy and charged at me, wanting my skull. I was ready and moved off, waited for him to change weapons and come at me with fists. I let him plant two angry jabs in my face before I made my exit, knowing I had done good and realizing we could never be friends again.

The boat was not to be saved. But Kincaid had enough money laid by to put a payment down on a larger vessel, something close to a real fishing boat. He set out to double, then triple our old catch while I went back to school, where I learned to recite Shakespeare's sonnets and read books by other dead Englishmen until I dreamed them in my sleep. John Kincaid didn't speak a word to me for over fifty years.

From *The Second Season of Jonas MacPherson*

*  *  *

And then the year came for all things to die, the year for me to rant against death, to establish eternity once and for all and to quiet forever all losses. November. The months are very important to me. Name a month and it rings inside me like a sound, a colour, a package of emotion and smell. Eleanor gone. November, pulling out the rocks from beneath the foundation of the hill, waves catapulting up the sheer dirt cliff and spiralling pirouettes of spray around to boil with the wind on a wild, grey night. Kincaid, finally dead. The news on the radio. Not one, but three boats from the harbour out at sea in late afternoon on a senseless, stupid ocean, blinded by instinct. Kincaid himself, refusing as usual to give it up, the tides good and high, the catch thick and heavy, no more debts to pay on any man's boat or mortgage, and his greed thick and running full-steam for a man my own age. Sixty-nine. Sixty-eight, actually. The reporter on the radio said he was sixty-eight. All those years. I could never have believed him to be younger than me. Kincaid. He never really spoke to me again since the hatchet work. He had walked the shore waiting for the boat but found only splinters with the right paint. The hand axe, by some uncommon, messianic whim of the sea, had made its way to the beach, and John Kincaid found it, planted it in the side of our house like any Indian.

It would have been the right night for John to die. A monster sea, the highest of tides and him a couple of miles out from here, tangled in kelp, a chance for the catch to get back at him. And my bloody trick had probably done nothing more than increase the agony, make it harder to die, which is to say give death more power. How many other blunders had I done in my life? How often had a well-meaning gesture caused a sufferer more pain?

I switched off the radio and calmed the kettle on the wood stove, then sat in dark silence staring again at completion. The tidiness of it all. Too simple, too easy. And I could at that moment fall on the floor and writhe if I wanted, alone on a sea cliff with my private hell. The loss. Eleanor, then John. The desire so great to wail, to pound my head against a wall or do myself in, to complete it once and for all. Yet I could also do quite the opposite now. And did. I could set it all outside of me and look it dead in the dark face and not be mad and not be terror-struck and not be unhappy at all. And I turned on a light and made room in the warm kitchen for us all.

It was then that John Kincaid ripped open the door and barged in, wanting blood.

"I could swim, you bastard. Look at me, MacPherson. The man saved. Twice saved is twice too many."

"Get over here by the fire, John. You're alive, I don't believe it. Thank God."

Instead of thanking God, he tried to kill me. It was perhaps the third time in my life he fully tried to do it. We were both old men now, but it was the same. He grabbed a piece of split hardwood and tried to bash my brains out, and I shielded myself only enough to feel the blunt weapon connect on bone but no meaty grey matter. I let him try to do what he had decided upon, but he was weak, and his own violence finally sent him flat to the floor, where he bunched up a rug and sobbed into its dust.

He had been in the sea two full hours, pounded by thirty-foot waves and groping from one stick of salvage to another. He had heaved guts into the cold sea three times and gone unconscious twice, only to come around for the last time with water invading his lungs and no feeling in his feet and fingers but his arms continuing to flap on their own as they moved like machines, long after he had wanted them to quit, long after he had schemed a will to drown himself, to end the stupid fight. He would have been happy. But instead he swam, his body worked the waves, not him. And then he felt a hand, something like a fist, pull him up into the air, then smash him down into the terrifying mass of white foam, a shudder-ing torment of water twisted him around and around until he couldn't tell up from down. His skull was nearly wrenched from his neck, and his eyes were stuck wide open. "I've seen hell, thank you. And it's white and it's grey and it moves like cold snakes around your throat and makes you scream inside your head."

From *The Second Season of Jonas MacPherson*

29

The grey and white hell had tried to break his back three times, lifting him and dropping him on the rocky stubble at the base of my hill until his dead fingers reached and found red mud. Then he knew he was alive and wanted to be dead.

Kincaid drank tea and then drank rum. He refused a trip to the hospital, and for that he later lost the tips of three fingers and two toes. In the morning he cried for over an hour, and I had to leave the house, hovering nearby for fear he'd slice his wrists, but he didn't. Nor did he go to sea again. He took the insurance money and holed up with a cranky bitch of a woman who kept three other old men. He was obliged to turn over to her all of his savings, and there he sat before a television with the smell of stale urine forever in the air. When I would go to visit him, he would say my name but that was all.

From *The Second Season of Jonas MacPherson*

# MURIEL AND THE BAPTIST

On the other side of Rocky Run there's a crooked finger of land that stretches into the sea. When the sky is low and grey and knifed clean by north winds, I look over at those dark red palisades of Penchant Point and think of Muriel, alone with her God and three towers. You can almost see the narrow strait of open sky electric with invisible communications. Muriel of the open Gideon Bible, Muriel of the unshadowed kingdom, speaker in tongues, interpreter of dreams, enemy of the Voice of America.

Once a year she would travel the shore and try to force truth into our souls, to save us from hell, to indoctrinate us with the law of a book. She could only ever half-read, but that was enough. Her eyes burned like hot coals, and there was always fear and mistrust of anything in this world in the flames. In brief flashes you could see love, a love we knew nothing of, a love for a tyrant God, a Giant MacAskill of a being who shouted to her in the wind, instructing her to remind the world of the fire below. It burned beneath her house in a damp secret flame at night, and no one could feel its heat quite like she could. Muriel was one of those women you could take a knife to and she wouldn't bleed. The flame had dried the blood in her veins and lit the torch in her eyes, and, like so many believers in such power, she was more than capable of murder.

\* \* \*

On a raw spring day, Muriel would show up just when I was finally set to paint the house, and she wouldn't let me alone until she had preached the full gospel, all pumped up with her own venom. She spit as she talked, not on purpose but because the fire inside wanted to get rid of the dampness and let the flame rule. Eleanor and I would weather her storm and invite her in for tea once she was worn out, which took some doing. It was dangerous to invite her in if she had not worn herself down. Once she kicked the sleeping dog underneath the table so hard that she cracked his rib, and we had to have it set. She apologized, knowing it wasn't her but the devil who had wrenched the spasm in her leg. The devil, she said, was often the messenger from God sent to let her know white by showing black clear as midnight. Eleanor would always say to me that Muriel was a kind woman, that it took a little to see beneath it all to the loneliness and softness that was barricaded up behind a skin like white bone itself. To me, she was like the lobster, the crab or the sea urchin: she wore her skeleton on the outside. Eleanor insisted that we should be kind to her. And we were.

Muriel was maybe twenty years above me and a pioneer of sorts, in that she preceded the rest of us who live our lives out alone on this coast of forgotten people, quiet strangers in a world of noisy crowds. Primitives left to live out what's left on the coastline of a forgotten fringe of a continent gone mad with machinery and power and empty promises. If I live forever, as planned, I will confuse the new generation with my very knowledge of the world of sail, of tide, of wind and wood. They will see me as a museum, and the public will pay good money to enter into me and become the past.

When Muriel's Baptist came to Penchant Point, we had never heard of Baptists in these parts. He wore work clothes and carried that book, the one she kept for her own. There was no bridge then, and I was the kid, greasing oarlocks by the inlet, who offered him the ride across to Penchant. He spoke the whole way, never thanked me, but said the Lord was to be my anchor, this to a person who then believed in perpetual motion. I would let nothing tether me to a sunken weight but preferred to swim wild with any current handy. The Baptist wore shoes the size of anchors themselves, and he had a curious pallor, a blondness in the skin with a blue-grey and soft tan just underneath. No doubt he was a mix of black and white. I wanted to know more about that, but he wanted to speak only of Guiding Lights and more so about punishment, not skin colour. His voice boomed as if it had been shaped out of rock, and, each time he spoke, he was throwing a hewn boulder at the sky.

"How did you get here?" I asked him. He seemed to me like someone who had come from a place very far away.

"A man walks," he answered. "A good man walks upright." He had such a cold, sure sense of himself. I would like to have untied the knot that held his tongue back, so when we reached the other side, I stood rather stupidly shaking his hand and asked him how far he had come and from where.

"Today I walked here from North Preston. Before that I walked as a child under the hand of the Lord with my daddy from Virginia. We did some walking in those days. My daddy had walked back and forth in a dirt field working for a sinner, but before him his father walked free in Africa, a pagan who had never spoken the name of the Lord. We are different now." He said the word *we* like he was referring to all three of them. Staring into his face, I suddenly realized how much older he was than I first thought and how unlike any man I had seen on the shore before. The Baptist had steel girders for shoulders and poured concrete for a body, so that when he stood up it was as if he pushed the earth down beneath him from his force.

The Baptist wanted to know about the people out on Penchant Point, and I told him his preaching might be better accepted elsewhere, since the families of Penchant were hard, untrusting creatures, tied down to farms of rock-strewn pasture and thin topsoil for generations. He smiled. "But I've come to speak to the people." So I offered to take him to the first house on the little trail that stretched like a crooked, injured spine to the ultimate narrow, steep headland that barely held out against the corrosion of the sea.

Lincoln MacQuarrie was the unlikeliest of candidates for the

From *The Second Season of Jonas MacPherson*

33

Baptist's kingdom of God. We found him behind his barn in his turnip field trying to pry a rock from the ground with a ten-foot pole, a contrary ox with one bad leg, and more cursing than the Baptist probably had ever heard in his solemn life. Years later I would remember that rock when my first dentist, a man with stale alcoholic breath and a shaky hand, tried to pull out a tooth he claimed was rotten. "It's only holdin' by the nerve root," he told me and pulled until my jaw would have cracked, but still nothing ever came out. That rock was nerve-rooted deep into the planet with the devil at the other end of the nerve holding on for dear life. A man with an ox can move mountains but not with MacQuarrie's beast, who looked starved and starry-eyed and better suited for sleep than work.

"Dirty Jesus, would you look at this?" MacQuarrie asked the wind as I introduced the Baptist, who held out his hand. MacQuarrie wouldn't take it, just kept wiping his bruised knuckles on a dirty handkerchief, his lower jaw quivering the way it always did, as if he was chewing air and turning it into something acid, his face all pinched up.

"Sir, I come in the name of Jesus," said the Baptist, towering over MacQuarrie. "Jesus, who showed us the way. Be not aggrieved by your tribulations here below. But cast out the demon within and kneel before the Almighty!"

No doubt the Baptist meant well in his own heart, but he was a trifle confused, having spent so much time walking, walking alone and making conversation only with the angels, for he appeared to lack the graces of idle shore talk in this land where men spoke at length on wind and tide and foul weather and the revenge of the North. MacQuarrie conceived that the giant mulatto was some sort of crazy lunatic who was asking him to kneel before him as a heathen god. For the Baptist, framed against the bleak, low-slung sky, sucked in his chest, and you could see muscles rippling like living serpents down the length of his almighty neck. Many men before MacQuarrie had confused the images of angel and devil, prophet and Satanist. And he had thought more than once that the Evil One would one day show his face and own up to the rotten tricks he had so often personally inflicted on this peninsula. So MacQuarrie grabbed the pole and was about to make good his revenge. There was nothing I could do but seek refuge behind the ox and let philosophers contend.

The Baptist saw the pole raised above him but stood firm, opened his Gideon, quoted slowly the words of Paul to the Thessalonians: "We are bound to thank God always, for you brethren, as it is meet, because your faith groweth exceedingly and the charity of every one of you all toward each other aboundeth."

The pole came earthward, and as if through a miracle or some magic of his huge frame, the Baptist dropped low in a wrestler's stance, bracing his hands above him in a mighty grip to receive the message of the unbeliever. He caught the pole and held firm while MacQuarrie chewed air and made good the whites of his eyes. And as Lincoln stood frozen, a man with irons locked to a circle of loose pebbles and goose tongue, the Baptist lifted the weapon and advanced to the stone, drove it hard beneath and executed a profound cantilever as the ox moved forward of its own accord. The rock moved up, then slipped back; then an unshaken Baptist heaved again, pulling up the earth for a full foot outside the perimeter of the unwanted inhabitant. With a shoulder he pushed it aside, and you could see the thing lying there. Underneath, it had been like an iceberg which fanned out in horizontal planes that had kept it solid in the earth.

MacQuarrie had fallen flat on his back. He leaned up on an elbow from the weeds to see the vacant hole filling with water from below. The Baptist hauled the farmer to his feet, brushed off the man's shirt and turned to go.

But on the road, the Baptist spoke in a slow, trembling voice. "The damned fools." I encouraged him to think that it might be easier from there on out but felt my own safety was not to be bargained with. I explained to the Baptist about the road and its absurd crooked path. It passed through "towns" marked on an official map with names, as if to believe that a town could be two houses less

From *The Second Season of Jonas MacPherson*

35

than a quarter-mile apart. Each town had been labelled with a binding, uncreative name — Upper Penchant, Middle Penchant, Lower East Penchant, Lower West Penchant and Lower Penchant itself.

The final house at the least habitable mile of the peninsula was where Muriel lived alone, with maybe twelve goats. I had been there once and seen a curious little hill, perfectly round and smooth like a bowl turned upside down, green as if it were a smooth-clipped cemetery and populated by goats and ravens, all perfectly placed so as to create some supreme balance and order. Two other hills, the same as the first but covered in stunted spruce and alders, followed, and, beyond that, a phalanx of stone pointing to the sea. By the first green hill lived Muriel Cree, a large woman herself, a full six feet, but bent at the neck and appearing as if she was always looking for something at her feet. I knew almost nothing of her except that she was the daughter of a Portuguese sailor who had washed up here and taken for his wife a dark, brooding Penchant girl who had been out berry-picking. Since the girl had always seemed odd, unexplainably dull-witted and prone to fits of madness and speeches in unaccountable animal languages, the family approved of the sailor. Muriel was their only child, and she grew up alone with rocks and gulls and a few goats. Then, when she was a teenager, her parents disappeared. It was said that a Portuguese ship drew in near shore, and the father flagged it down. The story suggests that they simply embarked, leaving Muriel all alone at the end of the earth to feed the goats, her with a bent neck and club foot.

I had turned back before reaching Lower East Penchant, but the Baptist found her at last, a woman with ears in the land of the deaf. He thundered away as he had before until she was convinced of his piety, then asked him to stay. The Baptist stayed on after he had washed away her sins in a cold sea and made her memorize all the names in the Old Testament. They would chant them together in late December, when winter braced its feet against a cold northern rock and pushed hard, only to feel itself unready to convince a stalwart ocean. The sea banked up its thick grey clouds to form swirling foothills in the sky, holding onto what heat it had dared to absorb through the warm months and not wanting to relent to the icy pitchfork tongue of the Arctic.

The few rugged fisherman left who slid their boats past Penchant heard the rattle of ancient names coming from shore: "Obadiah, Malachi, Manaseh, Ephraim, Abraham, Jacob, Isaiah, Zebulun, Helon, Milcah, Noah!"

It would not be for me to pretend an accurate reconstruction of what sort of passions went into their name-shouting or what it meant. I had heard, though, that the Baptist had stayed, that he had married her in his own way, with himself as the minister, with God his witness. With a vision of beginning a new line of Israel, repopulating the shore with a crowd of Christians carrying the names of Deuteronomy and literate in their hearts with the teaching of Jesus. It would have been a curious mix with the pagans on this coast.

Toward his end, the Baptist found himself one morning walking a ground of clean white frost that had sculpted blades of grass into a valley of scimitars. He walked to the top of the first hill leading the youngest of the tribe of goats that had populated that point for seven of their generations. It was a goat with a long white coat and one long mark across its neck like a black scar. To the Baptist it seemed like an instruction from the Almighty to cut along the line, to offer up sacrifice to his bloodthirsty God who had found satisfaction in seeing blood, even the blood of His own Son, seep into the earth for renewal and rebirth.

The goat had two marbles for eyes and, at the centre of each, a green diamond displaced from a night star. They were unblinking eyes that might have been borrowed from a god or a devil, for the Baptist had seen the goat stand upright in the wind on a November night beneath a full moon. Muriel had seen it, too, and without explanation she had taken a box of salt out and sprinkled it in a circle on the grass. In the morning she found a perfectly circular formation where the green grass had been ripped out and the few inches of soil dug back, so that nothing showed but a smooth circle of seamless bedrock that had been polished clean as if someone had licked the stone to a shine.

From *The Second Season of Jonas MacPherson*

For the Baptist, the sacrifice of the goat would help insure that the human race would begin new and fresh in the new year. The goat did not blink as he held out the gutting knife and sliced along the line, watching its own blood fall on the green frost-white grass and then, in a matter of minutes, begin to freeze in a widening dark pond around itself and the Baptist. With virtually no struggle at all, it was as if the creature had no qualms about giving up any rights it had on this earth. But when the last cup fell from the neck and splashed on the Baptist's shoes, the man found he could not move; his feet were frozen fast into the red ice, and he looked up to see his wife standing there, her head bent over as she stared at the blood and let out a mournful wail. As she walked back to the house, the Baptist had to take the knife and chip away at his shoes, without success. He removed his feet, leaving the shoes frozen stiff and stained red, then continued with his ritual, cutting alders and piling them in an arc toward the heavens, and then lifted the blood-drained carcass to the top.

With kerosene he doused the pile and attempted to send his offering above, but a cold, hard rain started, freezing instantly anything in its path. The pile glazed over in a matter of minutes, and the tomb was ice, not fire, and remained like that half the winter as the ice grew thicker but unclouded, staying perfectly clear and building up so that it acted as a magnifying lens, enlarging and distorting the impaired covenant. Had anyone found his way this far out to the point in January, he would have seen one gigantic green diamond eye fixed on the door of Muriel's house.

On that morning, when the Baptist had found his way back to the house, he was himself partially glazed, and his bare feet seemed to sweat blood. Muriel washed them in warm soapy water, then made a breakfast of oatcakes and salt fish.

On the third day of the ice storm, Muriel asked the Baptist to go with her to the basement and pray there upon the bedrock with bared knees, and he did, shouting in his solemn voice to the massive timbers that held up the floors above him, speaking in tongues Biblical and unknown but fearing for once that the words might have come from Satan rather than the Almighty, both having shared the same language once.

I relate this all to you as best I can by piecing together the fragments of Muriel's own story from her numerous visits. What happened next remains shrouded, but Muriel took the gutting knife to the Baptist, that is fairly certain, and she may have watched his blood slide along the rock floor and settle in tiny pools, and maybe she left him there for the rats to gnaw, or perhaps she did something else. I'm not one to speculate on that. But when she went back up into the warm house, she had made her own offering to the Old Testament God and consummated a difficult marriage beyond heaven's gates.

I was one of the few to have even met the Baptist and never once considered his absence until the following year, when Muriel had begun her own preaching along Penchant, condemning the MacQuarries to a burning pit and requesting in public the Lord to swallow up the men as they stood on the wharf. But to me she said only kind things and simply asked me to read a bit of Revelations to her out loud, which I did in my most proper schoolboy voice. For that she was grateful, and annually, wherever I lived, she would seek me out and ask me to read.

The loss of the Baptist was unquestioned, but so were a great many other things along here, and what we always said in public was this: "Probably fell off a boat and drowned," which was the way so many went that it was said in much the same way as someone might have said: Your neighbour is suffering from a cold, too bad. The goats increased and wandered all over the peninsula looking for better feeding ground. Many turned wild and found their way into the fields as far away as MacQuarrie's, and for years you couldn't head over to that end of the land without somebody or other saying to watch out for the wild goats. At least one hunter had been reported to have been gored by the curled horn of a snow-white goat with a long shaggy coat, but everyone said it served him right because he was an American come up from the Boston States look-

From *The Second Season of Jonas MacPherson*

39

ing for moose, and we didn't need his kind anyway. But the kids were warned off, and generally no one really wanted to trust a car on that winding stretch of ruined earth called a road to see how Muriel was faring with her farm. Not until the Voice of America, the radio people who wanted to send messages to Europe, decided that the three low hills out near the tip of Penchant were just perfect for their radio towers. They inquired of the government to discover the land's owner and found, to their delight, that Muriel didn't officially own any of her land anyway. And, oh, they were polite about it and said that she could keep her house and her little kitchen garden and the barn, but that the three gentle hills of such perfect geometry must go to the Voice, and so they did.

Some of the construction crew shot a few of her goats, and she tried to set fire to a bulldozer, but the RCMP came for the first time ever and said she would have to go if she didn't co-operate. So she went back to shouting names from the Old Testament at the sea as the radio people skewered the sky with three giant towers, each with evil blinking red lights, each sending invisible messages in foreign tongues to people on another continent.

Muriel realized that she may well have sinned in the eyes of the Almighty back there in the time of the Baptist and knew that the sinister blazing red light of the tower had a message for her, too. The Lord did move in mysterious ways and had taken his time with settling up accounts with her. And she was grateful for that.

Many years after the towers were built, she would visit us and explain how she prayed daily on her bare knees in her basement on a certain circumference of smoothed bedrock that, she said, she kept polished with her own tongue. She had shown Eleanor and me her knees, which looked misshapen and gnarled like old cat spruce limbs. The skin had a tough, leathery callus like the hide of some animal. She would ask if we would allow her to kneel for a while and pray on our own floorboards, and we would always oblige her. Afterwards she would thank us and compliment the softness of our boards. Then she would ask for a cup of tea, and we would sit quietly together like we were all the most civilized, gentle people on the face of the earth.

# DANCE THE ROCKS ASHORE

I think I love him more now that he's losing his mind than I did when I first married him. Pretty funny how things work out that way. He says he doesn't want to go to a doctor, and I don't blame him for that. Never know what they'll do to you. We never went to doctors much the whole time we have been married. Just the way we were, the two of us.

Hard to think ahead about what might come next. Tough enough to focus on the here and now. But I'll tell you, I can see every little detail of our past life together like it's right here before my eyes. The first time I laid eyes on Jim. Getting married before the judge, just the two of us before him in that big empty room. Of course we'd already been living together. Then there's all those pictures of him and me swimming around in my head.

Or sometimes I see pictures of just him. I can see Jim and the dog rolling around together in the yard. We always had a dog because we couldn't have kids. Usually the dog would come with us when we took those long morning walks to the wharf, with the sun just barely fending off the shivers with its thin, grey-silver light. I don't need to get out the photo album to see all that.

Of course I'm not a hundred per cent sure that it's him who's crazy. Could be me. Caught myself staring straight into the TV set the other day and it wasn't even on. I was entertaining myself, I guess, with my own reruns of the past. Better that way, maybe. No commercials, no interruptions. But I don't think that makes me crazy.

Jim's the one who wakes up some mornings, and, if I don't wake up myself, he'll be all done up in his rubber boots and sea pants, picking up his gear and heading out the door to his boat.

Only there is no boat. Well, at least, she can't go anywhere. She sits up on land now. The boat's too old and too dry to ever go back into the water. Jim said it wasn't worth keeping her in repair. Like us. Jim and me. Old, tired a lot, one or both of us crazy.

Jim started to lose a grip on things when the fish gave out. Oh, we'd seen it coming for a long time. Jim came home one day, and he sat down on that piece of lawn furniture he'd built out of alder saplings, and he just looked at his hands.

"What is it?" I asked him. I knew something was wrong.

"It's over," was all he said, but I knew what he was talking about. I'd been catching bits and pieces of it on the CBC radio.

"What do you want for your dinner?" I asked him, putting my arm around his shoulders.

"Nothing," he said.

I had to walk away then 'cause I didn't want to have to look at him. I didn't want him to have to see me watching him cry. You know what I mean, what I'm trying to say. About men and all. I went inside and closed the door and let out this big sigh of relief. I could never come out and admit to him that I was secretly happy that it was over. He'd be safe now.

Yes, he did cry. I know that. A man isn't supposed to cry, but I think he can handle it as long as he thinks no one is watching. Jim always cried when the dogs died. Trouble with dogs is that you outlive them. We outlived three, Jim and me. All died of old age, but they died just the same. We have three good dogs buried on the edge of the forest here. Don't know exactly why we never replaced Beauty. She was the last one to go.

I guess Jim never had any real thoughts about what he'd do once he stopped fishing. But it wasn't like he planned to die at sea. Jim had sense. He came home one day with a survival suit that the government helped to pay for. "A man could stay alive in this thing for days at sea if he had to," he said. "Got pockets for food and everything." He put the ridiculous-looking thing on, and then he put his arms around me and hugged me tight. "I'm never gonna drown like them other silly bastards. I couldn't bear the thought of leaving you alone. If my boat ever goes down, you better bet on me out there bobbing around like a cork, waiting for that Jesus helicopter ride. Just make sure I got plenty of sandwiches, in case. I'd hate to be out there without food. That's the only thing that scares me. The thought of missing lunch."

Jim was always a survivor. Nothing got him down. He had that suit ready to just jump into the sea with my sandwiches in his waterproof pockets. He even had radio emergency gear to signal the coast guard by way of a satellite in space. Jim was not a man prepared to go down with his ship. He'd never be that mean to me.

That suit is still hanging upstairs on a hook. Jim never had to use it. It was always with him on the boat, though, ready to save him and keep me from being lonely. It was the suit that got us both going on that conversation, you know the one. "If I go first I want you to . . ." Every married couple goes through that.

"If I go first, I want you to find some sensible, pretty woman and marry her," I said.

"Not possible," Jim said. "The two never go together."

"What's that supposed to mean?" I snapped back, pretending to be insulted.

"What I meant to say was that a man can find a woman with those two qualities only once in life, and I found it."

"You're a liar," I teased. I wanted more of the flattery. Jim never was good at flattery, never said a whole lot about how I looked or if he liked my hair or dress. I learned to live without the language of flattery.

"If I go first," he continued, "you have to do something you always wanted to do but never did because of me."

Funny thing, but right then I actually thought about a whole list of things we never did, things that maybe I would do if he was gone. Drive to Halifax and go to a symphony concert, eat breakfast some day in a fancy restaurant. The whole time we were married, we never once ate breakfast anywhere other than at home, and half the time we were eating it in our kitchen with all the lights on because the sun wasn't even up yet.

Jim saw the look in my eyes, dreaming up a list of things. "If I go first, I want you to do whatever you want. Just be sure to bury me out there with the dogs. I'd like that. They were good dogs."

All he had to do was mention the dogs and I started to cry, feeling awful guilty for even thinking about Jim dead.

"If I go first," I said, "I want you to take good care of yourself." That was all I could get out. Then he gave me a hug and went out to mow the yard with the lawnmower.


I need to explain about the place we live in. It's a house Jim built — well, I helped him build it, too — about thirty years ago. It sits on five acres of land that goes right up to the inlet, with a big lawn stretching down to the sand and the water. Jim has about ten pieces of lawn furniture out there made from those alders and young birch trees. Stick furniture it's called, although the name doesn't do it justice. People admire the chairs because they look like they are still wild and alive. Jim would mow the grass with a gasoline mower, and it would stay green right up into December. We'd go out there on one of those rare, warm days in late fall, and he'd say, "It feels just like summer." The grass was a rich green, the water in the inlet was a piercing blue. Those were good moments. Those were better than any old breakfast in a restaurant.


So hard to think of all the good things as being behind us. If we had kids like other people, maybe we'd have that way of talking about the future, seeing it in our children and grandchildren. But we don't have that, and I'm not gonna go worrying myself about what might have been. Like I say, I've got Jim to focus my worrying on.

It was a couple of weeks after the news that the cod were all gone. They might not be back for ten years, a hundred years or ever, that's the way the government man said it. Jim sat down in the yard on his chair with a pile of newspapers he'd pulled out of the wood shed. And he started to read them. Those papers were probably three years old or older. But he just sat down and started to read one after the other — the news, the classifieds with boats for sale, the sports. I didn't say a word about it. What was there to say, anyway?

Later that day when I was in the kitchen making a soup from an old ham bone and some stuff from the garden, Jim was walking around the house from room to room, like he was looking for something. He opened drawers and peered into cabinets, and when he was on his second circuit, I asked him what he was searching for. Jim seemed startled, and he looked at me with this odd blank stare on his handsome face. He tried to shape some words in the air with his hands, he stuttered, and finally he just said, "I don't know."

I saw the fear in his face, and it scared the living daylights out of me, but I didn't let on. I laughed and chastised him for being so absent-minded. "You'd lose your head if it wasn't held on by your neck," I said for the five-hundredth time in our marriage.


One night I woke up and touched him on the shoulder. He didn't notice, I'm sure. His breathing was so slow and steady, just like that of a child. I needed to talk, and I guess it didn't matter much if he was awake or not. I'd been feeling guilty for some time about the whole fishing business. Like it was my fault or something that the cod had all gone away. Jim, I said to my sleeping husband, when you said it was all through with the fishing and the boat and hauling off in the morning in the dark to risk your life at sea, I had to hold back from smiling. I had to hold back from going bloody wild with happiness now that I'd never have to worry about you at sea again. Pretty selfish, I know, 'cause I wasn't thinking about how you were feeling but thinking about me. I had you all to myself and wouldn't have to share you with the Atlantic Ocean ever again. Well, I got that off my chest. Knew I had to say it to him some day because it had been burning a hole inside me. But now I didn't feel so bad. Jim was safe, and I would have him with me twenty-four hours a day.

But I guess I was fooling myself somewhat on that. It was like I was going to be punished after all for my selfish, foolish thoughts. The next morning Jim woke up first. When I opened my eyes he was sitting bolt upright in bed, and he was looking around the room in a strange way. I knew already what the look was about. He didn't know where he was. I took a deep breath and sat up. Jim edged away slightly and turned his piercing blue eyes in my direction. I thought they were going to drill right through me. "Who are you?" he asked, his voice almost shaking.

I knew that this would happen sooner or later, and I had been practising in front of a mirror for my own way of dealing with it. I'd a read a little bit in the *Reader's Digest* about the disease that was affecting my poor husband's brain. I didn't understand it real well, but I knew there would be these lapses. His memory would go away, and it would come back, a little bit at first, a little more later. Something like the tide going in and out, but it would get more drastic over time. The tide would someday slip out and never come back at all.

"What am I doing here?" Jim demanded as I tried to get a grip on myself.

Here goes, I said to myself, putting into action my little plan. Now, the experts had said, stay calm and reassuring, slowly and carefully remind the person of who he is and where he is. But I wouldn't do that and rob my husband of whatever dignity still threaded its way through his brain.

Instead, I slapped him playfully on the leg, then tickled him under the ribs. "Don't be silly," I teased. "What games are you trying to pull on me?" Then I traced my fingers once through his thinning hair and ruffled it up like when we both had been twenty years old and he had had this big, shaggy mop of thick, curly brown hair.

Truth is I'm a lousy actress, always was. Couldn't recite a couple of lines from a play in school in front of a class, couldn't pretend to be anybody other than who I was in my whole life. This was a real test, I'm telling you.

I'm not sure Jim figured out much of anything in those few seconds except for the fact that he was safe and this was where he was supposed to be. If I'd have asked him, he wouldn't have known his own name, I think, and it would have scared me to the root of my being, but I wouldn't let that scene happen. If Jim was going crazy, then I'd have to go halfway crazy with him if we were going to work it out. One foot in crazy, one on solid ground, that was my plan.

"Let's not get up right yet," I said, and I tickled him some more and wrestled him down under the covers until I got him stirred up enough so that we made love. That was something we didn't need any talk for at all, and whoever the hell we both were right then didn't seem to matter much. Everything worked out just fine. It pulled us both back into some warm, secret world full of tenderness and light.

Afterwards, Jim reached over and flicked the shade on the window so it flipped up in a snap. The late November sunlight came flooding into the room like a big, friendly, happy dog. "What's for breakfast, woman?" Jim asked in his pretend-to-be-tough voice. I had always liked the way he did that, mostly because it was pretend stuff. Jim was tough, all right, but tough deep down in some strong way that few men on this shore would ever know.

"Anything you want," I answered, pretending to be the dutiful wife who only took orders.

At breakfast, Jim talked to me like there was nothing wrong at all, and I knew that I was going to be able to handle whatever the memory eater could throw at me. I even believed that, if I fed Jim enough of the right food and took good care of the old guy, everything would work out fine. That's why I fried up some of the cod tongues we'd kept hoarded away in the freezer for special occasions. Jim loved fried cod tongues for breakfast the way some rich people must love their caviar. But caviar could never compare with cod tongues done up just right. When breakfast was over, I checked the stock of what was left in the freezer. It was a hard case of reality coming back to haunt me. We had maybe a dozen more feeds of the blessed stuff in there. It dawned on me then that, with the cod all killed off, I might not ever be able to replenish the supply. I'd have to dole it out carefully and make it last as long as I could. Cook it up only on extra-special occasions like this.

Jim saw me standing there with the upright freezer door open and cold smoke pouring out over me like a spring fog. I quickly closed the door before he might begin to consider what I was worrying about.

"I'd like to go down to the boat," Jim said to me, and I didn't know if he was still thinking she was in the water afloat or if he could remember that those days were all over. But then he added, "Good day for a walk. Maybe you want to come with me."

"I'd like that," I told him, and began to take the plates off the table until Jim stopped me.

"I'll take care of this. Go get yourself ready."


Out on the road that morning, we walked the same path Jim would have taken every working day, winter or summer, whenever the weather allowed the boats to go to sea. Despite the cold, the sun felt hot on my face, and I felt young again like you wouldn't believe. Everything made me smile. Jim holding onto my arm, the McCarthy's big stupid dogs yapping at us as we went by, the sunlight sparkling off the ice crystals that grew like diamonds in every blooming pothole in the road. It was a day to be fully alive. It was a cold but clear day, not a touch of wind. I was all bundled up, but Jim had on nothing more than his old ratty wool pullover. We walked down the gravel road that leads from the highway to the fishing wharf. Beyond that point, the road dwindles off to nothing. It doesn't exactly come to an end, it just fades to nothing that looks like a road, just a patch of stubbly stones and a stretch of flotsam and sand. Further beyond is a stretch of rocks sticking up out of the water like broken teeth. That's all that connects what's left of Crofter's Point to the mainland. Still farther out is what's left of the headland where Jim had grown up, on a farm at the very tip of the land named for his family. Unfortunately, the sea has swallowed up most of the old farm. It's hard to believe that in forty short years the Atlantic could have been so hungry as to chew up a barn and a field and so much land. Every time I thought about that place through our entire marriage, I had this sneaking suspicion that the sea had stolen Jim Crofter's family farm and that it was anxious to snatch him away as well. Even though I loved the ocean for its beauty, I never trusted it once in my whole life. We were sworn enemies, she and I. Both of us had wanted Jim, but I had won.

Our home was halfway out from the highway to the wharf. For Jim, it had been a kind of retreat back from the high hill of the headland where he grew up, a safer haven along the less trouble-some, less greedy tides of the inlet, with its crystal clear water, its ribbons of eelgrass and its millions upon millions of underwater snails. We had a nice little house set back from the road and that big green lawn that he was always so proud of spilling down to the edge of Five Fathom Harbour. At the sandy shoreline, we had a grand view of every sunset of the year and all the privacy and beauty any-body could cram into a single lifetime.


When we arrived at the boat, Jim's own *Just My Luck*, it was like a big dark cloud suddenly came swooping across the sky even though the sun was still out bright. Jim sucked in his breath and reached up to put his hand on the bare, weather-stained wood of the gunwale. That touch and the look on his face was something I care not to translate. I was sure he was about to slip into one of his episodes and lose himself, either that or explode like some kind of volcano. Ever since the fishing had gone bad it was like everybody around here was ready to go off like a firecracker. Who the hell was to blame, anyway? Government, politicians, Spanish trawlers, the Russians? Was it us or the sea itself? Nobody could pin it down, and that frustration made some of the men go right crazy. Billy Jobb taking a hammer to the RCMP car one day for no obvious reason. Kyle McCurdy beating on his poor wife until she had to leave him and move to Truro. Stammy Woodhouse, who had always lived alone, just boarded up his house one day and took off in his four-by-four. Nobody ever heard from him.

Jim had his own way of dealing with it. He didn't hardly talk to me or anyone for about ten days. And then he started to lose his memory.

I pried Jim's hand off the side of the boat. We both looked like a pair of prize idiots, I know, standing there in the blasting sunlight staring at the side of an old boat whose paint was peeling badly. All that blue and yellow giving way to grey boards beneath. It seems that every damn thing along these shores of Nova Scotia  first turns grey before it eventually gives up the ghost.

Jim turned away from the boat finally and followed the track of where the boat had been hauled up from the inlet, skidded up on parallel logs leading ashore from the water line and the tidal zone, rich green with algae and slime.

"Tide's real low," Jim announced.

"Hardly ever gets that far down," I offered. When you live all those years as a fisherman's wife, you learn that any discussion of tide is a serious matter.

"It does. A couple times a year. Easy to make a mistake coming in past the point. When she gets this low, you don't want to trust the markers."

That's when I noticed Jim had turned his attention seaward. He leaned against *Just My Luck*, and I watched as he drifted off back home, to his first home, that is, on Crofter's Point. A lot of people consider it an island now, since the rocks that connect it to the mainland are underwater most of the time.

It had been a long while since Jim had gone home to what little was left of his old place. The last time he had gone there alone on his boat and rowed the skiff ashore. He never told me more than five words about his visit that time. I looked off to where Jim was staring, and I could see what he had discovered. "You could walk there today, if you don't mind high-stepping all those slippery rocks."

"And if you get there and back before the tide slips."

Once the words were out, there was no turning back. I hated trying to walk on slippery, stony shorelines more than anything else, and there was probably some ice on some of those stones today as well, but like I say, there was no turning back.

"I haven't been home in a long time. Maybe there's still something left."

It was a difficult trudge for me, a real battle of body and mind just to keep from crashing down and breaking a leg or an elbow, but Jim held me steady and had no trouble at all, except for the fact that I was slowing him down. It took forty-five minutes from the end of the road, and it wouldn't have been possible except for the extreme low tide.

Crofter's Point, once a hundred acres of beautiful green pastures just poised above the sea, was now whittled down to a third of that size. Barely anchored to shore by that backbone of boulders and stones we had just travelled, it was as if the place was prepared to let slip from the mainland altogether and drift off to some other continent. Where the hills once curved smoothly and gently down to the sea, now there were ugly, scalloped red dirt cliffs and, above, a dagger-shaped plateau of land that was being hacked away by every storm and wave the world could conspire.

Jim and I climbed up the lowest slope, him holding fast onto my hand as we set more stones free to rattle against their cousins beneath. Jim's parents were long dead, no brothers or sisters left. He still paid taxes on this place and had never argued to have them reduced because of the fact that it was shrinking. We both knew that it would disappear forever without a trace not too many years after we were gone.

The gulls were the true owners of this property now. They nested here on the grass in the early summer, their young ones grew, and those who survived took their first flight at the cliff's edge. They swirled and shrieked about our ears as we walked through the tall, brown grass and dead thistles. I smelled the crush of bayberry plants beneath our feet. "This was quite a place for a boy to grow up," Jim said as his eyes followed the swoop and flow of the gulls around us. Some looked like they were brazen enough to dip down and stab at us with their beaks, but it was as if an invisible barrier prevented them from getting dangerously close. It was obvious they didn't like us being here. They didn't trust us, and I could understand why. I'd seen fishermen shoot gulls for fun, a sickening game. Jim had gotten into a fight more than once with someone over that. He hated seeing anything killed without good cause.

"It was heaven or hell," Jim continued as we walked on to where the family homestead had been. "Heaven on a summer day with blue seas stretching to the horizon. Swimming in the pools with the fish and crabs, sometimes a young harbour seal slipping by right beside you like it was nothing at all. Other times, the storms came and battered away at the barn and the house, and a good blow might last three or four days, and you'd see the sun for only an hour before a new storm would come in right at you again until you thought you would crack. It was during those times my father would start to act like he wasn't my father. He'd bang me around for some foolish thing I'd done."

"He beat you? You never told me." I was taken completely by surprise. How could we have lived together all those years without him ever revealing this?

"It wasn't worth telling, I guess. Besides, I was afraid you knew what I knew — kids who grow up getting batted around by an old man with a temper usually grow up to be just like their fathers."

"That's what they say. But why didn't you ever tell me about it?"

"I didn't tell you at first because I thought it might scare you away from marrying me. Then I didn't tell you after because I thought you'd feel like I had somehow lied by holding it back." Jim was about to either laugh or cry. I didn't know which. "Then after about thirty years I figured it didn't matter anyhow because I turned out not to be like him at all, so what's the point in wasting words on it?"

"Then why tell me now?" I asked.

His face softened into a smile. "Guess I figured I didn't have anything to lose and should get it off my chest." His whole body seemed to relax as I shook my head and called him a big goof. "C'mon," he said, "I want to show you something."

"Something" was the cliff where the barn had tumbled right off the edge into the sea. "I would have liked to have been here during the storm where she let go," Jim said. "I've seen it fall in my dreams a thousand times and thought that if I had been here maybe I could have done something to hold it back. It's crazy, I know." Below us there was a scattering of loose boards, bleached greyish-white by the sun, salt and sea. Certainly not enough left to make a body think it had ever been a two-storey barn. And if the rocks were down there that had once been part of a carefully laid foundation, well, they just looked like all the other ones.

"The barn was right there," Jim said, pointing with his finger into some place that was now only air. I could almost see it suspended in space before us, floating on the light breeze. To think that the barn was gone, the foundation and lumber dropped below into the sea and the very land it once stood on evaporated to nothing. I felt small just then, and vulnerable.

We walked around the dent in the ground that was all that was left of Jim's family home and then crossed over the rim of lichen-covered rocks, and stood inside the old house. "Right about here was my room. The ice pellets used to beat against my window like machine-gun fire. Over there was the kitchen with the wood stove. When all the trees were gone here, I had to row softwood in a dory from up the inlet. Hard and slow work, but I liked it. If I didn't get there and back quick enough to my father's liking, he'd call me slow and lazy and sometimes take a belt to me until I bled." I could see the pain in his face as if the beating had just happened. Then he took a big gulp of air. "Doesn't matter now. All turned out okay. I still miss him as much as my old mother, who never did an unkind thing in her entire life. Funny, eh?"

"Not funny at all. Times were different then."

"I guess. Look at this. My father would never have imagined this could happen. He believed in this place and thought he had captured the best of both worlds — the sea and the soil, cod and cabbages. At least it was enough while it lasted."

"Nothing lasts forever." That was all I had to offer up, that sad, tired old phrase, as we poked around in the soil that had once been beneath the wooden floor. I expected to come across some old child's toy or an old shoe, but there was only dirt and stones and bricks shredded into fragments by the weather.

Suddenly, Jim walked from his old bedroom to the kitchen, for I knew the geography of this troubled home now, and across the threshold where the door had been. He walked straight out, turned left, and, with a sudden burst of energy, ran toward the cliff's edge, about twenty yards away. "Jim!" I screamed at him, afraid that the return trip down memory lane had rattled him badly. What was he about to do? My heart jumped up into my throat.

Jim knelt down on the ground and began to scrape away at the weeds, and I wasn't sure if he was looking for something real or imagined, but when I scrambled over toward him, I could see what he had found. I knelt down beside him. He carefully lifted a dilapidated wooden lid. Below was a dark, clear pool of water. "This well never went dry. Ever." He sounded proud and exuberant and that made me feel tingly inside. "We had the best, purest water in the county, my old man said. And it never dropped an inch."

Jim threw off the wooden lid and leaned over. The water was almost flush with the ground. He pushed his face right into it and drank long and hard. When he looked up at me, droplets of water streamed from his face and caught the sunlight as they spilled onto the ground. "You know something, Mary? I feel like it was okay that I had heaven and hell, both of them, right here. I had the best life. And it just got better when I left here. I feel so completely alive."

I held his face in my hands. The cold drops of water collected on my fingers, and I put them to my mouth. The taste, oh my God, the taste of it all.

To the gulls still spiralling above, we must have seemed like a curious pair of humans, kneeling side by side as if in prayer beside a hole in the ground. I looked up at those gulls, catching the updraft of air at the edge of the headland, and wondered at the amazing fact that this well, dug by Jim's temperamental father, was now only eight feet from the very brink of the cliff and a drop off of over a hundred feet.

The well was full to the brim with fresh, life-giving water, impossibly close to the end of the land where soil and stones gave way to empty air. A miracle of nature that could only result from this being the best well in the county, right here in heaven-and-hell land. But the miracle would be transient. In a year or two, five at the most, the land would give up, the rocks would be loosed by the wind, and the cold, fresh water of the Crofter's well would spill out into the air, cascade down the side of the red dirt cliff and wash into the sea.


"Tide's sneaking up on us," Jim said, helping me to my feet. "Time to dance you ashore." It was an old expression of his. Walking on rocks was always like a dance. Jim would lead, I would follow. It was as if his feet agreed to the shape of each stone, negotiated a perfect hold, while mine rebelled at every step. A fresh wind had come up off the sea, and it had the sting of winter to it. Halfway back to shore, the dryer rocks had given way to little slapping waves, and we were ankle deep before we had finished the dance of rocks back to the mainland. We walked home with numb toes and warm hearts. Jim fell asleep that afternoon, the first of many daytime naps that lasted frighteningly long — two hours, three. Sometimes I'd have to wake him for dinner.


The ice came but no snow. The inlet began to freeze over quicker than any year I had ever seen. While the back yard grass remained green but frozen stiff, the pans of ice heaved and hawed in the inlet, a vast glazed expanse, reshuffled each day as the tides pushed renegade islands of ice right up to the foot of the sandy little beach. On some days Jim would forget to stoke the stove, and the house would go cold. If he caught me carrying in logs or splitting softwood at the chopping block, he would feel terribly bad, beg my forgiveness and say he'd never let it happen again. I told him I didn't mind. I needed the exercise, and besides, this was better than doing like those ladies in the magazines who lifted weights or jogged around city streets to stay healthy. I didn't mind the work at all.

And there were days when Jim was with me and days when he was only half there. He'd lose his shoes or lose his coat or his boots, or wonder where he had left the money in his wallet. He'd try to tell me about a dream he had but lose himself in the middle of a sentence and only in his most desperate moments come right out and say, "I don't even know who I am," or, even more frightening to me, admit, "I don't know where I am."

Once or twice I caught him napping outside on his stick furniture, where he had gone to enjoy the view of all that inlet ice at sunset. I had to keep a close eye on him, all right.

I won't try to tell you these were the best of times, but they were not the worst. I just felt the weight of so much responsibility. At first it didn't bother me at all, but it soon began to wear me down, until one day, feeling exhausted and drained, and secure in the fact that Jim was napping soundly on the chesterfield near a warm wood-stove fire, I lay myself down on the afternoon bed and closed my eyes.

I opened them when a brazen goldish red beam of light from the west window shone straight into my eyes. I had slept to nearly four-thirty. The sun was going down. The house was cold. I shook myself awake and realized I was alone in the room. In the kitchen, the fire had gone out in the stove. The door was open. Jim was nowhere around. Panic shivered in my limbs and a knot of fear twisted into a tourniquet in my gut.

Outside, it was still but cold, bitter cold. I walked quickly to the road and slipped on the ice of a frozen puddle. I fell hard and scraped my shin on a jagged rock. I stood back up, steadied myself and made it to the road. Not a car, not a soul in sight. I retreated to the back yard and walked slowly across the frozen green lawn. Before me was Jim's high-back homemade chair. Each step was painful to me but not nearly as painful as something stabbing at my heart.

Somebody was in the chair. I advanced toward the dark, silent silhouette of my husband. The red wash of the December sun made the ice of the inlet go blood red, a screaming colour that invaded me with cold and fear that conspired into something hot and awful.

Jim had positioned himself here to watch the sun go down over the inlet he loved. He had even dressed warmly in the only coat he could probably locate — one of mine, a bulky blue winter affair with a hood. As I kneeled down in front of him, I knew that I was not at all prepared for this. His head was slumped over. I was having a hard time getting air into my lungs, and I could hear my blood pounding in my ears.

Fear had scissored big holes in my ability to reason and clamped shackles onto my arms and legs. I could not bring myself to pull the hood back off my husband's head and read the sorry news. Instead, I gave up on everything, my belief in myself, my hopes and my happiness. I put my head upon his knees and wept. No sound could escape from me, but my body quaked with convulsions of despair.

The next thing I knew I felt the lightest pressure of a hand upon my head. I felt a human hand stroking my hair and I looked up. In the dying winter light, I saw the face of my husband and heard the sweet song of my own name, "Mary, Mary, Mary."

I was unable to find a path back to the world of language as he lifted me towards him and wrapped his arms around me, repeating my name again and again, pulling us both back into the realm of the living.

"I was just sitting here," he said, "remembering summer. The sun was warm on my face, and I was enjoying it so much. I guess I fell asleep. It felt so much like summer. Remember what it was like?"

"I remember," I said. "I could never forget."

*Dance the Rocks Ashore*

57

"Nothing is ever really lost," he said, and continued to stroke my hair as if I was a little child, as if he was the one whose strength allowed me to cope with living.

"I know that," I said, realizing just then that I had come to grips with the eventual loss of my husband. During all our life together he had been building up my own strength, preparing me for the time when the water in the well would be released from the hill, greet the sky, then slip down the cliff of the faltering land and find its way back into the sea. Sooner or later I would be able to accept this absolute fact. But as I led my husband back into the house, I knew that first I would drink deeply from the well and appease the thirst that was in me.

From *The Republic of Nothing*

## EYE OF THE HURRICANE

My sister was born during a full moon in August, at one of the high-est tides recorded on Whalebone Island in the very eye of Hurricane Irene. I was five years old, and I think it was the first time that I understood my mother and father were in love. At five, you tend to think of love as something you feel toward favoured pets more than human beings. I had a one-winged seagull that ate cod scraps and a geriatric dog that had moved into the crawl space under our house. Like so many other wounded creatures, the one-winged seagull who my father had named Khrushchev and the flea-pestered dog that I named Mike had found their way to Whalebone Island and the Republic of Nothing for solace and refuge from the outside world.

What I am trying to say is, I loved both these creatures, and I think that what I felt toward them — the pity and the compassion and the downright joy of playing with each — I think this was the way my parents felt about each other.

Hurricanes bring out the best in creatures who love each other. At least that's what I learned during Irene. During a hurricane, how-ever, is not a great time to have a baby. The sea heaves enormous waves pounding with incredible force all over rocky parts of an is-land like Whalebone. Hurricanes pick up anything that isn't tied down and devise lethal flying weapons. Boats, the fisherman's live-lihood, become playthings in a maelstrom bathtub where they worry and smash against the wharves until wood gives up its sanity and becomes splinter. Hurricanes shred, suck, spit, stammer, scream, batter, bruise, beat, beleaguer, bend, moan, mangle and molest an island like Whalebone and its usually happy people until they feel they know something of war.

Maybe it was because the skies of earth were jealous that year (my mother would later say) because of that deadly weapon, that H-bomb equivalent to ten million tons of TNT that disturbed the Pacific sleep of the world over Namu islet in the Bikini islands back in February. "For the world has a single soul," my mother argued, "and such an offense might cause her to react — even on the Atlantic thousands of miles away. What is fifteen thousand miles to a soul as complete and round as a planet?"

For the most part, hurricanes do not batter Nova Scotia with their might. A hurricane is a southern thing, a warm water creature with a supple spine and catty mind that reminds the American east coast it is merely a whim of cities and scum. A hurricane stirs itself to fury in a spiralling soup of skies and crawls like a hungry galaxy toward land to devour houses and businesses and scrape clean the coast, to put it back to normal as best it can. And when the heat runs out, when the bite of the North Atlantic off New England reminds the hurricane that this is far enough, that above here the land is still pure, the glaciers have just barely left, the people are not quite as confounded and corrupt as southerners, then the hurricane usually veers east toward Iceland into a humble retirement of dissolution and repentance.

But such was not the case with Irene. We had boats on doorsteps by the time the quiet eye found us huddled in the living room. A hurricane like Irene reminded adults that something had been disturbed in the clean order of things. My mother, for all her affinity with the future, later admitted she had been misled by the stars, that she had miscalculated the arrival of the baby, for she had predicted the baby to be a Virgo, and a birth now would mean a Leo.

I was sitting in my bedroom with Khrushchev and Mike. The gull was on the windowsill eating cod tongues from a plate, and Mike was asleep at the foot of my bed. We had weathered the first blast of the storm, and I had almost become used to the sound of raging wind and maniac seas. I can't say I was scared of Irene. It was too much fun, since it was the first time I was allowed to have both Khrushchev and Mike in my bedroom with me. My father was preoccupied with other things.

Everett MacQuade was the ultimate disbeliever in weather reports. He saw the weather office as a sort of combined misinformation conspiracy and make-work project for know-nothings. We had listened on the radio about the approach of the storm, how it had ripped through several island communities in New Jersey ("That'll show 'em," my father said), and how it had carved a deadly trail right across Long Island and Cape Cod ("People should never have lived there anyway"), but when it was reported that the storm was regrouping its strength and gearing up for a full onslaught on the coast of Nova Scotia, that it was already reducing Sable Island to something less than sand and spit, my old man said that it wouldn't dare touch the Republic of Nothing.

So it wasn't until the winds gusted to sixty miles an hour that my old man started screaming at me to find every god-damn shred of rope I could lay my hands on.

My mother was sitting in a chair reading a book on phrenology when my old man relented and admitted that it was a lucky guess on the part of the weather service, a damn lucky guess for them know-nothings. "Sure, the wind is up a little. I've seen onshore winds much worse than this. It won't amount to much, though," he said, looking out at three inches of water in the front yard and a dory slipping by on the road. "Still and all, you better get your creatures inside."

That's when I knew my father was serious. I ran out into the pelting rain and found Khrushchev hunkered down on his roost by the shed. I had to wake up Mike who was still asleep in the water rising beneath the house. Khrushchev was under one arm and Mike, the big old mangy beast, was in tow by the collar as I went back in the front door.

My old man was headed toward the cove to lash down the boat more tightly when the door — a big square four-foot-by-four-foot

From *The Republic of Nothing*

61

contraption of one-by-six spruce all nailed together — flew off the shed. It took off like a flying island and sailed past my old man's head, within inches of knocking his brains out. Everett stopped dead in his tracks. Next, he saw a twelve-foot wall of water smash up over the granite rock that acted as a breakwater for our tiny dock. The flying door headed straight into the shooting spray and then fell to earth, smashing on the granite. When my dad came back in, drenched and looking shaken for the first time in his life, he said, "Now I get it. Just when the weather office so thoroughly perfected giving wrong predictions, Nature turns around and throws off their entire system by following up with what was predicted." My father had once again, in his own way, made sense of the world. "There could be a little damage to the republic," he told my mother. "We're in for a real blow."

My mother put down her phrenology book and looked at her husband. I was there in my bedroom doorway, my gull on my shoulder and Mike still in tow by the collar. What I saw between my mother and father had nothing to do with the weather. I saw worry and I saw understanding and I saw a kind of wonder, but most of all I saw between them love, something almost physically tangible, like a heavy silver thread that was strung out across the room from one to the other.

"I guess it was *supposed* to be a Leo after all," my mother said, suddenly grabbing her belly and sucking in a quick, almost panicky gulp of air. Just then the back door flew open and wet wind and tide sloshed into the living room.

Another contraction hit, and my mom let out a howl that roused Mike to howl in empathy. My father fought his way to the wooden door, shoved it closed, and, realizing that the lock was clean busted off by the brutal wind, shoved the chesterfield up against it. I probably shouldn't have been surprised to see that there was a smile on my old man's face. He loved weather of any sort, and the harsher it got, the more my old man admired the natural forces that were ready to put us in our places.

"Jesus, did you see that?" he asked me. "That's no ordinary

wind. That's a wind that wants to be everywhere. It's not satisfied to stay just outside. You've got to admire a wind with such audacity."

My mother let out another long, low moan. "Something's wrong," she said.

"Not necessarily," my father said. "It's just Nature's way of re-establishing her set of values, testing us to see if we're strong and ready for the challenge." My mother was lying flat on her back in the bed, and I could see her grab onto my father's hand and squeeze hard. Now he clearly understood. The love and concern for his wife cut right through the fascination with the hurricane's political will. "Hang on," he said. "We'll get Mrs. Bernie Todd."

I know that he meant that *he* was going. As I stood there in my bedroom doorway with my gull on my shoulder and my old dog at my feet, it never occurred to me that I was about to head out into the terrible storm. But as my father tried to pull away from my mother, she pulled him back. "You're not supposed to go. I don't know why and I wish it was that simple, but you can't leave."

It could be that my mother was just so scared that she was hiding behind her visionary powers, using them as an excuse to keep her husband by her side. And had she thought it through, did she really think it sensible to send a five-year-old boy out into a raging hurricane? Didn't she care about me? All I wanted was to crawl under my bed with Mike and listen to him snore through the hurricane. I was in love with the sound of my dog snoring. It was all I needed out of life just then. Things had been whittled down to that simple bit of familiarity.

Khrushchev was back on my window sill, ducking and bobbing at the flying debris that would have been assaulting him had it not been for the window glass. I crawled under the bed, sneezing several times at the dust and amazed at the lost socks and spare toy parts. I had dragged Mike with me, and I started singing "Old McDonald" when I saw may father's gumboots before my eyes. "Ian, I need a word with you, son."

At five you believe that if you just close your eyes and pretend

From *The Republic of Nothing*

you're asleep, nothing bad will happen. At least that was the lesson that I learned from Mike. Since he slept almost all the time, very rarely did anything bad happen to him.

"Ian, son, your mother needs your help. She says I can't leave right now." His face was level with me now, parallel to the rough slate-grey floorboards. Underneath us in the crawl space, small waves crested and broke. As I lay there, face to the floor, I felt as if I was on an old sailing ship, far to sea.

"I know," I said. "I'm scared."

"You should be. It's not fit out there for the likes of you. But your mother's having some problems with her contractions." My father had become quite a literate man and had read books Bernie had loaned him, books on everything from alchemy to gynecology. My knowledge on these matters as well as my vocabulary was much more limited, so I assumed he said, "trouble with her contraptions," contraption being a favourite word of my father's concerning problems created by governments around the world. With a five-year-old's knowledge of anatomy, I could not begin to imagine what sort of machines were involved, biological or otherwise, in the delivery of a human child. Nonetheless, it revived in me a curiosity that caused me to open my eyes, convincing my father I was fully awake and aware of what he was asking.

"Your mother thinks the baby is coming out the wrong way. Nature'll do that to you. I don't know enough to help her. We can't go anywhere in this weather. Mrs. Bernie Todd will know what to do."

"Right," I said, crawling out from under my bed, still reluctant to let go of my sleeping dog, who I skidded out on all fours along with me.

"You've got to leave Mike here. He's too slow." Slow wasn't the word. Immobile and unconscious was more accurate. Reluctantly, my hand let go of the dog's collar, and he slumped to the floor, oblivious to the human drama.

As my father dressed me up in boots and rain gear, I could see that his hand was shaking. I could feel his ragged breath on my face and saw the worry in every inch of him. It's funny, but the fear in him somehow had the reverse effect in me. I felt suddenly adult, responsible, important — more important than I'd ever felt before. I was either about to help save my mother and her new baby or I was about to be swept up into the sky, never to return. My father rooted in the closet and found an old life jacket that he tied onto me with a piece of rope, tight under both armpits until I could feel the bite of the rope even through my oilskins.

My father began to slide the chesterfield away when my mother let out a piercing note of pain. "Wait. Not yet."

"What the hell do you mean, not yet?" my old man said.

But she just held up the flat of her hand and then motioned me to the bed. I went in to her. She held my head between two uplifted hands as if she was praying with my brains sandwiched between her outstretched fingers. And it was more than that. She was pushing back her own pain to use her special skills to determine for certain if I would make it or not.

I can still feel the way her hot palms felt against my ears and the way it made me hear my own blood pounding within my skull. I don't think I had heard my own heartbeat until then and wondered at this incredible magical drum that was beating in my head. Suddenly she relaxed her grip and lay back with a brief smile on her face, her eyes closed.

"Wait five minutes, then go," she said, sounding strangely matter-of-fact and certain. A spasm of pain gripped her, and my father grabbed onto her hand. He offered her a wooden spoon with a dish towel wrapped around it to put in her mouth, but my mother shook her head from one side to the other.

"Better get going, son," my father said, pointing to the door, unprotected now by the chesterfield and rattling at the hook that held it. It sounded like a madman was outside wanting to get in.

"Wait!" my mother screamed. My old man looked down at his watch.

"Your mother knows what she's saying."

The waiting was hard. I've never been good at waiting and never

From *The Republic of Nothing*

will be. Neither is my old man. If a thing needs to be done, better to do it than to stew over it. Still, my mother had an understanding of things. We had an old grandfather clock in the kitchen that ticked away. Five minutes, five years, it was all the same. I was growing older, more frightened, more certain that we would all die in the storm. Why couldn't I just go outside, get launched into space and be done with it?

"Four minutes," my father said. My mother was having more difficulty with her contraptions. Only four more decades to go before I could leave and do my duty. Just then a gust of wind, stronger than anything we'd felt yet, slammed into the house like a runaway truck. I looked out the window just in time to see the entire roof lift off the shed and catapult out into the road. The very house itself, stationed as it was atop loose stone and held to earth only by the basic contract with gravity, lifted up, I believe, ever so slightly. It was enough to wake Mike and make him howl like the living dead.

"It's a girl. Her name is Casey," my mother said. "It's turning out all right because Mrs. Bernie Todd is here."

For a moment my father was stunned. After their many years together he was still having a hard time adjusting to my mother speaking of the future in the present tense. No baby had been born. No miracles performed in righting the position of my little sister. *Little sister?* God, now the pain had a sex and a name. But there was a big unsaid *if* in there, and that was Mrs. Bernie Todd. And the *if* depended on me, my legs and my ability to fend off a hurricane. My father looked at the clock. My mother seemed unable to talk. She tried the spoon in her mouth but spit it out right away and bit hard into my father's wrist, drawing blood. The time had come for action. "Go!" my old man shouted.

I was like a cannonball fired out of a cannon. I vaulted for the door, threw it open, gave myself a quarter of a second to survey the nightmare that was once my yard. "Run!" my father shouted at me, as he rushed for the door and shoved it closed behind me. I took a big leap to get off to a good running start, fell headlong into a foot of seawater, lost my bearings and came up sucking for air. I cleared the water from my face and rolled over, only to find that the life jacket made my body float, and I was being carried across the ocean of our yard to who knows where. My old man was halfway out the door to help when I righted myself, got my feet on the ground beneath the water and leaned hard into the wind. The harder I leaned into the wind, the more it held me up. I was momentarily overcome by the exquisitely terrifying and beautiful vision that if I leaned far enough, my feet would simply leave the earth and I would be in flight. I convinced myself that I was about to be turned into a bird and swept away to some distant world, never to be heard from again. I tried to walk and couldn't. I tried again and again. My father was inside, at the window now, shouting something to me through the glass, but I could hear none of it.

The roar of the wind and the pounding waves was a sound beyond anything which I had experienced. I found myself stuck, tilting ahead, locked against wind, afraid to lean back, afraid to fall down and float off. My mind wrestled with this impossibility until the wind slapped me with a smack of cold seaweed and turned my head. There, ten feet away, was a granite outcropping. It was behind me but created a ridge against the sea, a jagged buttress of stone that ran an erratic but inevitable course from our house to that of my grandmother. This path had been left here, devised long ago by the glacier, designated for no other purpose than this, so that a small boy in an evil storm could save his mother and his sister from a tortured death.

I leaned left, began to tack towards the rocks. A gust hit me. I fell, as before, onto my back and floated upside down. I scrambled over onto all fours and crawled through the shallow water. At last I made headway, and finally I found my granite shelter. As soon as I tucked in behind the ridge, I felt some semblance of control. I ran, stumbled, slipped and floundered onward, not stopping again to look back.

I had never felt so fully alive, so fully human, before that moment in my life. I could barely breathe, the very wind stealing oxygen away from my lungs. I tore up the rain gear, bloodied my

From *The Republic of Nothing*

67

knees and elbows and was sure I was blinded more than once by the salt water and rain. Minutes or hours, who knows? But I made it. I raced across a final open space with the wind at my back, ready to drive me like a spike into the side of the house. I slammed hard into the heavy wooden door of the great stone house, having been lucky enough to aim for the only available wood of an otherwise impregnable wall of stone. Jack Todd heard the encounter and looked out, saw me slumped at the doorstep. Together, he and Bernie shoved open the door against the weight of my body and pulled me in.

I said nothing. Mrs. Bernie Todd asked her husband to find her medical bag. He ran to another room as I sprawled on the floor, dizzy, possibly delirious. I believed that I was still out racing and fighting the wind, and I felt as if I was looking down at my body contorted on the floor of this place. Bernie did a strange thing. She uncorked a bottle of rum, measured out two tablespoons into a glass, sat me upright against the wall and forced me to drink. "Your grandmother insists that you swallow it hard." This was the first time that she had ever actually called herself my grandmother. In the other room, rattling through a closet, was my grandfather.

It was my first encounter with the demon rum, and I assumed that someone had just lit up a fire on my tongue and sent boiling oil down my throat. Had it been anyone else but Bernie, I would have spit it out, but Mrs. Bernie Todd was not a woman to mess around with. She made quick and absolute decisions on her behalf and for others and did not tolerate complainers. As my mind reeled and my stomach burned, I felt the alcohol eventually light fire to my brain, where it burned bright as a summer sun. I stood up, saw before me my grandmother and grandfather. "The baby's coming out the wrong way," I said.

"Breech," my grandmother said.

"If you get there in time, it will be a girl. Her name is Casey," I told her. She immediately understood these to be the words of my mother.

"Good, let's attend to your little sister."

My grandfather shoved open the door. It flapped back hard

against the wall. My grandfather, with a far-away look in his eye, held hard onto my hand, and we followed my grandmother out into the blast, never turning to try to close the door. As Bernie started for her car, I instead pointed to the ridge, for I knew that the road must be even deeper in flood. And it was a longer drive as well. My route was a shortcut. She immediately knew I was right. Jack held on hard to my hand, his eyes fixed firmly on the back of my grandmother.

Almost the minute we were inside my home, a curious thing happened. The wind abated and a brooding, unnatural quiet began to settle over us. The seas still boomed baritone in the background, of course, but the battle of our house to hold itself together against the blast had subsided. Bernie was not two feet in the house when she saw my father's desperate face. My mother was screaming and my father was bent over her, between her legs. The sight of a woman in labour from any angle is a startling vision for anyone, but especially startling for a five-year-old. My father had his arm up between my mother's legs, which were spread wide. His hand was inserted up to his wrist, and the pain on his face almost equalled that of my mother.

Bernie went immediately into the room, saw the crisis. At my mother's instructions, and fearing we would be too late, my father had inserted his hand into the uterus to try to turn the baby around. "Let me take over," Bernie said in her confident, clinical manner.

"I can't," my father said.

She nodded. Bernie pulled out the bottle of rum, gave my mother a sip and one to my father. "Everybody just relax," she said.

By then we were dead centre in the eye of the hurricane. "Stay or leave the room as you see fit," my grandmother said to both my grandfather and me. Jack took my hand and we both sat off to one side, not leaving. Bernie put her hand on my mother's belly and studied the opening that would bring my little sister into the world.

Something new hit our front door. Not wind this time but wave. The door held, but water gushed in over the doorstep, and, if that wasn't enough, the wave rolling under the house forced water up

From *The Republic of Nothing*

69

through the floorboards with such intensity that the room was alive with veritable fountains of seawater.

"That's not important," Bernie said, pulling a scalpel from her bag, shoving it into the flame of the kerosene lamp and cleaning it with rum.

My grandfather saw what was about to happen and tried to distract me with a story. "Sometimes, Ian," he began in a soft, controlled voice, "in the nineteenth century, ships out to sea for months in the Indian Ocean would be so dry that the boards would begin to separate and the corking would not hold. They would begin to leak at every seam at once. Just like this. And sometimes the ship would simply pull itself apart, board by board, until all her sailors would have to swim for it. Of course, you don't last long in the Indian Ocean with so many sharks. Not unless you can surround yourself with a pod of dolphins or come upon a sperm whale willing to give you transit home."

But the story was not enough. I twisted my head around to see that the scalpel had made a slit and the blood had begun to flow. My mother's face told the story in greater depth. She was tired now, pale, panting hard. Whereas before she was pushing during her contraption, now she looked weak, defeated. "Keep your hand on the baby," Bernie insisted, even though she saw later that she had also cut hard into the flesh of my father's wrist. The blood of my family was everywhere on the bed in pools of red that began to drip down onto the seawater on the floor. Another wave hit the house, this time with amazing force. My grandfather seemed quite calm, or maybe he was faking it, for it was his job to keep panic at bay. "They had storms like this all the time in the nineteenth century. Things were much tougher back then. Men had to be able to rig a mast in a hurricane and single-handedly sail a schooner in a typhoon wind."

Bernie was helping my father shift the baby around now. My mother gave one final, feeble push, but then sank back, I'm sure unconscious by now, exhausted. It seemed almost as if they were wrestling little Casey into the world, that she was refusing to come, that nature was against us every step of the way and unwilling to let her waiting soul depart from wherever she was at.

And then I saw her arrive, bottom-first into the world. "Don't pull," Bernie shouted, as my father tried to pick her up, blood still dripping heavily from his cut wrist. "The cord is wrapped around the neck," Bernie said. "Be very still."

The baby was barely out as Bernie began to unwind the umbilical cord that could yet strangle my sister. Bernie then immediately put her fingers inside the mouth of the child and turned her upside down, holding her from the heels, and spanked a gentle but firm smack on the bum. My father sucked in his breath, heard the baby cry and fell backwards into the water on the floor. As Bernie cut the umbilical cord with the scalpel, my grandfather picked up my father, discovered how badly he was bleeding from the wrist and began to wind a bandage tightly. He staggered back to his feet and up to my mother. He kissed her cheek, found it clammy and screamed. "Bernie, I think she's dying!"

Bernie handed me the baby, wrapped only in a single, bloody piece of ripped sheet. She was coated with blood and mucous, and, despite that, I held the tiny, bluish face close to my cheek and began to sing, "Old McDonald had a farm."

When the next rolling wave, more powerful than the last, slammed into our house, I saw my grandfather trying to stop the bleeding of my father while Bernie was pushing air into my mother's lungs with her own mouth. My father, at that minute, looked out the window and, with a vision of pure terror in his eyes, pleaded with some unnamed, unseen force to allow his wife to live.

The eye of a hurricane is an incongruous event in the middle of such turmoil. Even as the next wave, weaker now than the last, made a dull thud into the walls of our house, the sun broke through and sent down a single shaft of light into our yard which was now part of the Atlantic Ocean. The light spilled almost gently into the water of the front yard, and little Casey ceased her crying and fell asleep in my arms, perfectly contented, it would seem, to have been born amidst this holocaust.

My mother coughed and vomited and began to breathe, and my father sat down beside her and put his arm around her. Bernie

From *The Republic of Nothing*

pulled out needle and thread and began to stitch my mother back together. I had to turn away. I could not watch, but I held tightly onto the little bundle of flesh and life that was my sister.

And when the hurricane returned and we were all, in varying degrees, alive, I gave my little sister to my father to hold, and he could not stop himself from smiling. He began to tell her that she had been more than a little trouble, but that it's probably a good sign of a busy, challenging life to come. Bernie and Jack made some tea, poured some more rum and kept vigil as I curled up under my bed, even though the floorboards leaked water, because that's where Mike was still sleeping through it all, like it was no big deal. I rested my head on Mike's mangy back and listened to his sad, soft snore and fell asleep through the next blast of wind and wave, wondering if this was the normal way of the world, wondering perhaps if it would be like this every day from here on, if the easy times were behind me.

From *The Republic of Nothing*

# DRAGON'S BREATH

So Delaney O'Neil was alive again. The great gaps in his memory concerning his life as Duke and his life as Grandfather O'Neil seemed insignificant. If he was crazy, then I suppose he was no more or less so than the rest of us. Once school had started up again, I'd swing past Gwen's house to walk her to the bus, and her grandfather would be standing outside their door, his arms out in a welcoming V toward the sunrise. If I asked him what he was doing, he'd only say he was "embracing the star that feeds us light." A poet he was. The words were stored up inside him, and the beauty of them leaked out in aphorisms and metaphors, but his true identity was a cocoon inside his heart. When his granddaughter kissed him goodbye, I thought he would take wings and fly into the sun.

"Step only on the light-coloured rocks," he would offer for advice. "This is what I call the Lesson of Nova Scotia. They won't teach you that in school, though." What he meant, of course, was that if you were walking along the coast at the tide's retreat, the light-coloured rocks would be dry. The darker stones were likely wet and covered with a film of sea algae that could dance you to your death if you weren't careful. And, thus far, the dark rocks were all that Duke Delaney O'Neil had found to fear on the island, for he had tumbled twice and tapped his skull on stone as a result. This was when he had learned what he called his Lesson of Nova Scotia.

Despite my part in the heroic retrieval of her grandfather from the dark realm of nothingness, Gwen and I remained only friends, not that other unspoken thing that should have been. Gwen was taller than me, and her true shape was finding her. The other boys noticed, and I could not shelter her from the attentions of the older ones, the landlubber no-goods with hearts like fists who talked of hunting and killing for fun, the ones who lived near the highway and bragged of television in their homes, of frequent family shopping sprees to Dartmouth, the boys with metal-toed boots who carried knives and, on weekends, ran chainsaws to cut cordwood for sheer machismo pleasure.

Gwen could probably have leaped three grades ahead of me if anyone had ever tested us, but she held back, for me perhaps, and never showed off her great intelligence and hidden wealth of wonderful but seemingly irrelevant knowledge. Only after a gruelling, boring day of school, after the tedium of memorizing math, after the competitions of seeing who could accumulate the most spitballs stuck to the high Victorian ceiling, after the stares of monster boys at Gwen's beautiful features, after the afternoon lectures on improbable inland provinces like Saskatchewan and Manitoba, after the final spelling quiz with words like "diaper" and "envelope," then and only then, released from the regimented torture of the classroom, would Gwen walk with and only with me to the bus, point up to the nimbus-covered remnant of the same sun her grandfather had embraced that morning and remind me: "Ninety-three million miles." I knew precisely what she meant and exactly why she and I had been positioned in a perfect synchronization that far from a medium-strength sun wobbling around somewhere in the suburbs of the Milky Way.

My father had written two letters, both short, both disturbingly skeletal. The first:

Dear Dorothy, Ian and Casey,
   Sorry for the silence. Very busy times as I find my footing here. Powerful men all around me who need

taming. I haven't yet found the tools I need here for the job. Coming home soon with a surprise.

Love, Dad

"He's bringing home a dragon," Casey said. Lately she had been having a lot of dreams about friendly, fire-breathing dragons and lonely dinosaurs. She missed her father desperately — the gruff voice, the flaming red hair, the brush of his coarse unshaven cheek against hers like a store-bought rasp file, rough enough to leave her scratched but bubbling with love.

"There might be dragons in Halifax," my mother would answer. "If there are any there, I'm sure your father could find one, and I'm sure he would bring it home to you."

The second letter was much like the first. It arrived two weeks after I returned from New York.

Dorothy and Kids,

I trust Ian made it home from New York. He never stopped to see me on his way back. I was looking forward to it. No harm done. The boy's changing. Growing. How's Casey? Any leaks in the roof? Be home by the end of September. Let me know if you need anything. You'll all like the surprise.

Love, Dad

My father arrived home at nine a.m. on the thirtieth day of September. He was driving a dragon, or something close to it, a burgundy red '57 Buick with a bumper and grill that could only have been fashioned in a dream by Casey herself. She recognized the car immediately; much to her delight, the dragon was accompanied by smoke. The second he arrived, my father had to pop open the hood, and a black cloud of smoke issued forth.

"Just a fanbelt, nothing serious," he said as we breathed in the acrid, exotic smell of burnt rubber. I think I'll always remember that smell coupled with the sight of my father, the new man. Most things

From *The Republic of Nothing*

new and unexpected seemed to fit in easily on our island — the washed-up clothes and furniture, the refugees, the resurrection of a dog or the arrival of a replacement grandfather. But this was different. My father was wearing a suit and a tie. My mother, standing behind us in the doorway, had turned to stone. Casey stopped in her tracks as she ran toward the man who must certainly be her father. Even when I had met him coming out of the sooty Halifax Legislature building, he had not been wearing a suit. Now this. *What had they done to him?*

Reaching his arm down into the smoky engine pit of the car, he lifted out a black snake that had once been the fanbelt. But it wasn't the car or the snake that had stolen our ability to speak. It was the change in the way my father looked that shocked us. I decided that it was up to me to break the spell. "Need a new one of them, I reckon," I said, taking charge of the morning panic, wanting to grab the source of the crisis by the tail and whip reality back into place. Reading my message, my father looked at the fanbelt, then down at his clothes. He loosened his tie and flipped it up over his head like a sloppy noose, like a man trying to decline the offer of a hanging. Then he tossed me the fanbelt, which landed, still hot and smoking, in my hand. "Here, Ian," he said. "A souvenir. We'll make another one out of rope and lash it on to get me to the Irving station in Musquodoboit."

I smiled. My old man took off his coat and vest, threw them back into the car. He tossed me his tie. "Didn't mean to scare you. Just a little costume I bought for the job." He was looking at Casey now. "Y'know? Like Halloween."

"Yeah. Like Halloween," Casey answered and now ran to her father, who raised her to him and hugged her breathless. My mother unhinged herself from the doorway, and everyone acted as if things were back to normal. Perhaps they were. I held the fanbelt in one hand, my old man's tie in the other. The dragon was cooling off. I ran my hand along the sleek, bulging fender. It reminded me more of a sexy woman than a dragon now. But it remained an alien thing, certainly not something of our shore.

My mother did not reveal her loneliness, I don't think, to the man who had pulled her from the sea so many years ago. At supper she spoke of the unusual alignment of Saturn and Neptune and how we had just had a full moon fall within the same month coupled with the highest tides she had ever seen. "It was one of those times when you just wanted to hold your breath and wait for the world to be swallowed by water," she said. "I could see it in my mind as clear as daylight in July."

"You should see what a full moon does to the men in the goddamn legislature," my father said. "I've seen two men actually start barking at each other right in the middle of a debate concerning taxes on a pulp mill in Pictou County. Barking, I tell you."

"A dog is not so much worse than a man," my mother responded without surprise.

"I saw the face of the man in the moon," Casey added, wanting to get in on the dialogue concerning lunar effects. "He talked to me. He told me that he was very sad for everything on earth because he could see us all down here night after night, but we were too far away to talk to. He said he was happiest, though, when the sky squeezed him down to a sliver, and he could shut one eye and go to sleep."

It's funny that I hadn't been paying much attention to the moon because I was, by nature, a tidal person. I knew almost without looking if it was high tide or low tide. I knew it sitting in school even miles from shore. I had spent so much of my life around the cycles of tides. I knew their patience, their unquenchable thirst for shoreline, their resigned retreats. I knew that a certain moon pushed waves higher, a certain moon of another sort slipped the sea edge far out to lumpy, kelp-laden rocks and left the old shoreline high and dry.

A silence pursued us at dessert. It had been chasing us like a wolf all through the meal, but we had been fending it off with small talk. "Do you like the car?" *Uh huh.* "How's the well holding?" *Fine.* "Anything new?" *Not much. The usual.* Finally, my father met the wolf head on, leaning from the table to sneeze from too much pepper. He always shook pepper onto a piece of crabapple pie. His sneeze sounded like a yelp, and after he had launched the air out of his lungs he said, "What would all of you think about moving to Halifax?"

It could have been worse. He could have said that we would wake up tomorrow and the sun would never shine again, that the moon would never show its sad, expressive face to Casey again or that the sea would dry up for good. I think I had believed that my father's brief infatuation with provincial politics would end as abruptly as it started, that he would shake himself like a dog shaking off seawater on the beach, come to his senses and retrieve himself from Halifax. But I had never expected this.

"No," my mother said. Her voice was barely audible. I don't think my father heard. Or wanted to hear. *No*, I tried to shout but nothing came out. I was thinking of the island, of Gwen, of Hants, of Ben Ackerman. I was thinking of me.

No, he had not heard a thing, not even the wolf silently howling at the door. "I was just thinking," he continued, "of all the opportunities there for Ian, and of course there's better schools. And we'd have more time together — when I'm not in caucus or dealing with constituency problems." He might as well have been speaking Arabic. I don't think any of us knew what a constituency was or what sort of problems it had. Dandruff? Injured limbs? Mental disorders?

"There comes a time in a man's life," he proceeded to orate, "when his perception shifts suddenly and new light comes at him, light he's never seen before . . . and understanding."

"Understanding," my mother repeated now, her voice a bird that had flown about the room, flapping frantic silent wings until it had found its way back to the cage of her mouth, where it sang a troubled tune. "Understanding is knowing what is true."

Did the words mean anything? Casey stabbed her pie with the fork and began to disembowel it. I shifted uneasily in my seat. *Understanding*. What did I understand about anything now that my father was trying to pull us off the island with him?

"John G.D. took me to have a private lunch with the premier, just the three of us. The premier had some news. He said the party — that he himself was behind it — was grooming me for leadership." Here was that strange word that I had heard before.

"Grooming?" my mother asked.

I thought of horses or girls with long soft hair. I looked at the new man, the groomed MLA. Yes, his hair was more closely cropped and his cheek more finely shaven than before, right down to a red, almost polished neck where all the hairs had been pruned down to the skin. The top button on his shirt was still tight, tight up against the red, ruddy skin where a razor had lopped off what God had grown there.

"The premier is going to take a senate seat soon in Ottawa and they'll need someone new, someone fresh. Someone with a vision."

A grey pall fell over the room. How had the change happened so quickly? It was hard to tell. My father, an anarchist with a fishing boat a few scant months ago, a man who had carved an imaginary country off of Canada and set us adrift in a happy peaceful kingdom, was now turning Haligonian, turning landlubber, turning into a politician, a Tory, a man being "groomed" to be premier.

"Why is it you have to become premier?" I asked. I wanted more information, some key to understanding the change and why my father was willing to uproot us and destroy our happy lives.

"I told John G.D. and the premier about my ideas. The premier said they were good ideas, but that the public wasn't quite ready for them. Perhaps, though, he said, there would come a time when I could put them into practice. In the meantime, all I would have to do was keep my loyalty to the party, and do the best I could at my job."

"What *is* your job?" my mother asked, staring hard into the window beside her, at the old, almost liquid pane of nineteenth-century glass that had actually distorted itself as a result of gravity. Perhaps she saw the wolf that we all felt to be haunting us at dinner.

"My job is to help people. I can help a whole lot more people if I'm in Halifax. Look, I haven't changed anything I believe in. I'm just learning the ropes so I can be effective. You'll see." He was sounding defensive now.

From *The Republic of Nothing*

"I'm not sure I understand," my mother said.

"The ways of the outside world are not the ways of Whalebone Island," he said, trying to explain. But it explained nothing. For the first time in my life, my father's words sounded hollow to me. I watched my mother for a response. She continued to stare at the pane in the window. If I hadn't followed her glance at that second, I would not have seen it and said it had been there all along, but what happened then was real. The glass cracked, a thin, diagonal line ran southeast to northwest.

"I asked the moon once," Casey said out loud, "why you were in Halifax, Daddy?"

"And what did the moon say, Casey?" my father asked, happy to be distracted.

"The moon said that you were tired of being happy, and you went there to look for something to make you sad."

My father laughed. "The moon likes to play tricks on you," he said. "I'm happy in Halifax. Would you like to live in Halifax, Casey?"

"No," Casey said. "I don't think the moon would talk to me any more if I lived there."


That night we dreamed of dragons breathing black smoke and wolves with long saliva-dripping tongues and a moon who spoke truth to us through a shattered pane of very old liquid glass. In the morning there was no sun, just a ceiling of low grey cloud fringed in dark blue-black lace. I heard barking and howling and finally the shot of a gun which jolted me awake. My father was out the door before me, and I was behind him as we ran in the direction of the second gunshot. "It's coming from over by Hants's place," my father said. I could see now that it was my old familiar father who had returned, for he had forgotten altogether about the car, which would have made our journey quicker, fanbelt or not.

When we got to Hants Buckler's wharf we saw Hants standing in his long johns in front of what was left of the skeletal elephant.

He had blood dripping from one leg in a steady stream, and he held a shotgun aimed straight at the sky. "Sonsabitches tore it apart," he said. We could still hear yapping dogs in the distance.

"What did it?" I asked.

"Dogs from the mainland. Big German shepherds with eyes given to them by the devil and teeth stolen from a god-damn barracuda." He looked down at the wounds on his legs. "They went for the elephant bones first, and after that, I guess they wanted a taste of fresher marrow."

"How many were there?" my father asked.

"Ten. Ten dogs the size of hammerhead sharks. Mean mothers too. Look at what they did."

The dogs had truly managed to ruin the great work of elephant bones. They must have jumped up and wrenched the ankle bone from the elephant and then gone crazy enough to rattle the thing down, the great monument that had been Hants Buckler's pride and joy. Bones were scattered everywhere. And at Buckler's doorstep were the remains of his pet seagull, Gilbert. The dogs had surprised the poor thing and torn it to bloody pieces before it had a chance to get out of the way. Hants just shook his head. "When I opened the door, they jumped me, the sons of bloody bitches, and tore into my legs. They had teeth like ice picks." He showed us his leg, and my father stopped to look at it, but Hants pulled back. "I wanted to kill them but couldn't," Hants said. "Once you start to kill a thing, even a brute like one of them beasts, you never know what happens to you. It takes restraint at time like this. But I fired the gun to chase them off."

We helped to patch up Hants and get him settled down with a cup of tea mixed half and half with rum. We offered to take him to Mrs. Bernie Todd for a more perfect, professional repair, but he'd have none of it. "A body knows how to repair itself, " he said. "Can't blame the dogs," he said. "Can only blame the master."

We all knew who owned the dogs. When we left, we took the inland route back to the house. We skirted the bog, and my father pointed to something, a freshly pawed hole out in the middle. We slogged through it to where the Viking had lain asleep so many years. Sure enough, the dogs had dug here, too, and the leather of the face and a section of the shoulder had been chewed off. It seemed incredible that dogs would sniff out a dead man after so many centuries. The Viking was still to remain our secret, and so we shovelled the mud and peat back over him, somehow believing that we were still protecting the lost legacy of the island.

"Burnet's old man raises them for hunting but doesn't hardly feed 'em," I said. "He kicks 'em about and teaches them to be vicious. This was the first time that I know of, though, that they came on the island."

"They'll be back now. We can't let that happen. I'll go talk to Burnet McCully."

But I could have told him there was no talking. The Burnet McCullys were the kind of people that took whatever they could from the world, gave nothing back and then dumped what was left out their back step. I insisted that I be there when my father confronted Burnet's old man. They lived together, father and son, the two of them without a wife or mother.

The next morning my father and I went to confront Burnet Sr. The dogs were in the back yard now, all chained to a single post, snarling and biting at each other. Mr. McCully looked like he had maybe slept the night with the pack of dogs in a bed, he looked so dishevelled and disoriented. My father played it cool. The damage was explained with a clinical, unemotional tone, for it was clear that my father had learned a trick or two of emotional control in the legislature. "What do you think we can do to prevent this from happening again, and how do you plan on repaying Hants Buckler?" my father asked with the greatest decorum. McCully just stood mute. Burnet Jr. was awake now and pushed out the front door, past his old man, and began to piss on the ground alongside of where I stood. Mr. McCully had one wild eye that just sort of roamed about while the other was fixed like a vulture on my father.

Burnet Jr. was zipping up his fly and snickering like my father had just told some great joke. His own father was coughing and calling up a big wad of phlegm that he spit directly on the ground with a reptile-like hissing sound. "Not my problem," he said. "Just the nature of a dog. I ain't doing a damn thing."

"There are laws that deal with this sort of thing," my father said. Inside him a volcano raged, but on the surface he was the Halifax diplomat. Here was the ultimate anarchist speaking about law and order to a Neanderthal.

Young Burnet picked up an axe from a chopping block and began to split kindling with such malice I expected the wood to cry out in pain. My father studied the vile face of Burnet Sr. a minute and then looked down at me, as if waiting for me to suggest some alternative. I had nothing to offer. I was scared. Something about Burnet and his old man had always scared me — they were brutal, stupid and uncaring. Nothing on the island or in nature rivalled them. At that minute, I hated them both to the bottom of my being.

"Get out of here. And take your skinny kid," McCully snarled.

But my father was not to leave so easily. His face was a study of cool intelligence and reason. "I'm sorry you'll have to see this," he said to me and walked toward the dogs chained behind the house.

Without so much as blinking an eye, my father walked into the midst of the pack of them, picked up the biggest, meanest German shepherd and yanked its leash from the stake. He held the dog's head as he carried it towards Big Man Burnet. He had one arm fixed across its squirming body, the other hand gripping the head tightly with an arm across the neck. I thought I knew what he was about to do. It seemed like a terrible thing, an inhumane thing for any man to do even under the circumstances. My father had always been a powerfully strong man. His days in Halifax had not atrophied his solid muscles; they could not undo years of hauling nets, loading lobster traps and doing the work of the island and the sea.

I wanted to say no. He was about to snap the dog's neck in half right in front of Burnet. Like Hants Buckler, I suddenly felt sorry for the beast. I didn't believe it was the fault of a whipped, maltreated dog that it did what it did. Old man Burnet looked my

From *The Republic of Nothing*

83

father straight in the eye, daring him. A faint, sinister grin seemed to appear, and as his mouth cracked open, a thin bead of dirty, tobacco-coloured drool slipped out of the side. He was pushing my father to do it. He wanted it to happen and wanted to watch the powder keg of violence set off in uppity old Everett McQuade. "Do you care what happens to this dog?" my father asked. I could hear his voice quivering ever so slightly now. There was anger and hostility pent up in there.

I watched Burnet Jr. pick up the axe now and wield it like a weapon in front of him, ready to pounce, to lop off my head, maybe, or chop my father and me in two.

"I don't give a shit what happens to that dog," Burnet Sr. answered, taunting, trying to push my father over the edge so that he'd have cause to rip into the bloody politician with his own teeth and tear him limb from limb.

"Seems to me all this dog needs is a little something to eat. He's half-starved," my father said. And with a quick, sudden motion, he wrenched hard on the dog's neck, pushing it forward toward Burnet Sr. until the creature's muzzle was square in Burnet's crotch. Then, quick as lightning, my father let go of the dog's head as it chomped down hard on the first thing in its vicinity. McCully fell backwards as his son ran to pull the dog off his old man, who lay howling on the step. As we walked away, my father repeated the words of Hants Buckler. "Can't blame the dog," he said. "Can only blame the master."


My father seemed particularly rejuvenated as we stood on the little bridge after the incident. "In a true anarchy, Ian, you have this problem about freedom. If everyone is free to do what they want, every once in a while you have some asshole, like Burnet there, whose *freedom* causes trouble for someone else. Then somebody has to set things straight or you have an unfair system. Otherwise you have to start creating a bunch of laws and good people start to lose their personal independence."

I guess I didn't realize just then that my father was himself a law-maker — that was what the legislature was all about. Up until that minute I don't think he had ever seen himself as such. He got elected on a fluke and wanted to change the world. He didn't want to make a bunch of laws.

"Without laws, though, who decides on the punishment?" I discovered that I was unconsciously holding onto my crotch, still imagining what it must feel like to have a full- grown, razor-toothed German shepherd lunge at your privates and take a deep bite.

"Me," my father said. "Somebody had to do something or those damn dogs might have gone back one night and killed Hants Buck-ler." He seemed almost smug now. Even at my age, I could see through his logic. Something was wrong. We both looked down at the clear, cold water flowing toward the sea beneath the bridge. It carried a beautiful mane of long, flowing, green, gold and reddish seaweed. "Necum teuch," my father said. "That's how the Micmac would have described this stream. Meant 'hair of the dead.'"

As I looked into the water, I could see what the Micmac had seen. Long flowing hair in the channel, long-gone remains of their ancestors, still with them or trying to find their way back to the surface of the earth.

"That doctor friend of yours?"

"Ben. Ben Ackerman," I reminded him.

"Think he knows how to stitch up a man's pecker?" I thought that my father had lost his conscience in Halifax, but something in the little creek reminded him. The dead Indians were speaking, maybe. *It's not fair to let a man die because he doesn't take good care of his dogs.*

"He's a doctor," I said, shrugging.

"I wouldn't want even Burnet to bleed to death."

Ben was meditating in his kitchen when we got there. My father was a little uneasy around him at first, just like before, but I could see that they liked each other. My old man told him what had happened. "I guess I got a bit carried away," he admitted.

"We better get over there quick," Ben said.

Back at the Burnet house, my father and I stood out front while Ackerman knocked on the door, explained who he was and went in. Burnet Jr. let him in and scowled out at me. I knew I was going to pay for this somehow, on the bus or at school. It's one thing for fathers to feud, another what kids have to live with and suffer.

Afterwards, on the walk back, Ben said that Burnet Sr. would be okay. "Gonna hurt like hell to piss for a while though. Couple places the teeth went clean through."

My father hung his head.

"Don't you think your measures were a little strong?" Ben asked.

"It was a political act," my father said. "Besides, those dogs don't even get fed proper."

Ben laughed. They did like each other. I had a funny feeling about it, though, as I slipped behind and watched the two men walk ahead of me. My mind was conjuring up a comparison of the two, and it occurred to me that I knew Ben Ackerman, with all his well-intended lies and half-true past, better than my own father. And it scared me more than staring down Burnet Jr. from thirty paces outside his doorstep.

The dragon was asleep and didn't wake until after lunch, when my father had lashed his tie around the pulleys and started up the car. No smoke this time. And then the dragon took my father away. He had said no more of Halifax, of moving. My mother was resolute about that, and there would be no persuading her. None of us wanted him to go. We all hoped that it was just a phase of madness, that he would quit, give up his seat in the legislature. I wanted things to be like before. We were island people, ready to welcome the refugees of the world but reluctant to lose a father to the mainland, to the world. The dragon was a promise that he'd return more often, that we'd see more of him, but it was also a reminder that he had joined another society, one that spent time behind the wheel of a gasoline-powered machine, that ate in restaurants and slept in homes rented from strangers.

Later that night when the manic yelping began, I thought I was still dreaming of the day's events. I opened one eye as I lay in bed and saw the full moon through my window. There were howls and barking. The dogs were out there again, prowling the island despite my father's lesson. I thought of my old pup, Mike, who had survived the hurricane with me, that gentle, dumb dog so full of loyalty and happy for a scrap of anything. He'd been dead for several years now, and I wondered how a dog could be so corrupted by its master to become like these creatures of Burnet's.

My father was gone. We were alone: Casey, my mother and I. The barking of dogs came closer. Would they go after Hants again, break down his door and attack him in his sleep? Or had they found their way to my home? At least one had tasted human blood, possibly more. Could dogs with strong savage motivation kill one of us? I was sure that these dogs certainly could. I wanted it all to go away. I wanted to slip back into bed and fall asleep, but as I peered out into the moonlit yard, all at once one of the monster dogs lunged at my window with a horrific yelp. It smashed its face right up against the glass until I could hear its teeth click hard on the pane. It scared the living daylights out of me, and I fell backwards off my bed onto the floor. My heart was racing.

There was no gun in the house. My mother refused to allow one. Suddenly, Casey burst through the door and ran over to me, threw her arms around me and hugged me with all her might. She was crying. The dog threw itself at the glass again. It would find a way in. A window wouldn't stop it. I stood up, sat Casey down in a chair and threw on some pants. I surveyed my room for weapons. Not even a baseball bat. A collection of beach stones was the best I had. I picked up one the size of an orange and tried to borrow strength from it as I held it in my hands. Looking out the window,

From *The Republic of Nothing*
87

I could see someone standing outside. Not a man. A boy. Burnet Jr. This was his doing, not his father's. And now I realized that this one was my battle, my test. My father was gone. I felt helpless. I didn't have his politics, his strength or his courage.

My mother was in my doorway now, wearing her long blue gown, her nightcoat. She saw the rock in my hand and my other arm around Casey. There was no fear in her eyes, only indignation. I stood upright and wanted to say something. I wanted to say, "I'll take care of it," but I wasn't as good a liar as Ben Ackerman, and I was scared. Scared of the dogs, scared of Burnet as I realized that my father's ability to settle problems in the Republic of Nothing had diminished to nothing in his absence. It was not a place for part-time presidents and simple violent solutions. But then there was my mother.

My mother in the moonlight is a vision of beauty and power — strange, maybe even dark power. She speaks little to us, but you get the feeling that she is in communion with distant voices, maybe the dead Micmac below the streams, maybe the unnamed voices of her confused past. To some strangers, my mother is so frightening in her ethereal presence that they simply leave without speaking to her. Others, like Ackerman, are drawn to the dark beauty and power that she carries.

The dogs were crashing at the door now. It sounded like the thrashing of monsters. I was reminded of the wind during the night Casey was born. A hurricane of dogs was assaulting our house. Typically the door was not locked and was held in place by a simple hook. It sounded like a battering ram was pummelling the wood. "Fear is always the worst of it," my mother said. "Once you're past the fear, things begin to fall into place."

And with that she left us, closing the door to my room behind her. I heard the ranting, growling, thirsting-for-blood madness of the dogs; I heard her footsteps across the kitchen floor, and I heard her unhooking the latch. The door creaked open, and then I heard nothing. The dogs went silent. In a panic I went back to my window. I couldn't see anything but a cold white moon and the silhouette of Burnet. Damn!

I opened my own door, closing it behind me with Casey still sobbing inside. My mother was nowhere in the kitchen. The outside door was wide open. I walked cautiously across a path of blue moonlight on the floor, expecting to feel teeth at my throat at any second, terrified that the dogs had already pulled my mother down. And then I was outside. She was there. Twenty feet away from me. She held her hands out, palms upward. They seemed white, glowing, but it was just the powerful light of the moon on her white skin. And the dogs were all lying down on the ground surrounding her, all ten of them. They might well have been dead for all appearances, but I knew they were simply asleep.

I would not speak and break whatever spell she had put on them. Burnet was now stumbling backwards, his mouth agape. He was watching my mother as she bent down and petted each dog ever so gently. I kept an eye on Burnet, afraid he might do something — throw a stone, a knife, pull out a gun, but he soon disappeared behind some rocks and was gone. He had been let off easier than his father.

I walked over to my mother, but she waved me away. Her eyes were cold blue fire in the moonlight, and I felt a severe chill creeping up from my fingertips. My mother saw my dread and gave me a warm, soft smile and waved me back towards the house. I said nothing. As I walked back, I heard a man running, panting in the quiet night air. It was Ben Ackerman. He had heard the dogs barking and come. When he saw my mother petting the sleeping dogs, he stopped in his tracks, didn't say a word.

The door to my house found me and I slipped back inside. I went to my room to tell Casey that everything was okay, but she was gone. In a panic I ran out to the other rooms, the kitchen, the living room. No Casey. Then I threw open the door to my parents' bedroom. Casey was in my mother's bed, asleep, and my mother was fast asleep beside her. I froze and tried to sort out the facts. It

From *The Republic of Nothing*

was simply impossible. But I would not wake them. Returning to the door and walking outside, I saw the dogs, gently loping away from the yard toward the bridge, toward Burnet's house. And on the dry cold stones of the driveway, I saw Ben standing all alone, peering straight into the moon, like Casey does, as if the man in the moon could offer him some satisfactory explanation.

# THE WRECK OF THE *SISTER THERESA*

Spring was in my old man's blood. He'd look out to sea and tell me that he couldn't stay here on shore another minute, that the world looked inside out when he was standing on a shoreline instead of looking at it from the sea. I was nine years old at the time, and I had learned how to look out at the blue horizon and give a long, plausible sigh, just like my father.

"What you see out there, Ian, is a man's dream taking form. Look at the thin, hazy edge where sea and sky melt together. You always try to find that place, but you never get there. I've almost touched the horizon with my finger once or twice, but it always found me out and sneaked off further to sea. I stopped trying once I married your mother. Your mother swam around in the sea once and said it was enough for her. She'd prefer a desert. That's why we got all them damn cactus."

I had understood about the cactus long ago. It was more the old man's palm tree growing in the rum barrel in the front room that worried me. "It's just a symbol," he told me.

"What say we go make a visit to Lambert and Eager," my father suggested.

I knew he would finally get around to it. And this year I would be allowed to go along. "Sweets," my old man announced to my mother, who was sitting in the kitchen sewing a new star onto the flag, "we're going over to see Eager and Lambert, maybe help them out today."

Mom looked sullen. But she knew she couldn't stop him nor me neither. "Just don't come home drowned and all bloated out like seals," she said with sandpaper in her voice.

"I'll make the boy wear a life preserver," my father announced. We didn't have any proper life jackets, so he harnessed a round cork life preserver onto my back. I didn't dare complain.

It was nearly seven-thirty when we arrived at Lambert's boat. There were maybe five hundred sea gulls asleep on the cabin. All the other skippers were already gone to sea. My old man knocked loudly on the door to the cabin, and in a few minutes out stumbled two of the hairiest, smelliest, arguingest men I'd ever seen.

Lambert and Eager were both short, stocky men with bloodshot eyes.

"I hope I didn't wake you," my father said.

"We've been up for hours," Lambert said. Lambert was the skipper. It was his boat.

Eager was second in command, but you could tell he was a professional complainer by trade. "I never seen such rotten weather," he said, looking up into a pure robin-egg-blue sky.

"Goin' out today?" my old man asked.

"Hell, we've been and back," Lambert said, a cold-blooded liar. Fishermen like to pretend they're always several steps ahead of anyone.

"That's too bad. Ian and I thought we might go along to help out."

Eager looked at the life preserver on my back. "What the hell is he supposed to be?"

"He's never been very far offshore before," my father replied, "especially not in a boat as big or fancy as the *Sister Theresa* here." He knew how to suck up to a guy like Lambert if he wanted to get his way.

"I suppose we could go out a second time for the tourist trade." It was an insult to my father, but he tried not to show the sting of it.

Instead he felt obliged to remind Lambert of his status on the island. "I've been thinking we don't have enough holidays here," my dad said, reminding them of who he was.

"That's right," Eager said. "Sonsabitches like Lambert here would work the balls off a mule deer if he could. Bastards like him gonna have labour unrest if'n we don't get a few more good holidays."

"I'll have to come up with a good occasion," my father said.

Of course, they hadn't been at sea yet that day, or possibly the day before, from the looks of things. "Fire up the engine. Then make some coffee," Lambert instructed Eager. "And don't forget to retard the spark."

Eager looked at me like it was all my fault. "What the frig you lookin' at?" he snarled.

I walked over to the rail and pretended to be studying the water. Someone in one of the fishing shacks flushed a toilet and a pipe nearby gave forth like Niagara Falls.

Lambert squinted at the logs of shit that hit the water just astern, plopping down like bombs dropped from a B-52. "Pretty soon that whole ocean'll be nothing but a cesspool. Got a mind to hook up the new power bilge to the end of that pipe and fire back a cannonade of sea water. There should be some kind of law."

My father said nothing. He was a devout anarchist, and, while he favoured creating holidays for events no more monumental than field mice having babies, he shunned the idea of too many limitations on human behaviour.

"Start up that damn thing and get us out of this septic tank!" Lambert yelled to Eager, who was still apparently intent on retarding the spark.

The engine coughed, gargled, backfired, then roared into life. Almost at once, the boat lurched forward. Lambert had only a split second to pull the coiled rope off the bulkhead.

My old man felt the first tweak of a sea breeze begin to tangle his hair as the boat moved south. His face lit up like a cherry bomb, and I knew it was going to be a good day.

"Caught over three ton of hake last week," Lambert lied. "We donated most of it to charity. The rest we sold for three cents a pound. If we wanted to we could retire, but the sea's in our blood."

Possibly there was sea water in there somewhere, because a lot of the fishermen around had a habit of mixing rum with cold sea water to take the edge off a day.

"Head her out past Rat Rock, Eag!" Lambert shouted.

"Aye aye, skipper," reported the helmsman, although I could see that the wheel was lashed onto an upright pole, and Eager was trying to light a fire under a soot-black coffee pot. The boat seemed to know where to go, and nobody was surprised too much about anything.

My father was looking back at the shoreline. I stood beside him, and he put a hand on my shoulder. "That shoreline has freedom written all over it." You could now see from one end of the island to the other. You could see Hants's old shack toward the east end, my own house at the west. In between were some other houses and lots of grey, jutting rocks and scrub spruce trees that pretended they belonged there to ward off the elements.

"Pretty as a picture," Lambert observed.

"Probably the only truly independent country in the entire world."

"Don't know," Lambert said, feeling argumentative. "I used to ship out to Africa on the steamers. Ended up in a place near the Equator where the women didn't wear nothing and didn't care who did what when. Figured that was independence."

My father nodded. "All depends on what's in the heart of a man," he answered. Lambert stuck his tongue in his jaw and shut up.

"Coffee's ready, skip," Eager called out. He poured a cup for each of us. It was stone cold and tasted like vinegar.

"Nothing like a good hot cup of java in the a.m.," said Lambert.

When it came time to drop the nets, it turned out they were in pretty bad repair, what with tangles created by Lucifer himself and dry rot to boot. So we dropped a few hand-lines with bacon and cod scraps tied neatly to each hook. My father was in a meditative mood and just gazed back at his beloved island from beyond the gull-splattered ledges of Rat Rock.

"Been talk of turning this island into a sort of resort," Lambert said, pointing to the Rock. It was a low, granite ledge of maybe three acres inhabited by several thousand sea birds. The rocks were bleached calcium white by the gull shit. A broken-down duck hunter's cabin stood on the west end. Lambert pointed to it. "A man would fix up a place like that and retire there. Have an easy life of it away from the maddening crowds."

In truth, I could see the romance of Rat Rock. There were deep, dark, mysterious pools all along the edge. Seaweed swayed back and forth in the shallows. Seals dipped up and down just a few feet away. It was an expansive blue world out here on a day like this. And time had ceased to exist.

Eager cracked open a bottle of home-made beer and pulled up a crate beside me. I was having no luck with catching anything.

"I'll tell you something, Ian," he confided. "Never go to work for nobody. A man can answer to only one boss and that's himself. You take Lambert there. He thinks he's God almighty 'cause he got this bucket of a boat. If it weren't for me, he'd have lost his shirt years ago."

Lambert pretended not to hear.

Just then the engine stalled. "Jesus Christ on stilts!" Lambert roared.

Eager set his beer down and propped open the engine cover. I peered in and breathed the smell of a red-hot, oil-soaked engine. "What do you think she needs, boss?"

Lambert stuck his finger down the throat of the carburetor. "Crap in the needle valve again. Only thing for her is a good splash of gasoline straight down the throat."

They had played this scene before. Eager grabbed a coffee cup and filled it with fuel. Lambert stood back as Eager splashed the gas half in, half out of the carburetor.

"Give her some ignition," Lambert ordered, but almost as soon as Eager pushed the starter, a flame shot out of the carburetor high up into the sky. It was like the devil coming up from the centre of the earth, right through the sea and the centre of the engine. A six-foot yellow-blue flame. I swear I could see a face in it. Everyone jumped back. Just as suddenly as it had flared, it sucked back into the carburetor and the engine backfired. But by now some of the spilled gas had caught fire. The engine was burning.

My father heaved a bucket of sea water onto it, and it seemed like it would go out, but there must have been a leaky fuel hose there, too, because it flared up again, the flame growing wilder.

The men tried to pour on more water, but it didn't seem to help. The wood around the engine had caught fire. My father, ready to admit that things were already out of control, was pulling on the rope of the dinghy that trailed behind. He told me to climb in, and as I did I noticed that all of our hand-lines were tugging at once. Finally we had caught something, but it didn't matter now.

My father went back to trying to help, but it was a losing battle. Half the deck was on fire. Lambert and Eager were screaming at each other. Soon all three of them were up to their ankles in sea water, and a dark plume of smoke filled the air. Then they, too, were in the small boat, and we all said goodbye to the Sister Theresa. It had all happened so quickly that I could not believe my eyes.

"Well, ain't that a handshake in hell," Lambert said. "A man's livelihood headed for the bottom of the sea. Just like that."

Eager was sulking. "There was a case and a half of good home-made brew on that boat."

My father appeared stoic. "Perhaps forces in the universe greater than us conspired this moment for a good reason."

"Just the same, it's hard luck," Lambert said, sucking snot back up his nose.

"That it is," my father admitted.

"But no one got hurt," I chimed in, trying to put a good face on it.

"No one but my pocketbook. I had close to a quarter-million tied up in that boat," Lambert lied.

"What about my beer?" Eager complained.

I grabbed one oar and my father the other. We began to row. After a few minutes, the bitterness of the loss seemed to fade.

"Reminds me of the time the steamer went down off of Cape Race. I was in the water. There was just me and these three beautiful women. All around us were maybe twenty or thirty sharks. I told the ladies not to be scared. One of them was right upset, though, and she grabbed onto me like I was her heavenly hope. She went and wrapped her legs around me, felt just like lobster claws, the bite was so intense. Then after a while, we were bobbing up and down in the water, and she starts to moaning. Heck, I didn't know what it was, but then I seen she had a smile on her face. Pretty soon she got tired, and one of the other women give it a try. Then finally the third one.

"Well sir, by the time the coast guard feller come by, I was plain tuckered out. The women, well, at first they said they didn't want to be rescued, that they liked it in the ocean just fine. But me, I wanted to get back ashore and get some sleep."

"That so?" my father said with beneficent disinterest.

"Well, I suppose we're not going to be lucky enough to just drown," Eager began. "I never did mind the notion of drowning. I just hope this doesn't turn into one of them ordeals. I never could stand an ordeal. Like when you get up in the a.m. and you can't remember where you left your shoes. I'd rather drown outright than have to go through all the contortions of figuring out where I lost my shoes. Yep, a watery death would seem just like a holiday compared to that.

"Or waiting in a line. I waited in a line once down in Halifax. I think it was a movie house that some fool had persuaded me to go into. I waited in line for over twenty minutes, and I swore that nothing was as bad as that. That's why I moved down the shore. I just didn't want to have to wait in no more lines."

With all the excitement and confessions, I hadn't kept an eye on the shoreline. I had just rowed my one oar. I guess my father was steering. I just assumed we were still a long way at sea, but when I turned around I saw that we were pulling into a tiny cove of sorts on Rat Rock.

"Why don't we just get out and stretch our legs before we row on ashore?" my father suggested.

Lambert seemed elated to finally be setting foot on the Rock.

"I been to islands before not much bigger than this one. Down around the Canaries, they were. Nothing but big-breasted women and a few wimpy little men. Could never understand what so many big-chested women were doing on such a tiny little island. It gave a man pause to think about that."

"I know what this is," Eager said as he put his feet on the Rock. "This is hell. We have already died and gone on to the next place. Nothing could be worse than this."

"Every man makes his own heaven or hell," my father told him.

"That's true," Lambert added. "I seen men at sea go mad from loneliness, and others turn into friggin' saints."

"I ain't no saint," Eager said. "But I guess you're right. It could be worse. Could've pulled up in front of a movie house and be told by the devil we'd have to stand in line. I couldn't handle standing in no line. Not after going through that once."

My father and I did some exploring and found a tiny, rusted-out stove in the deserted hunter's cabin. There was one good match on a shelf, and the old man's luck held. He torched a year-old copy of the *Halifax Herald* and lit up some scraps of driftwood. He found one old pot and put in some sea water. Then we went down to the pools and found sea urchins, clams and quahogs. He set them to boiling, and we gathered up the other two survivors, who were sitting beneath a canopy of angry seagulls.

A few minutes later we were inside, eating a minor feast of seafood. "I can picture this whole island as a resort for rich people," Lambert said, the quahogs warming the lining of his stomach. He spread his arms out across the entire three-acre bare-stone-and-birdshit island. Above us the gulls screeched and roared.

"I like it better the way it is," Eager countered. "If a place like this got developed, soon there'd be movie houses and possibly crime. A man could wake up in the morning and find someone had stolen his shoes. I couldn't handle such a life."

The talk went on late into the afternoon. Lambert decided that it was good fortune, after all, that his boat had gone down. He was tired of fishing, he said. "Besides, this is the best time I've had in years."

"I've seen better," Eager complained, lying back on a sunny rock and falling asleep, his shoes tucked deftly under one arm.

Then Lambert fell asleep. It was nearly four o'clock when my old man woke them up. We had been exploring every inch of Rat Rock and even gone swimming in a beautiful blue grotto that was carved into one shore.

But we had to get home. My mother would be worried. The final half-mile row to shore was a quiet one. Lambert had begun to talk of a salvage operation to save the goods on board his sunken ship.

"It's too late," Eager countered. "Them beer bottles would explode from the pressure down below. Ain't nothing worth saving out there."

My father said that it was his duty to see that Lambert and Eager came up with a new boat. He said he'd talk to Ernest Cowley about building one, and everyone on the island would chip in.

"That's kind of you. In the meantime, I guess I'll go stay with my sister in Halifax," Lambert said. "She was about due for a visit. She's got thighs thick around as tree trunks in the Amazon, but she has some mighty nice petite lady-friends. Eager here is welcome to come along to town if he wants."

Eager sat up straight in the boat. He seemed insulted. "Might as well cut off my hands and feet with a chain saw, then stuff the rest of me inside the jaws of a lion. That'd be kinder."

But a few days later I heard that Eager went along anyway for a week or two. When he returned to our island, he treated himself like a man who had just seen the end of the world and had survived. He swore he'd never set foot off Whalebone Island again.

# The Road

# IT ALL COMES BACK NOW

It's night now. The small towns blink on and off as you head away from one coast toward another. When morning comes you know what you will see.

There will be a stretch of road, no houses. Trees will be crumpled up along the side from when the highway was built maybe twenty years ago. Never burnt for wood, never cut up. The ground that slopes off from the raised, well-drained road will not fully recover from having been scraped clean of plant life. Red mosses, tires, mostly infertile soil. The spruce grow beyond, though rarely more than thirty feet high and never all that healthy-looking, but somehow stately with all that funereal fungal growth, beautiful but draining the life out of the wood.

And when you approach town, there will be a house, a basement really, a full basement rising maybe four feet above the ground and then finished off, a flat, tar-papered roof where the owner intended to build the real house but ran out of money. There will be one junk car in the yard. A good body, but you know some engine or transmission crisis stole the life out of her a while back and at the most inopportune time.

As the sun tilts up over a crest in the road, you see several hastily cleared lots where mobile homes are parked. What was once natural to the land is bunched up in a pile at the back of the property where the bulldozer operator shoved the goods. Things in the way. The mobile home looks exactly like every mobile home you've ever seen. You wouldn't want to see the inhabitants for fear you'd recognize them. Even if the sun is in your eyes, you know there's a bunch of old bald and blown-out tires on the roof to keep the noise down in the wind. Aluminum skins are noisy mothers. Two junk cars in the yard. One's an old four-wheel-drive vehicle of some sort. A man's dream, his hopes of trekking endlessly through the interior of the province, buggered up just days after he bought her at a steal from a guy in the next county.

One driveable wreck, looking in worse shape than the two derelict cars, sits as close as possible to the door of the house. Mobile home owners avoid walking, the carrying of groceries over any distance.

The husband has built a wonderful platform and pulley system for the wife to dry clothes outside. The platform looks as if it could be used for hanging. The victim would walk the steps and put his head in the noose and step, or be pushed, forward. Instead, the wife will use multicoloured plastic clothespins to attach sweet-smelling, clean clothes to a blue plastic-covered wire. The pulley system allows her to send the wash out over the frozen, muddy yard. The pulley at the opposite end is attached to a lone stunted spruce tree, now dead, left standing near the corner of the forest. In cold weather the clothes freeze on the line, and they can be hauled in like lumber, piled near the furnace outlet to melt and then dry. In warmer months, the fog may be thick, and it will take days, often a week for the clothes to dry.

There are several more mobile homes. Quicker, cheaper than building a wood frame house. Less work. You get a package deal. Furniture included. Insurance companies make owners put plywood around the bottom to cover up the axles and the wheels. That way they can be insured as homes. Otherwise, they'd have to rate them as vehicles, cars.

There are two or three absolutely empty and final homes sitting alternately along the road before you hit town. The glass is out of the windows, the centre brick chimneys have fallen or were pushed over. The porches sag. They are small homes, all with wood shakes, one still has a pile of rotting firewood on the porch. If you looked closely you would see the loose stone foundation has shifted, rocks have fallen into the basement from the heaving of the spring frost. Or you could be wrong; the foundation could be perfectly intact as if set into place yesterday by a master builder of stone pyramids.

An apple tree still grows, bent and gone mad with sucker branches, in the front yard. It still flowers in summer, and the small red apples fall to the ground in the autumn and rot while the bees extract their last harvest of the year.

You won't stop to go inside any one of the three. God knows it will be hard enough to stop at all when you arrive. But you are sure that if you were to walk into the run-down house closest to town, you would find in one of the rooms one of the two: broken rum bottles or dog-eared copies of *Playboy* and *Penthouse* magazines. These old falling-down homes have become indoor parks for necessary evils that young folk can't get away with in town. They are full of all sorts of mould. Plaster walls have become wet and bloated, and ancient wallpaper is stained beyond belief with years of neglect. Should an American summering in the province drive by, he would stop and enjoy the houses in his own way. He would go into town, ask a guy at the Irving station, Who owns the land? Is it for sale? He would like to restore the house.

You feel your foot easing up on the accelerator, almost instinctively. You are coming into town. You are sure you are not lying in saying that this town looks like at least four hundred others just like it. You are neither pleased nor despondent over that. But there would be something to say if you could claim it looked different, unique.

The Irving station has gone out of business, although a Fina remains open farther down the road. The church is white, stark, impressive in its size. It's larger than would seem necessary for the town. Sundays, it always feels empty even when the whole congregation is there. But on Christmas and Easter many have come home, and it seems bright and full. There is a looming hardwood tree in front of the church. Without leaves you couldn't name it, although memory should serve you here. You'll say it's a maple. A wooden sign with a triangular peak labels the church, names the minister and indicates that the sermon this week will be "Tithing: Is 10% Enough?" Oh, well, these are times of inflation, and perhaps the Bible writers did not take into account double-digit inflation.

And of course, finally, the place to stop. The house itself should be familiar. It has changed, though. Tree roots knuckle up the hard-packed soil in front of the house where you are sure grass once grew. You drive up the path past the house into the back yard and stop alongside a wooden flagpole more grey than white. There is a chain tied to the pole and a perfect circular area of absent grass where the dog once ran its circumference. The chain lies rusted and wrapped tight around the foot of the pole.

Familiar landmarks, though. An old refrigerator with brownish snow drifting up along one side of it. A cement mixer by the shed, and a small rock foundation where the outhouse once stood that was torn down even before you left. Through a broken pane of glass in the shed door you see the neat uniformity of bicycle spokes from a wheel hung on the wall.

You turn off the car, not wanting to get out quite yet. It's been a long trip. So much sameness. Perhaps it will be so here as well. You feel the heat leaving the car with the engine off. Soon you can see your own breath. As you watch it rise and freeze against the glass you notice smoke coming from the central brick chimney of the house. Someone is at home. You look at the worn steps that lead into the back porch. It would be hard to fit your feet into those ancient depressions. You decide to use the other door. Walking along the side of the house toward the front, you feel uncomfortable. It isn't predictable. The wooden clapboard siding has been repainted a light green colour, and already the paint is removing itself in great curved chips.

An aluminum storm door in the front. Intimidating. Should you knock?

It's unlocked. You walk in, opening the wooden door as well, which rings a small bell, but there's still no sign of life. You must make your way to the kitchen. Someone will be there. The path through the house seems strange, alien, different. Maybe walls have been torn out and moved. The wallpaper is recent, the ceiling stuccoed. Your feet shuffle across carpet, not wood.

For a moment you close your eyes and try to close the gap between the years, but it yawns wider and wider.

In the kitchen, a familiar sound. The oil stove is running, pots of water boil on the surface. A woman is sitting with her back to you reading a magazine, the man is bent over looking out the back window at your car. They both turn at once, startled. The faces show fear, mistrust. Your father walks around the table squinting at you, picking up his glasses. His face changes. He's astonished, he smiles. Your mother drops her magazine to the floor and begins to get up.

In an instant he's shaking your hand, patting your back. "It's good to have you home, son." Your mother has her arms around you and is laughing and crying into your shirt.

You wonder if you still could turn around and get back to your car, drive on to the next town, predict exactly how it will look ahead. Things are not as you left them, not as expected. You're frightened, you'd like to run.

# THE CURE

I guess I'm one of those guys who believes in miracle cures. I don't mean the religious kind, but, like, if my car burns oil, I'll go buy a pint of STP, or if the radiator leaks, I buy some other stuff. When I bust something, I'll try to stick it together with some sort of glue. When my kid cries, I buy him a Battlestar Galactica game, and last week when my wife decided that our marriage was on the rocks, I took her out and bought her eight hundred square feet of purple shag carpet. It's what she always wanted and damn if it didn't make her happy.

The guys came and tacked it all down, and she just stood in the kitchen (the only room that didn't get the purple flush treatment) and sipped a cup of coffee, and she beamed. I had to take out a loan to pay for the rug, and as I sat downstairs in the den figuring what the interest ran up to and listening to the hammering (over a perfectly nice hardwood floor yet), I realized something was wrong.

The kid, Derrick, is in his room miming to a record of some rock group. I bought him the record when he said he was mad at me for not owning a Corvette.

Now here's the rub: I keep buying STP and glue and purple shag carpet, and it all works for a couple of days, and then you're right back where you started from. Problems. My old man realized that, and he just stopped trying. Twenty-five years' fishing down the Eastern Shore. One bad season and he said to hell with it and quit. He left my mother and me and moved into his shack down on the Causeway. Took the radio and nothing else. I went to visit him all the time. He'd be smoking his pipe made from an old bottle cap of some sort, and he'd nod like he was listening to me. He wasn't nodding at me but at the guy talking on the radio. He ate salt herring and blue potatoes while he lived there. How a soul could survive on that I don't know. He let us keep all the welfare cheques, and he never touched any of it.

I rode my bicycle out there once during the worst hurricane we'd ever seen, and there was my old man sitting by the radio. A window was busted open, and the curtain (just a muslin rag, actually) was blowing in his face. He was nodding at the radio as usual and wasn't at all surprised at my feat of pedalling out through the storm. I told him I was gonna go fishing with him next summer. We would start over, him and me, fix up the boat, catch us some lobster and drive them into Halifax. We'd get a good run of haddock and barrels and barrels of mackerel.

He said one thing to me. "Ain't no fish left in the whole damn ocean and that's that."

I sat out the storm with him and pedalled home in the morning. My father had made up his mind that there really weren't any fish left, and he believed it. To him it was truth, and like many an Eastern Shore fisherman, once he found his own peculiar truth, there was no changing his beliefs.

When I went out there again, I saw a couple of broken boards in the side of the boat. It was beached, and the breaks were clean and simple. Nothing much, just a few pieces to replace. When confronted with the damage, the old man just said, "She'll never sail again." Truth, I suppose.

My mother became the same morose person as my father. "Your father ain't never comin' home," she said. She turned the oil stove up a notch, which the old man would never have allowed her to do, thinking it far too unfrugal. She planted herself by the stove like the old man by his radio, and that was that.

I quit school, moved into town and later got into the business school where I learned bookkeeping. I vowed never to move back Down East.

But the truth was that this purple rug thing was too much for me. The city trucks were trundling by, spreading salt on the icy roads. I thought of my old man throwing the same salt on his barrels of fish. I thought of how the street salt had rusted through both front fenders of my Pinto, only two years old. I thought of all the work involved in trying to fix those fenders, in trying to fix the kid's mini-bike and in trying to satisfy my wife's next craving, which was for a heavy-duty Filter Queen vacuum cleaner that would loosen dirt from deep down in the pile of the carpet.

So, late one Saturday morning in January, exit one disgruntled suburban accountant. Sylvia's on the phone now and thinks I'm just stepping out. I wave once and close the door, snug against the weather-stripping, behind me. The old Pontiac station wagon is in worse shape than the Pinto, but I take that. I drive straight to the rotary in Dartmouth, and then I go round and round the thing. I do fifty consecutive trips around the perimeter. It's great because I never see the same people and they have no idea that I'm in this orbit. Every other driver shoots his vehicle off on a tangent to the new bridge or the airport or downtown Dartmouth or the Eastern Shore.

There it is, the route (Number Seven) back Down East. The sign looks more appealing each time around. I think of all the poor buggers like me looping their Toyotas and Fords around the rotary morning after morning on repetitious trajectories to jobs in Burnside at unheated building supply warehouses; jobs at the north end of Halifax for book distributors; jobs at downtown offices where the same old jokes are told over and over; jobs selling pantyhose in Simpson's, where customers pride themselves on belittling the sales help. Three more orbits and my station wagon cuts loose down the old Number Seven. I swear it was even hard to break the wheel out of the locked-in pattern. It fought against me as I carelessly sliced in front of a cement truck whose driver lay hard on the air horn.

*The Cure*

I wait impatiently through the lights and traffic by the cluttered Dartmouth shopping centres, then zip up the hill past the vocational school and east as the clouds begin to shed the first flakes of yet another snowstorm and the wind whips up from the northwest.

Damn if I don't just get beyond the last string of cigar-box vinyl-sided houses and a Mountie slips in behind me, starts flashing high beams, and I have to pull over. I think back to my more passionate days of adolescence, and, caught in a momentary panic that somehow the cop knows exactly what I'm up to, I kick the accelerator to the floor. The engine coughs and backfires, and I look at the fuel gauge. The needle is drowning below the E line. (Curses on you Sylvia. You had the car last, and why do I have to put gas in it for you all the time?) I pull immediately over to the side of the road, hitting my brakes almost too hard. I see the police car tilt forward as the driver, ready for a chase, brakes hard to keep from smashing into me.

I calmly take out my license and registration, imbedded in the hinterlands of my Genuine Simugrain wallet. Stuck to the license is an absurd ancient picture of my father and mother hugging on the sunniest day imaginable at a wharf in Murphy's Cove . . . that was when we actually took short trips down the coast together fishing, just for fun.

"Sorry, the accelerator sticks sometimes. I've been meaning to get it fixed but . . ." I look up meekly at the attending Mountie, and for Chrissakes it's a woman.

"You wanna come back in the patrol car for a minute?" she asks, not really waiting for an answer.

Inside her car, she tells me that she was parked back at the A&W stand and saw me doing my merry-go-round on the rotary.

"Just what the hell were you doing?"

"Indecision," I tell her. "I just didn't know where I wanted to go."

I stare across the highway to the big glass windows of a furniture store. They have a display of tartan chesterfields in the window. "A Family Tradition," reads the big gaudy sign over the assortment. People are filing out to their cars in the dirty snow of the parking lot. They look across at me with the cop. Poor jerk got himself caught for something, they're thinking.

I remain very cool — I can do that under pressure sometimes. I listen to static messages on the police radio. It's like someone trying to communicate from a distant galaxy.

"You were speeding, too, you know."

"Sorry, I still haven't adjusted to the kilometre signs." A poor excuse; I've used it far too often. I rambled on. I changed the subject a dozen times. I complimented her on her astute observations and asked her what it was like to be a woman cop. I sympathized when she told me that sometimes she'd stop a drunk and he wouldn't take her seriously. She knew how to use force, she said. Karate, judo, she was nobody's fool and had busted a few ribs of those who thought she was. She was from, of all places, Sober Island, sixty miles east. She liked being a Mountie. We talked about someone who was a friend of someone that we both vaguely knew as kids. In the end, no ticket. We even hit a quite genuine feeling of liking for each other.

When I arrived at my old man's fishing shack, it was bitter cold. I had been the only car out the Causeway since the snowstorm several days ago. I liked the way my tires sounded on the crusty snow and the deep clean impression they made. Only problem was that I wish I could have covered those tracks. Like they did in the old cowboy films.

But I was still convinced to go ahead with my plan, dumb as it was. At least it was a plan. I had bought ten cases of beer in Sheet Harbour — the only Liquor Commission store for seventy miles in either direction. I'd hole up in the old man's shanty and drink 'em, one after the other, until I made some sense out of things. Now this might sound ridiculous, but I swear it's a very sacred old tradition down this shore. Some men died from it. Some claimed they learned from it. Some ended up working for the government, and some went nuts. My uncle Cally did. Went right crazy. Swore he'd seen

God, and they packed him up and sent him to the nuthouse, where he seemed to have quite a following the one day I went to see him.

But my old man never went in much for drinking. He'd always get into fights, and only with his friends. Finally he realized that he didn't have any friends left. Claims he gave up drink 'cause there wasn't anyone left to fight with. But he's long dead anyway.

If this had been another part of the Shore, men would have been out here every day checking their boats like worried mother hens. But this set of shanties was stark and deserted. Nobody fished these waters once the Russians started dragging the bottom, killing the seaweed which in turned killed the small fish which in turned killed off most of the larger stock. My father had been a kind of pioneer in failure. He'd seen it coming and had given up altogether. A real doomsday prophet. And looking at his old shack, I realized what doom looked like.

It was a tired little one-room board cabin. The winters had painted it a grey you'd never find a paint to match. The unboarded windows were unbelievably intact, too far a trip for any vandal to bother with. I wrested open the heavy plank door, one rusted hinge busting in rebellion. It wasn't until I was inside that I realized how frigging cold it was. The wind was lancing through various cracks in the wall, and little thin highways of snow were creeping toward the centre of the room, driven by the restless wind.

Hell of a place. Clean, though. Almost no dust anywhere, even though nobody had touched it since my old man died. Even a neat stacked pile of hardwood under the bed. (My old man said he couldn't sleep at all unless he had a full load of wood under where he slept.) I tore off some old wallpaper — newspaper, really — and heaved it in the stove, an old forty-five-gallon oil barrel that had been patched a hundred times with can lids and metal screws and homemade stove cement. The walls of the thing were paper thin but allowed the heat to come quickly as I threw some kindling, bone dry, onto the paper. I caught one quick glimpse of the headline, "Newfoundland Joins Confederation," before it blistered with flame and I had to plop the lid down.

I immediately regretted having burned the document and tramped back out to the snow to haul in the beer. Waves pounded an old ice-covered wharf, gulls clung for mercy on the roofs of other buildings, and the car sat quietly rusting in the salt air. (No block heater to plug into you tonight, sweetheart.) I kept telling myself I was home.

Without dampers to cut down the air, the heat from the stove moved rapidly through the house despite the drafts. I could see the smoke being pulled down by the wind and off across the ice of the inlet toward a graceful tear-shaped island that looked to be the very heart of peace in this bitter winter torment.

I stared at the island a long while. I think my father had called it the Parson's Nose. I can't remember why. I thought about it as I jimmied the first beer cap off against the door latch. I settled in front of the fire, angry all of a sudden that I still wasn't satisfied. I had come this far . . . I was away from the agony of the purple carpet, the civilized life, and I still wanted to go further. Halfway was still defeat to my blood. Only the cold leaking through the walls gave me the contrast I needed. The assurance that the winter could still claw at me, challenge me, make me feel half alive.

Then, on the third beer, someone was at the front of the shack. The door swung open and a stark figure of a man with at least ten devastated thin jackets on came in. He was laced with snow in his hair and beard, and he hobbled on crutches. A foot was missing, which accounted for the supports.

He closed the door and shook himself like a dog, sending melted snow droplets spraying around the room. Reaching inside one of the battered coats, he pulled out a transistor radio, set it on the window sill and turned it up to a distorted full volume.

"That'd be a bit better," I heard him say. "Reception ain't a bit good at my place." He motioned out the window to a tiny fishing shack made of green aspenite and bits of loose tarpaper. "Hockey game. They're playing the god-forsaken Russians." The radio crowd let out a blast of cheers — a Russian goalie must've taken the puck in the guts.

"Oh, really? So who the hell are you?" I asked him. It seemed ludicrous that anyone else was alive here, but then it felt good to be talking to a local again.

"Oh, sorry, me boy. I forgot me manners for sure, livin' here all these years. Last bugger to move out lived right here in this place you're in. Didn't move, though. He died. But to answer your point, name's Chopper. 'Cause of me foot, ya see." He dangled his stub in the air. "Got drunked up and fell asleep one February. Forgot to stoke the fire. Would've lost 'em both if it weren't for the helicopter come and carry me away. Chopped me left foot off . . . frozen just like a chunk of salmon. Oh, well, so she goes."

"You mean you live out here? Thought everyone was gone with the fish. Here, wanna beer? Moosehead."

"Nope. Sorry, can't accept the offer. I only drink once, maybe twice a year, and every time I drinks for a month straight. Ain't got the money to do that now. Besides, she be cold out and alcohol can make that dangerous."

"Yeah, I see. Oh, well, what the hell." I killed the third bottle and moved on to the fourth. Four beer hadn't even given me a buzz yet. I was disappointed.

The old guy drifted off toward the radio for a minute or so but then got up and wandered toward the stove. "Most snow I seen this year. But the wind is a good one. Bring in more fish by spring. Wait and see."

"I thought all the fish were gone. My father thought so when he was livin' here."

"No lie? That was your old man who holed up here for so long? I knew him well, but we never got along."

"Really. How could that be?"

"Well, you see . . . he lived here to hide from somethin'. Never did figure out what. I moved here to find somethin'. Come to think of it, though, I never figured out what, neither."

He paused and smoothed the wetness out of his grey beard.

"But I'll tell ya this. When your papa died, there were more herring in this cove than you could shake a stick at. I salted down

a decent ton that year and could have done more if I had the spirit."
He spied a wooden barrel over in the corner and sort of hopped
over to it. Without asking he pried open a cork in the top.

Then, Jesus Christ, this foul smell like the very armpits of hell
filled up the room. I had never smelled such an odour in all the
polluted civilized world. He quickly popped the plug back in. "Bit
over her prime, I reckon. Salt herring. Shame to see it go to waste.
I give it to your father 'cause I worried over his health. Don't think
he ever ate a one. Said to me, 'No damn fish left on this whole shore.'
Barrel just sat there all them years, I guess. Sorry about unleashing
such a worrisome stench on ya."

By the time I was finishing my first case, I didn't care much about
the smell and had got into a long explanation about my family and
living in the city and all. Then I went outside to take a pee and found
myself staring at the island. It was long and majestic, the spruce
trees carved by the wind to provide the outline of a perfect dome.
Maybe I needed to get out there, but not just yet.

Inside, Chopper had fallen asleep by the stove. I turned off his
portable radio and finished the case of Moosehead but then decided
to quit. No need to get drunk and freeze to death. I liked the winter. It wasn't my enemy, and I wouldn't let it do me in.


Chopper stood stiffly in the morning sun, leaning on the shack and
squinting across the inlet. "I'm telling ya. He was an odd sort. I
thought I'd have to stay just to stoke the fire, ya know, but he got up
half a dozen times and done it himself without the slightest com-
plaint. Right careful he was not to bust the sides of the old stove."

"But when do you remember seeing him last?" It was the young
female Mountie. For her, a first, this sort of interrogating.

"Well, I got up at about seven. Me joints stiff as knots, ya
know. The wind was gone, and this strange kind of winter fog had
come in. The room was empty, but the fire had just been stoked."

"I went out and there he was, walking out across the ice to the
island, confident as could be. I was a bit worried, so I went out and

blew the horn on his car. Didn't do no good. Just kept on. Don't think the ice give way, though, not even on the inlet."

"Did he take anything? Guns, equipment?" The young woman felt weak and confused by the story. She knew that on the TV shows all the women detectives knew how to sort out these strange bits of information. But she was a twenty-four-year-old girl from the Eastern Shore, and this sort of thing made only the barest bit of sense.

"The only thing he took, other than his coat, was a couple of old hand-lines — some fishin' stuff that I'd seen him foolin' with. He even left the keys to his car. Otherwise I'd never of been able to contact you. Put the bloody thing off the road twice before I got to the highway, too."

"You sure that's all you can tell me? There must be more." She was doing worse now. She had looked at the car again and realized this was the guy from the rotary. She felt panicked, the missing man no longer a name but also a human being.

"Sorry, miss. Made up his mind about somethin' or other and set off to do it. He could be out on the island here, or he could have walked the ice on down the coast to a thousand other islands. I liked the boy, though. Had a sense of purpose you don't always see down here. Sorry I can't help ya more."

# CONVENTIONAL EMOTIONS

It took me less than six months from the time I left Mulgrew to begin seeing things differently. I guess I had my moment of satori when I was sitting in MacDonough's anthropology class. He was explaining something about the Achilpa tribe, who lived in the deserts of Australia. Up until then I hadn't been all that concerned with anthro. In fact, at that exact moment I was hard at work studying the geography of Carolyn MacCormack's sweater. That terrain was complex enough without moving off to parched landscapes in the Southern Hemisphere.

But I guess I must have been listening to the professor with half an ear. He was an arrogant intellectual, too young for the job. When I left Mulgrew, I expected all of my mentors at the university to be ancient. MacDonough looked more like an excuse for socialized medicine. Yet this thing about the Achilpas hit some strange chord. I turned my attention from Carolyn country to hear this: "You see, the Achilpas are nomads. They wander around in the desert, never remaining in one place for long. How do they figure out where to go?" (A we-could-care-less silence issued from the half-slumbering class.) "They place a sacred pole in the ground each time they stop. It's a connecting rod between man and the heavens. They have a direct line to the guy upstairs." (More silence.) "And then they wait for the pole to tilt. Whichever direction it tilts is the direction they move toward their next destination. For them the system is perfect."

Absolute belief in a direct line to God. No big decisions as to where to go next. The decision was always made for you. MacDonough went on to explain a variety of rituals that involved the pole. As usual, he never passed up his chance to explore the very phallic nature of this structure, "an instrument of man having veritable intercourse with the heavens." I shot a quick glance over at Carolyn, squirming uncomfortably in her seat.

"Only one problem with the system. For one Achilpa tribe, there was a crisis. They went out one morning to find the pole broken in two, rotted away from years of use. No direction. No direct line to God. It was devastating for the village. No one knew which direction they should move in next. Without the heavenly mandate, they were inextricably lost. They wandered for years in a quagmire of spiritual bankruptcy and finally destroyed themselves from within.

"I leave you to think about the obvious cultural parallels. And think on this as well: the role of the anthropologist is to see man as he really is, to skim away the surface trappings and understand man the primitive and man the civilized. Detached observer or willing ritual participant, the anthropologist must come to grips with all members of the human family."

It could have seemed like some cornball religion in itself, but I was really taken. And for a guy hot out of the cultural myopia of Mulgrew, intellectual pursuit all of a sudden seemed like the most exciting thing in the world. As I reached out and woke up, I was even then remembering the last time I saw my father. He was heading off to work, to do his daily route delivering stove oil. He put on his green jacket emblazoned, "Jessup Bros. Fuel Oils — providing warmth since 1898." It was my last morning in town before catching the bus to Halifax and university. My old man's jacket smelled as if it had enough spilled fuel on it to heat the house for a week. The smell never bothered him. It was like putting on aftershave in the morning. Before he left, he graced me with a last short dose of his own wisdom. "Kenny, look, when you said you were going to school in Halifax, I thought you were gonna take up a trade or somethin'. But no, you want to go off and stuff your brain full of useless crap. I think you're wastin' your time. But two words of advice: don't take up no strange religions, and don't shoot up no drugs. And one more thing in case you're still listening: steer clear of communists and labour organizers."

So far, his advice had been followed, although not on purpose. I wondered what he'd think about anthropology.

Over the next few weeks, there wasn't a primitive desert tribe in the world that I didn't become acquainted with. At first, I had a hard time getting beyond my attraction to primitive women — the perfect black skin, the composed faces and the marvellous parading breasts the photographers for the texts seemed to linger on so gratuitously. Perhaps it was Oscar Hemmings-Hume, though, creeping around the Kalahari with yet another nomadic desert people, who helped me get beyond my adolescent obsessions and on the track to deeper meaning. He wrote with eloquence:

> Such intelligent survivors as these have rarely graced the planet. The bushman of the Kalahari have achieved an almost perfect symbiotic relationship with their cattle. To the man, a woman is not nearly as significant as his cattle, from which all nourishment comes. In his ability to strip himself of familial sentimentality, the Kalahari bushman is to be applauded. Yet in his personal attachment to his beasts, he applies the same maudlin conventional emotions that are the intellectual sacrilege of male/female relations in the western world.

I was struck by the phrase "conventional emotions," and I could see what the guy was getting at. Look at the mess people made out of their lives back in Mulgrew. All in the name of love and honour and family crapola. There was, after all, obviously something deeper to be gained from life — an understanding of the true nature of mankind. I had no intention of being duped into a conventional belief that I was in love with some girl just because her body attracted me, only to find myself stuck in a conventional marriage with a couple of screaming kids and a mortgage. A life dedicated to the pursuit of anthropology would provide me with a vision of the human experience that no one back on the Shore could even begin to comprehend.

After a while the library wasn't enough. To study the deep-down meaning of man, one had to move into the jungles, the deserts, the veritable hinterlands of civilization. I started at the Public Gardens. I studied an old man eating a sandwich, a creature for whom time was like a trained pigeon: it could be taught to stay put in one place. The old guy ate so small a morsel at a time that I thought he might keel over before the ritual was completed. Finally I approached him. Nodding at the sandwich, I asked, "What does it mean? To you?"

He looked up bewildered and then down at the sandwich. "Mock chicken?" He claimed only to be eating a sandwich; no more, no less. I scoffed at his unwillingness to divulge his interior logic. "Man does not live by bread alone," I chided him, and he got up and left. A great anthropological lesson had been learned: don't butt into private rituals. I would henceforth remain the passive but attentive observer. Soon I grew bored with listening to women discuss the white sale at Woolco and men outraged at the price of gas. Kids all seemed to be intent on feeding squirrels and pigeons or watching ducks copulating. It was all too, well, ordinary. I needed foreign cultures desperately, and the best I could shoot for would be down toward the docks.

I was hoping for a few strange characters from a Libyan freighter but had to settle for a couple of sailors coming my way from a Russian naval vessel. I figured that if I could watch them watching our culture, I might learn something about both. They saw my interest and stopped for a chat. Unfortunately for me, they knew only two words. "Liquor store?" one of them grunted in pretend friendliness. Any breakthrough in establishing contact with foreigners was valuable, I figured, so I led them off toward Hollis Street and the Liquor Commission. They shook my hand, indicating that my services were no longer needed, and one of the sailors placed three black cigarettes in my hand.

*The Road*

Back in the dorm, I lit up the first of the strange-looking things, hoping to get blasted out of my gourd, but it turned out to be an evil variety of tobacco and not some incredible Russian hybrid weed. "Ask for some caviar next time, instead," my roommate chided me. Mel Dorton was a kid from Digby. His very existence persuaded me that evolution probably had by-passed that part of the province altogether. I suspected Mel of borrowing my *National Geographic* for autoerotic stimulation, and I eventually gave him the whole collection rather then remain privy to his personal indecencies. Instead, nights would find me absorbed in reading up on Australian primitives, Hindu marriage customs, Micronesian puberty rites and Nubian migrations. I had positively devoured every word that Hemmings-Hume and his colleagues at the World Studies Institute had produced.

The year flew by. I ignored Christmas and spring break and held fast to the urban life, milking it of every drop of available intellectual insight on primitive cultures and anthropological wisdom. I remember the night that Oscar Hemmings-Hume himself came to town. He was giving a lecture, "Circumcision among Amazon Tribes: The Knife Rarely Slips." It was part of a pop-culture series held at the Myra Cohen Auditorium at the other university in town. This was a big year for trying to make academia look interesting, and there were grotesque posters of a huge knife held up to the male organ plastered all up and down Barrington Street. It wasn't really my idea of anthro. The posters were obvious drawing cards for a multitude of cultural platitudes that appeared on the posters like night-blooming flowers the first evening they were up.

But when Hemmings-Hume arrived in town, he, too, was in the fever of it all, and when he realized that the Cohn would be packed to the rafters with an assorted horde of local citizens whose prurient interests only peripherally touched on anthropology, he went for broke with the opening of the lecture. Standing a spear's-length away from one of the said posters on stage, he proceeded to throw a knife directly at the artist's colourful conception of the organ. It was a large triangular knife. The blade caught the printed member head on (so to speak), and at least one mournful, sympathetic groan sounded from high up in the balcony.

"That, ladies and gentlemen," began Hemmings-Hume, "will give you some idea of the accuracy of the lowland village medicine men — the Jacussi — in performing this delicate but culturally critical manoeuvre. The Jacussi are a little-known people, and their numbers are few. They alone perform circumcision in the Meganon Basin of the Amazon jungles. And they alone were subjected to the visitation of Helmut Vensgar in the early part of this century. Vensgar, educated in the study of primitive cultures, left Germany after shedding his Jesuit robes and espousing the teachings of the Talmud. He fancied himself a Jew but retained the missionary evangelical zeal of the Jesuits and finally found himself deep in the Amazon heartland, where he altered once and for all time the future of the Jacussi . . ."

I began to see even more clearly this problem of anthropologists becoming overly involved in the life of a naive ancient culture. And later, when I had the odd fortune of meeting Hemmings-Hume's wife, I vowed to be wary of women anthropologists as well. I somehow had wangled my way into the reception for the notable chap and ended up in a corner near the over-juiced punchbowl with the over-juiced Mrs. Hemmings-Hume. As I learned, she had been involved with monkeys while her man was off in South America watching disgusting rituals near the Amazon. She said that she and "HH" had a wonderful relationship, that they were always at one with each other as long as they were on the same side of the equator. Mileage was irrelevant.

Her fascination with killer apes had led her to live in close proximity with one in a rainforest for six months. I asked her what close proximity meant, and she looked at me, rubbing her hand up and down her neck, and responded, "Don't be childish." After a dozen or so glasses of punch, I found her steering me irrevocably toward the coat closet with several unusual body movements, reminiscent of dancing on the early *Bandstand* shows.

I successfully escaped, thanks to the arrival of Professor Mac-

Donough, who came looking for his coat. He seemed a bit miffed that I was getting on so well with famous world scholars, while he had been ignored at best. He left with the advice that I could spend my time better in the library. I agreed and slipped somebody's muskrat coat into Mrs. HH's arms. I departed.

I could go on with this, tell you about the incredible void in my life that anthropology had filled. I mean, the books all made sense, even if their authors turned out to be loony-tune material. Eventually I even saw the joy I'd get out of becoming as eccentric as the planet would allow, once I'd copped a graduate degree in my field of endeavour and had snooped around a little-known micro-culture in Micronesia for a few years. But they cancelled summer sessions because of the new budget cuts, and I had nowhere else to head for the moment but back to Mulgrew.

On the bus ride home, I found it impossible to fantasize that I was on the outskirts of Timbuktu, and I was continually reminded of my destination by the loud chewing of gum coming from a hulking woman behind me. Blowing bubbles, she would let them burst at periodic intervals, breaking whatever reverie I could lull myself into and riveting my attention on the present. Her eight-year-old son, who sat beside me, eventually threw up on my pants after downing a half-dozen Vachon cakes. The man across the aisle, whom I recognized as an old-time resident of Mulgrew, was tipping back some Andrés Port and asked me five time if I had a light. He finally asked how my father was doing. I told him I didn't know as I tried to fan my pant leg near the heat vent to dry off the puke. I said that I hadn't spoken with him in eight months.

That's when I learned that my old man had had a bit of a hard winter. He had been fired from Jessup Brothers after he accidentally forgot to shut off his hose at Esther MacMurphy's house. In fact, about two hundred gallons of the stuff must've overflowed, ending up in Esther's well, before the old man could himself shut her down. According to my informer, my old man must've been fooling around with Esther somewhere inside while his pump was working overtime outside in the cold. Esther had always had a foul reputation with the other women in town, but I still can't see my old man getting involved with her. I suppose that it doesn't matter all that much, since fiction is as good as fact in Mulgrew.

When I arrived home, he was trying to fix the lawnmower. He looked up at me and, without a bit of surprise or welcome, said, "Have you seen my god-damn five-sixteenths wrench? I got every one but that one, and that's the one I need." Then he threw the mower into a depression left from where the outhouse used to be and took me by the shoulders. Looking straight into my eyes, he asked me if I was straight. "What do you mean, straight?" I responded. He pulled out a folded-up page from a glossy magazine he had stashed in his pocket and held up a colour picture of a young naked woman in cowboy boots.

"I mean, does that do anything for ya?" He shoved it into my face, too close even to focus on. It smelled like stove oil . . . or maybe it was gasoline, I couldn't tell.

From my newly civilized manners, he couldn't figure what to make of me. When he finally gave up asking me about college girls and whether I had been approached by any homosexuals, he started in on drugs, then religion. But sex bothered him the most. He had read some article about Halifax gay rights marchers in the *Chronicle-Herald* and feared that I had been abducted into the movement. I tried to explain about anthropology, but it was like trying to explain chess moves to a wombat. I gave up.

As usual, my mother always went along with my father and believed him to be incapable of any wrong or any mistake. She remained silent for the most part, the way he liked her, and I settled in for an uncomfortable summer with a night job at the fish plant, where I was supposed to cut fillets off cod for eight hours straight.

The old man let me use the car to go to and from work, and it wasn't long before my interest in work disappeared and I found myself sneaking off on occasion with Debbie Conrad. Debbie was a packer and I was a cutter, and we found ourselves attracted to each other during a brief stint that we had together working in the freezer. We agreed that there were better things in life than fish packing, and as long as we made it to work at least four nights a week, we wouldn't be fired.

She and I had grown up together. But she left school at fifteen to marry Bart Kinsmen. Bart had since gone off to sea with the armed forces and not written in three years. Debbie told me how she had always admired my brains, and I admitted that I had often admired her body, so we hit it off on that note. I could see that the summer wouldn't be a total loss.

We spent our one stolen night a week in the Rambler parked out near where the old wharf used to be, before the hurricane of '62 ripped her off. There was a cozy little clearing in among the alders and plenty of room in the old man's '62 Rambler, a car he had kept all these years. I silently thanked him for this small luxury the first night that I noticed that the front seat went all the way down, making the interior of the car a sort of playground area for our nocturnal rituals. In fact, I soon learned that Debbie liked the ritual to be exactly the same every single time. Nothing fancy, nothing new. Just the basics. But then who was I to complain? I admit that once or twice I would get worried that some of the other local ne'er-do-wells would sneak up on us at night as we were all wrapped around each other in that steamed-up car with the radio on. So I kept a baseball bat in the back seat just in case.

Meanwhile, the old man was getting a bit edgy about why I missed work at least one night a week. News always travels in Mulgrew, but he only heard part of it. He kept plying me at dinner time with questions about political beliefs, drugs and screwy fad religious movements.

Now, the sad part is that he would have approved of my surreptitious activity had it been clear to him and had I the sense to tell him. But in the end it had to come to this:

It is a Thursday, full moon, warm as it ever gets on this shore. I'm out in the Rambler with Debbie, and I have the radio tuned in to an opera on the CBC, *The Mikado*. I hear a noise near the trunk of the car, like someone's climbing on the trunk lid to look in. Debbie looks panic-stricken, her moans of ecstasy transformed into whimpers of terror. I don't know what she thought was out there, or what I thought, for that matter, but somewhere deep in the DNA of my brain, a signal went out. I was overwhelmed by a protective and even somewhat violently aggressive urge. Without trying to piece my clothes back together, I jumped out of the car screaming and wielding the baseball bat, ready to take on whoever was out there. My pants fell down to the ground, and, still snarling, I kicked them away into the bushes. Debbie, scared out of her wits, leaned out the door and pleaded, "What's happening?" She, too, was less than thoroughly clothed.

And just then there was a blinding flash of light and then a click, and then a series of blinding flashes. I was still holding the bat aloft, Debbie was hugging my rib cage, and we didn't have the slightest notion as to what the hell was going on. And then I heard my old man say, "Well, I'll be damned. I'm sorry to interrupt you like this, boy. If I'd a know'd, I guess I could have saved the film."

We never said a word about it to each other after that. He'd just wink across the dinner table once in a while. I thought he was satisfied, but I guess the loss of his job had given him more time to think about his family and the future of his son. When I returned to university in the fall, I wasn't there but a day before I was summoned into the dean's office. Sitting before me were the dean, Professor MacDonough and someone introduced as head of the university ethics committee. Professor MacDonough held out a series of four photographs to me, and the case was presented that, whatever I had been up to, it indicated an uncertain mental stability and, at the least, a lack of moral fibre. The ethics board had decided that for the good of the institution I was to be denied permission to attend school any longer. MacDonough indicated that not only was I lacking the common decency necessary to attain any academic achievement, but that a career in anthropology for me could set back the field a hundred years.

Completely baffled and humiliated, I turned to go. The dean handed me the photographs, and MacDonough added, "And when you see your father, would you try to convince him that he should learn to spell. This is a civilized country, you know."

# THE RECONCILIATION OF CALAN McGINTY

Calan McGinty's cabin faced north, away from the sea. He was only five miles inland, but he felt as if the ocean must have been a thousand miles off as he faced the still, deep waters of Lake Ibis. The first perfect wafer of ice had developed overnight, creating a profound feeling of order. Calan knew that the wafer stretched the full twenty-three miles north from the base of the lake where his home was. The disruptive sea winds rarely ravaged the long narrow lake set between two ridges.

As he sat down by the edge of the water with a cup of tea in one hand, Calan could feel the sun climbing the hill behind him, finally breaking the crest and sending new volumes of colour to the valley.

Calan had been born no more than five miles to the south by the sea. It was a ragged, broken-down house that he was born in, just yards from the heave of the Atlantic. The old cedar shakes of the house were years beyond repair from the time he was born.

As a young boy he had studied how the sea and wind had conspired to fray the once-straight edges of the wood shakes. The cracks in the covering revealed the horizontal planks, which had more cracks and which allowed the winds of winter to bite into the heart of his childhood home. The whole of the two-storey house was covered with a green mould which slowly consumed what was left of the place. This bothered Calan immensely. He blamed his father for letting the place rot. His father blamed the sea.

"That damn stinking ocean. She'll tear her down altogether one day. I seen what she could do. Calan, never trust her. She'll cheat ya. I mean it. Look at the bitch." He was already staring out the window in disgust. Calan looked out at the boiling cold maelstrom. The November winds churned it up and around. It could have been seething with snakes. It jumped the seawall in front of the house and splashed across the hood of an old hulk of a car that had once been driven by Calan's father. The sea had jumped the wall on another day, drenched the engine, stealing the life from her for good. Now the sea had gnawed away at the fenders and frame, slowly, year by year, like a greedy cancer.

Calan's father had worked on the sea once. Worked on freighters out of Halifax and on trawlers out of Sydney. Saved his money for all those years and then bought a Cape Islander brand spanking new and lost her within a year. It wasn't until after he lost the *Margaret Elizabeth* that he married Marie Doiron and settled back into the house that had once been his father's. He was fifty when Calan was born and long past trying to make anything out of anything.

"Don't do one bit of good, son. Sure I'd fix up the outside of the house. But what for? The government'll charge me more taxes, and the salt water'll creep under the paint as soon as the tax man leaves the premises. She'll look the same in a year's time. To hell with it."

Calan's mother, a young woman whose parents had moved down from Anticosti Island, had tried to create a semblance of order in the kitchen. Calan would sometimes open the drawers to the cabinets just to see how orderly all the forks and spoons were, piled in their proper places. Old McGinty sat in a room just off the kitchen smoking a pipe made from a tin cap and a hollow piece of wood. He carved delicate little canoes out of spruce wood with a knife fashioned from the jawbone of a whale. As far as Calan could tell it was the only pleasure the old man got out of living. That and spreading a litter of wood chips and tobacco ashes all over the house for his wife to try and clean up. Sometimes the wind leaking through the winter walls would spread the stuff to all four corners of the first floor and into Calan's room, where he, too, fashioned miniature things out of wood, always careful to capture the wood shreds in an old tobacco tin.

The second floor of the house wasn't used, a household rule established by McGinty. "It ain't safe up there. Them beams might give way. B'sides, the rooms take the wind much worse. You'd likely freeze t'death." Nonetheless, every once in a while Calan's father pried out the nail that sealed the upstairs door closed and went up by himself, when he thought no one else was around. It would usually be sunset, and not always summer, and the old man would sit by the south window facing way out to sea. And the sea would be flat and still and not a bit like the madhouse he usually tried to ignore. And old McGinty would be smiling to himself as if he saw something a million miles out. Calan, lying low on the stairway, realised that it wasn't cold up there, between the sun streaming in and the heat rising up from the cookstove below. And he'd lie there for as long as he could without being discovered.

Calan's mother died before his father. His father died the winter they took his house for taxes, and Calan lived in a number of nearby households skirting the harbour. They were all relatives, or people who claimed to be relatives, of McGinty. When he was sixteen he took up working in the woods. Cutting pulpwood mostly. He worked in a crew of cursing, spitting, heavy-drinking, hard-working men for a while, till he saved up enough money to buy a rusted out pulptruck. He holed up in a barn for two months of one of the most bitter winters and rebuilt most of the truck body out of wood. The wood came from trees he'd cut and finished himself after hours of painstaking labour. Using blades more than saws, it was as if he had restored the body to one piece, the workmanship was that fine.

He enjoyed working alone the best. When he was nineteen he began hauling eight-foot lengths of firewood by the truck-load to families near the city. With five hundred dollars in his pocket, he bought a piece of land at the foot of Lake Ibis from Charlie Conrad.

Conrad thought the offer was too high. Only a couple of acres of spruce, no road access, not another soul living on the lake. Calan insisted and Charlie accepted.

The house was built very slowly and methodically. He planned every detail well in advance and hauled firewood only when he needed money for hardware. The house was fashioned from trees standing on the land. The walls of logs were made double, two walls instead of one, and filled with dried moss to keep out the winter. There was fulfilment in creating order and perfection. When the lighting was just right, the log home could be seen reflected in the still waters of Lake Ibis, as if in a painting.

Calan finally felt in control of his life. He didn't work more than he had to to make money. At fifty dollars a cord for wood, he figured he only had to sell fifty cords a year to get by. He appreciated the symmetry of his plan and had no trouble getting customers, who would watch Calan meticulously measure height, width and length of a load of wood for them when he delivered his goods. The rest of his time was spent in making cabinets or furniture or what he called "wood pottery."

He would no doubt have been content to continue according to his plan had it not been for Janine. He was making a delivery to a home in Waverly when she approached.

"I hear you live out near Inglis Harbour."

Calan smiled politely. "That's right."

"I, uh, just bought an old place out there and wonder if you'd mind selling me a cord of wood for the old cookstove in the house."

"Sure. Next week. You be in by then?"

"By Wednesday. About noon, okay?"

And she walked off across the street, forgetting to tell him where to deliver or what her name was. This made Calan feel confused and a bit angered. He didn't like uncertainty. At first he thought, to hell with her, if she's too dumb to tell me where to deliver. But then he knew that the Harbour was small enough that somebody would know who she was and where she was living.

Then his Waverly customer came out of his house yelling and waving his arms. "Stupid bastard! Look at what you're doing. You ruined a dozen rose bushes. You think I wanted six cord of wood piled on top of my wife's roses?"

Calan was embarrassed and insulted. He apologized and only took half of what was owed him for the firewood and drove home, feeling anxious and uncertain.

When he found out that the girl's name was Janine Desjardin, and that she had moved alone into the house he grew up in, he almost decided not to keep his promise. He didn't want to go back there, though it was only five miles away. He walked around his own completed hand-built home and studied every notch and groove again as if rebuilding it. He admired his own work and wondered what the girl would think of it if he showed it to her and let her see how different it was from the house by the sea. Why would she want to move in there? The place must be ready to fall down. And why did he find the thought of her so annoying? Or was it intriguing? He tried to remember what she looked like. Like wind chop. Like waters rushing against each other. He went out and proceeded to cut up the cord of wood into neat twelve-inch lengths and split them into perfect quarters, so he was certain the wood would fit in the old cookstove at the house.

Janine was sitting by the seawall when he pulled up in his truck. She was looking off at the horizon, a line which seemed to dip and rise incoherently where it intersected with sky.

"Great day," she said, walking over to greet him. She seemed so full of life, overflowing with it. But the abundant energy seemed to control her. She didn't know how to handle it. "Nice wood. Look, here, put it right here in the porch, some under the steps . . . some . . . over there . . . ah, hell, put it anywhere."

Calan unloaded an armful but held it against his chest, uncertain where to set it down. His bewildered look made her laugh. She buttoned up a couple of buttons that she had forgotten to do on her flannel shirt.

"Is that a beaut of a house or what?" she asked him, ignoring his indecision as to where the wood should go.

"A little worn, I guess, but not bad." She had walked away from him even as he answered, and he followed her into the kitchen.

"Say, could you help me get this stove operating right? I don't seem to have the hang of it. Grew up in a city, you know, Montreal. Good place to be from. Great place to leave."

"You should open that damper in the back. Like this." The stove was rusted shut in half a dozen places, and it took him a long time to get it operational. "There. Pretty rough shape, but she'll do for now, I guess."

Janine was flitting around the kitchen. The place was a disaster. All the old things from Calan's past, all the new clutter of this girl from Montreal. The worst of both worlds, he thought.

"You lived here, didn't you. They told me. Whatever could have possessed you to move away from the sea?"

Calan walked over to the doorway to the upstairs. Nothing nailed shut. No door in fact. The rust-frozen hinges must have broken off when someone tried to open it.

"You'll need this fixed, I reckon."

"Not really. I like it better without a door."


When the really bitter wind of February blew down off the ice pack, it ignored the valley of Lake Ibis but tortured the village along the coast. Calan suggested to Janine that she come move in with him. It wasn't unexpected to most of Inglis Harbour. It didn't even surprise Janine, who seemed to accept all things. It was a surprise to Calan, though, to hear himself asking her. The thought of this strange young women had so disrupted his comfortable life of routine that he often wished that she hadn't ever arrived. Nonetheless, when he asked, she was sitting by the cookstove huddled for warmth and burning the last of the wood she had bought from Calan. She told him how happy she was to hear the invitation but admitted she was satisfied with the old house as it was. In fact, the place looked much the same as when Calan had first seen it.


Calan made a few new calculations: sixty dollars a cord and sixty cord a year. No big deal. That would cover having electricity put in and the costs of the baby and, he figured, whatever else came along.

He had had every intention of getting Janine to the hospital that next October, but the doctor or Janine had somehow miscalculated and everything started happening too fast. The lake had just formed that first perfect wafer of winter ice that imposes a carpenter's level on the surface of the world. The morning light had just brought colour back to the valley.

Calan was out splitting wood, and the labour pains were well under way before Janine yelled for Calan to come at once.

"Too late for driving, Cal. Stay here with me now. I need you."

The pains came at irregular intervals, closer and closer together but then further apart. "Calan, what's an ibis, anyway?" She winced.

"A black water bird, like a crow on stilts. Not all that common, but we see a few here on the lake every few years."

She gulped for air. "Didn't think crows lived near oceans."

"They don't, usually, but we're five miles inland. Feels like a thousand sometimes. Do you like that feeling of being far from the sea?"

Janine didn't have a chance to answer. The pains came in persistent waves now, thirty seconds apart, then right on top of one another, and Calan, who was scared and feeling helpless, comforted her through the delivery and at last held up a baby girl for Janine to see. He cut the cord with the knife he had sharpened to a razor's edge and boiled for a half-hour.

And through the whole thing, Calan was in awe of what he saw, yet it seemed to have none of the clean, refined elements of the act that had started the process. It frightened him. The blood, the fluids, the seemingly misshapen child that emerged from an opening far too small for the task. The pain, the tears, the complete staggering chaos of the event. It didn't make a bit of sense for it to happen this way. And when he held his new daughter near the fire for warmth and the mother slept, he himself cried at the perfection of the child and laughed as he spotted a seam in the wall that had cracked and was allowing the now-gusting wind to intrude into his house.

In the spring, the ice dissolved and the lake overwhelmed its banks, pushing its excess waters into the narrow stream that linked it with the sea. The sound of the torrent was like the crying of the child when things weren't quite right.

Janine asked Calan to walk down the tiny river to the ocean with her, and Calan agreed. He enjoyed the cool spring air and the wind that grew stronger as they walked southward. At the harbour, the waves lapped nervously against each other and against the sand, distributing foam that drifted off across the salt marsh like diminutive clouds. Calan walked along the rim of the sea, carrying his daughter and watching Janine let her hair float in the sun. His feet followed the very edge of the most shoreward tidal advance, until once, looking up to see some exotic item that Janine had found, he allowed his feet to get soaked. Janine laughed wildly and came down to push Calan even farther out into the tiny breakers. Calan decided that he liked the biting cold of the water and continued to walk along, allowing the waves to lap around his ankles. His daughter slept peacefully in his arms, despite the roar of sea and waves. Calan felt perfectly satisfied to allow his feet to get soaked to the bone. He could thaw them out later. It was only a five-mile walk back to his home on the lake, and that didn't seem so very far at all.

# COMING UP FOR AIR

Dan had spent most of the night on the phone talking with a forty-year-old woman who had lived a classically horrible life and was finally getting around to teasing herself into thoughts of suicide. She had just that evening discovered the existence of Halifax's own twenty-four-hour hotline for the depressed, disturbed, disheartened and disenfranchised, but she waited until two o'clock in the morning to call. She sat down with a fresh cup of Nabob's and dialled the number she hoped would save her. She kept a half-full bottle of vitamins by the receiver just in case her listener turned out to have a short attention span, so she could rattle the bottle a few times to reassure him things were serious.

Her name was Gloria, and like most of them, she wasn't serious at all. But she was, for the most part, crazy, and had trained her neurosis well over those forty years, so that she was reasonably proud of her ability to gain mileage from it. Dan could tell from the tone of her voice that it would be a long one. He was determined to help her see the night through. He would not hang up unless, as he warned her, another call was coming in; then he would have to put his sympathies for Gloria on hold to make sure the other caller was not a rape victim, brutalized wife, overdosing teenager or near-comatose vodka gargler. But unfortunately no such calls came in. So, for Dan, it was a long morning with a truly unfulfilled woman, who confessed that the high point for her during an average week was finding fudge for sale at Kresge's or more than two available dryers at the Henry Street laundromat.

Dan was often amazed at his ability to listen and console. Only to himself he confessed that he was good at faking it. And all too often, faking it seemed to work just fine. In three years, he hadn't lost a caller. None had abruptly hung up in anger, none had actually carried out a death wish (at least none that he knew of), and many had written to the centre to say that one phone call with a gentle-voiced guy named Dan had changed their lives and put them on the psychological mend.

But all Dan could think about on his drive east — away from the grey night of Halifax and toward the blue sky, red sun and rising headlands of the Eastern Shore — was surfing. The north wind would make the waves hollow; there was always the chance of getting inside the wave, to angle across a five-foot face of water and fade close enough back into the lip that it would leap out over top of him as he crouched down into the tube at just the critical time. He saw himself immaculately locked in. To make it, even for a second, was to be able to frame the outer world in a watery halo of green and blue, to crystallize at once the immediate business of being alive.

And to surf the North Atlantic in Nova Scotia in late December was to be alone with a clean, hard blue sky, a stone-cold sea and a relentless, cold, antiseptic wind.

Dan turned down the gravel road leading out to Power's Point. The road was thick with potholes, and each one was paved back to surface level with a sheet of white or clear ice that snapped in two and crunched beneath the wheels as he drove over it. He thought again about all the Glorias in the world, all the men and women who became baffled as to exactly why they should keep on living. Maybe that was why he was so good at his job — he had never even once questioned the validity of being alive. He was fearless in his dogmatic belief in the insistence of survival to the point of being smug.

Dan's success at mock-selflessness in his job was due to his ability to keep a distance; he never allowed himself to fade too far back into the throat of someone else's despair. A lot of counsellors had cracked doing just that. When you wanted to save someone too badly, you tended to screw up. And Dan refused to wallow in someone else's dementia. But he never, ever, hung up on anyone, and, as far as he knew, he always left his clients better off, somehow.

Still, he had paid his dues. Back in university, Dan had taken a course from a fairly well-known American poet, a guy named Barry Walker, who taught creative writing. Dan became very involved in the course and felt a strong personal bond growing with Walker, despite the fact that the other students ostracized him for his loyalty to the somewhat eccentric writer.

Toward the end of the term, Walker had started drinking before classes. He arrived late and would read three of his own poems, then try to lead directionless discussions. But while he seemed almost affectionate to some and indifferent to others, he became antagonistic to Dan, who tried to share some of his own efforts with the class. Dan rationalized it all as a battle of wits and fought hard to hold his own ground.

On the last day of class, Barry Walker arrived blitzed out of his gourd and asked Daniel Alger to read two of what he thought were his personal prize accomplishments of the term. Dan read. Walker sat in silence, growing morose, and said finally, "So this is what we have accomplished?" and he promptly dismissed the class. Walker looked pale and something less than alive. Dan, however, had produced a volume of Walker's that he had just purchased, a National Book Award winner called *Inside the Domed Sky*. He wanted the poet to sign it for him before he was gone.

Barry Walker sank into his seat, hastily scratched off something, and tossed the book back across his desk. With a noncommittal voice he said simply, "I'm glad you were in my class."

Outside, alone in front of the Student Union, Daniel read the inscription: "You'll never be much of a human being. Only your mind can save you now." Then the scrawled signature.

Three years later, when Dan had read about Barry Walker's battles with madness, the trips in and out of the New York hospitals, he wondered if the man's morose behaviour in creative writing had simply been the first signs of a deep-seated malady. Dan became fascinated by the diseases of the mind, in fact; and when Walker's tortured creative brain had finally driven him beyond the world of the living, Alger, halfway through an MA in modern poetry at Fordham, decided to write his thesis on the late Barry Walker. He wanted to understand how Walker had translated such an unhappy life into such graceful, sensitive and inspiring poetry. And he wanted to try and understand why Walker had been so antagonistic to him. Daniel hoped for some insight, not only into madness and creativity, but into why Walker saw each of them to be "not much of a human being."

Almost anyone that Dan talked to about surfing, about surfing in Nova Scotia in the winter, thought that he was nuts. The cold, brutal Atlantic frightened most of his friends, who preferred civilized, indoor sports. Dan had even been out surfing late on the afternoon before the *Ocean Ranger* oil rig went down. He had surfed out the daylight alone on ten-foot powerhouse waves until he couldn't see the rocky shoreline and had to listen for the sound of waves crashing on rocks to lead him back to land. At home he heard on the radio about the fantastic storm farther out at sea that had produced such magnificent waves. Dan was thankful for the storm, glad he'd been able to tap such exuberant energy. The next morning, however, he heard about the oil rig disaster and felt guilty. The storm that had advanced graceful, cold tunnels of sea for him to ride alone had turned brutal in the night and ruined eighty-four lives.

Two nights later, the mother of one of the men who had been on board the *Ocean Ranger* called the hotline. The oil company had finally admitted that there was no hope for her son, twenty years old, a cook on the *Ranger* for only three months. "It was my idea," she told Dan. "I convinced him he'd make good money on the rigs.

I told him to get a trade, to study cooking, so he could work inside. It would be safer."

She wanted to blame somebody or something. The sea. The oil company, the rig owners. The government. But in the end, she could only direct the fury of her anger at herself, and it was tearing her apart.

"I think you should get in touch with your clergyman," Dan heard himself say to her in his best professional voice — sincere, compassionate.

"I don't have one. Why do you think I'm calling you?" She was sobbing uncontrollably, but Dan knew she wouldn't hang up. He was there for her, to help see the crisis through. It was his job and he was good at it. "They kicked me out of the Catholic Church when I married his father," she told Dan. "Now his father is gone and my boy is dead. God don't want to hear from me now." Daniel listened to her let out a long, frightening scream. Then she threw the receiver at a wall, and it fell to the floor. But the line was still open.

Dan had only asked the phone company to trace calls perhaps a dozen times. His supervisor had admonished him for at least eight of the efforts. But four of them had paid off. This was not a clear suicide attempt. Life wasn't in danger, and he had no clear imperative to instruct the phone company to trace her down. But something felt different about the call. He took a chance, asked her to hold the line as he put a call through to the MT&T switchboard.

The operator refused to begin the search, even though it would have been so simple with the woman still on the line. Dan insisted, but the operator refused the request, said the phone company had to protect the privacy of its customers.

Dan tried getting his caller to come back to the phone, but there was nothing to hear except a desperate woman sobbing alone in a hollow, empty kitchen. There was nothing further that he could do. No real reason to conclude that she would attempt suicide. But he couldn't let it be. He felt responsible. He had been surfing, out having fun, tapping his source of private ecstasy, while her boy was about to go down in his ocean, killed by his hungry waves.

Dan called up Mobil in St. John's, where they had set up an information line for media people and relatives of the dead rig crew. A harried woman on the other end had little trouble pinning down who the boy's mother was. She was more than willing to give the Halifax address.

Later, when the Halifax police arrived at Alger's request, they received no answer to their knocking. The door was locked and bolted and had to be almost fully smashed off its frame before they could get in. What they found was a middle-aged woman, scared out of her wits, sitting up in bed with a baseball bat. Grief and fear gave way to outrage, and later that night an ambulance took her to the Victoria General, where she had to be heavily sedated. Two days later, she filed a lawsuit for the violation of her privacy for no good reason. The story had become every journalist's favourite sidebar to the *Ocean Ranger* story, and the city police had taken a black eye for it all.

Daniel parked two feet away from where the road gave out, where it had been washed away by the sea that had been pounding the glacial land for centuries. Once there had been railroad trestles here across an inlet too shallow and unpredictable for most fishermen to pass safely to sea. Now the tracks·were gone, stolen by a storm fifty years ago, and the rail line had been rebuilt inland to avoid more trouble. Two rusty steel rails still jutted out into mid-air from the abbreviated headland. Dan walked to the end of one rail, poised himself in the gentle, frigid offshore wind as gulls silently skimmed past him to catch the updraft along the upper edges of the ragged hill.

The sea was a bright blue. Six-foot-high waves were peeling perfectly, left to right, away from the peninsula and into the finicky inlet. It would be easy to forget about the Glorias, the mothers of drowned sons, on a morning like this. He ran back to his car, grabbed his gear. Still standing outside in a deepfreeze wind, he stripped off his clothes and began to put on his wetsuit.

The wetsuit was his second skin — half-inch neoprene, black, warm, slightly stiff until it got wet, but secure. If the men on the *Ocean Ranger* had each been issued one of these, some at least would have made it to daylight and salvation. His body cocooned in the black suit, Dan pulled on the boots and gloves and then snapped the hood down over his head. With the tightness of the wetsuit hood over his skull, his ears pinched in tight against his head, he felt a special kind of privacy. Even though the morning was a bright explosion of colours and sounds of bursting waves around him, he grew more absorbed in himself, fading back to the inside place beneath the neoprene. When he surfed the waves, it would be his vital, inner self creating on the moving canvas of the sea. He unhitched the board from the rack on top of his car. It was a seven-foot contraption of foam and fibreglass, made by hand by some dedicated surfboard designer in Australia, on the other side of the planet from here. Like automobiles, surfboard designs had names. This model was called simply "Alibi."


Fordham never allowed Daniel Alger to finish his master's degree in English as intended. He had started the thesis on Walker but grew restless, spending all of his time locked up with the twenty-odd volumes of the poet's work and one blatantly harsh critical biography.

He started wandering the moonscapes and ravaged streets of the Bronx at all hours of the day, feeling perfectly at ease among the street people of the night, as if he was protected by some invisible armour, some second skin that kept everything else away, all the danger, all the pain of this city at war with itself. He sat in bars and greasy spoons and listened. It felt like a newly discovered drug, just to hang around this sort of life and absorb it all, to live through every night like this and arrive at dawn unscathed, untouched and always cleansed. In literary terms it was quite simple to explain:

catharsis. And it worked greater miracles for him than writing endless pages of wasted words over a dead poet named Barry Walker, who had, his work suggested, spent all his life cultivating a private agony created solely for the purpose of creativity. Walker had convinced himself that he had to suffer in order to create. He believed the psychic pain was essential to be a good writer.

Dan's thesis advisor — a dapper, pin-in-the-tie, mid-career professor named Larry Cagney — had been away on a sabbatical, researching in the labyrinthine libraries at the University of Texas while Dan Alger was losing touch with academia and learning about life outside the gates at Fordham. Cagney returned, positively charged with intellectual energy from his research. Dan couldn't see how seven months inside a library could possibly bring out the best in a man.

"Walker's widow gave me this," Cagney told Dan, setting down a pile of dog-eared typed pages thick as a Sears and Roebuck catalogue. "It's yours to work on if you want. I haven't touched it. Barry Walker is your baby. Let's screw that bloody sotfaced biographer, Turkle, to the wall. Go prove that he never even began to scratch the surface of Barry Walker."

It was a hodgepodge collection of notes, a randomly compiled journal kept by Walker of the final eight years of his life. Loose ends, notes, fragments of poems, bits and pieces of everything, jotted down and saved, then donated to a library as a tax write-off; now, somehow, they had found their way around to him. Daniel pretended to be interested, but he knew it would probably take more than this to pull him back to literary criticism.

On his way back to his apartment, for the first time during his tenure in the Bronx, someone grabbed him at a street corner and pulled a knife. A scared teenage kid in sunglasses and a fedora hat said, "Give it to me, sucker." Dan handed over his wallet. "Give me the box, too." The kid grabbed it from under Dan's arm and then plunged off toward the subway stairs. What fascinated Dan was that he hadn't felt frightened in the least. And now he had a good excuse for forgetting about the Walker thesis altogether. Cagney would be disgusted. Walker's widow would probably be livid. The papers would undoubtedly be thrown away. Lost. It wasn't exactly his fault. People just kept walking by. No one had reacted while the drama took place. If anybody had seen the incident they weren't about to ask any questions.

Out of curiosity more than anything, Daniel followed in the direction of the thief's retreat. He walked slowly toward the subway. He took his time going down, not really wanting to meet up with his assailant and press his luck. Damn, there it was. Discarded in a pile of trash by a water fountain that hadn't worked in years. The box was torn open and the papers scattered around. But it was all there. The kid had been hoping for anything he could pawn. An expensive jacket, something electrical, a cake even. Instead, he found a pile of worthless papers poorly typed and reworked by hand in the scrawl of a maniac. Dan's wallet was, of course, nowhere to be found. He gathered up the pages and walked home.

It would be next to impossible to put the pages back in order, but it was all there, like Walker's genius itself: inspired, inventive, insightful, but also cynical, uncontrolled, cluttered and confused. Words and images spiralled in a round, ruthless vigour, choking real life with the work of the imagination. Just from commuting through the disorganized fragments, Daniel had concluded that the poet could not see himself as anything but his work, and his work was so intensely private that it wanted to shut out all compassion for anyone or anything. It was about eleven at night when Dan came across the passage:

And I never knew exactly what the problem was until this smart young punk in my class started showing off his own poems. Namesake of the late Horatio, Alger picks up his crooked little pen at night and writes stuff as worthless as mine was at his age. Kindred spirits of the examined life. His poems stink but so did mine. I want to make sure he gets a job as a bank clerk; his soul is already lost. Maybe his mind can save him. I've seen people before with miniature souls and large brains get by in life and cause only minimal damage. There's a little hope left . . . for him. I shall discourage him from ever trying to be creative, for ever trying to do the world any sort of "good."

The rest of the page had been tramped into the remains of a candy bar, but it wasn't important. Dan got up to go out. He turned off the overhanging gooseneck lamp, walked out into the night and down the street to sit in a favourite haunt, the Express Lounge, a place where people moved fast enough to burn out their lives in a matter of weeks. He sat down to a rum and coke and very loud juke-box reggae. Why would someone like Barry Walker have singled out Daniel Alger to be such a paradigm of the wasted life? It didn't seem fair. And yet it was Dan who had gone looking for reasons behind Walker's death, wanting to write about the great, dead, unhappy poet.

A young Hispanic woman walked in carrying a bundle of something. All the Blacks and whites and Puerto Ricans sitting at the bar turned to look. She ignored their attention. Instead, she slowly marched between the rows of tables, looking for something, someone. Near the end of the long tunnel-like Express Lounge, she found Daniel staring up at her. She was maybe sixteen. Her dark eyes revealed fear and pain. Daniel almost thought that she, too, was about to pull out some instrument of destruction and do him in. Instead, she put the bundle of blankets on the beer-soaked table, knocking off a heavy glass ashtray. Then she turned and fled.

Daniel undid the blankets slowly, as if he was prying apart the petals of an unfurling flower to get to the centre. He knew what was there. The baby was sound asleep until Daniel's finger stroked its cheek. As it awoke, it cried a loud, single wail that overtracked even Peter Tosh. The music stopped and the bar went dead silent.

A Black man nearby, sipping a tall glass of something green, turned and said, "Hey, man, ain't you ever heard of contraceptives?"

The place cracked up. They all gave him one good laugh and then turned back to whatever they were drinking — all except one short, fiery-faced Puerto Rican who stood up, angry, ready to come after Daniel on some ethnic principle. But his buddy grabbed him and pulled him back to his beer. "Give the brother a break," he was advised. "The man has personal problems enough." And after that they all ignored him. Daniel discovered that letting the child suck his finger kept it quiet; so together they made their exit as quiet as could be.

The kid wasn't his. He had never seen the girl before. She had picked him out, a young white man who obviously had not grown up in the neighbourhood. He was her long shot that her kid might stand a better chance. (The dead poet's least favourite student.) In his apartment, the baby boy slept peacefully. He put the child into his own bed, the only soft piece of furniture in the place. Next, he changed the kid's diaper, putting on a clean dish towel. Finally, Daniel went to sleep himself on the floor.

When the kid woke him up at five in the morning, Daniel succeeded in getting the baby to drink some lukewarm evaporated milk; then he took him for a ride in his old Mustang. He took the Cross Bronx Expressway to the Major Deegan and then went east, out the Long Island Expressway to Jericho. He was going to ensure that the night deposit left with him would end up in a safe place where it might gather the most interest. So he picked a ritzy neighbourhood in Jericho. A sign on the freeway took him toward a recently built community hospital with immaculate lawns and tasteful contemporary architecture. Dan pulled straight up into the emergency entrance. Having kissed his foster son one final, gentle peck on the forehead, he walked in through the front doors, found a starched nurse at the desk and said simply, "I think he's looking for a good home." Then Daniel ran out the front door and sped off into the anonymous suburbs before a security guard could be called, before anyone could ask a pertinent question, and before anyone in Jericho would know that the child was from the Bronx. It had been important for the kid to have a clean break. No one would ever trace him back to the Express Lounge.

On his way back into the city, Dan found himself stuck in the morning snarl of traffic headed for work. He hoped now that, whatever happened, the kid wouldn't end up like these automatons in their automobiles stalled all around him. Two hours later he was back in the comfortable squalor of his Bronx neighbourhood. In front of his apartment house, the season's first cold snap had prompted some local truants to build a fire in a trash can, and they stood around enjoying the flames while listening to music blast from a gigantic portable radio with a cracked speaker. Daniel went inside and, for the first time in months, dug out his surfboard. He carried it down and tied it on top of his car with a piece of rope.

"Check out the white dude," said one of the kids. "He thinks he woke up in California." Daniel smiled at him, sat in his car and turned the key on. But he realized he was forgetting something. He ran back up to his apartment. There, he gathered up the Barry Walker journals and all the notecards for his thesis, shoved them into a grocery bag and bounced back downstairs and out into the street.

He poured the entire contents of the shopping bag on the dying flames in the trash can. "Just thought you could use a little extra fuel."

Far Rockaway beach on a fall day can be surprisingly decent. The crowds gone. The sea, despite the raw, smelly wastes dumped down its throat, tries to pretend it is as it always was, and the chilly north wind makes lively three- and four-foot waves look like miniature pipelines. Daniel parked by a gargantuan condominium block, untied his board and ran across the boardwalk past the old men playing checkers and some teenage girls sniffing glue out of paper bags. Up above, jets thundered in low, ready to land across Jamaica Bay at Kennedy Airport. They seemed like dark, intelligent birds, skirting low and big enough to cast awesome shadows over the sea and skyscrapers. The water was still over sixty degrees, and the sandbar offshore was the place to sit and catch wave after wave on a fine fall day like this.

The best part of it, Daniel realized — after ten fine tuckdown, scrunched-up little snappy rides — was that he felt hollowed out and clean. Out of breath, he sat for a minute to let the comforting rhythm of the sea and the sun's warmth overwhelm him. He had almost shut out the annoying rattle of descending jet planes when he heard something else. A thunder that was so deep, so loud and so violent that it seemed to be coming from everywhere at once. He looked around, but the sky was empty even as the roar grew in intensity. It was deafening and unlike anything he had ever heard. It just kept growing, a low throaty growl that made Daniel cover his ears as the noise reached painful thresholds. And then it finally struck him that this explosion of sound might be the last thing he would ever know. He looked toward Manhattan, fully expecting to see the first mushroom cloud that would signal the end. He was sure this time it was happening. All those other false alarms he had wondered over as a kid were nothing compared to this. And yet everything around him seemed perfectly normal except for the deafening blast. What exactly would it be that he would feel in the next minute? Suddenly he remembered the baby, out there in the purified, sanitary world of Long Island. On his drive to Rockaway, after the fact, he had named the baby Joshua, just so he could forever hold the name as well as the face in his mind. Now, after all the bad luck that Joshua was born to, after the glimmer of hope, the kid would be blown to dust like the rest. Stupid ironies. It was the one thing he couldn't shut out of his mind. He really didn't have the slightest grief for the rest of civilization, but he felt deeply saddened thinking of the loss of that one tiny life.

Daniel sat bolt upright on his board, still waiting for a shock wave to hit him as he looked to the northwest where the centre of the city lay. But, instead, the roar kept growing from behind him. From out at sea, it crawled down on top of him until he felt that he could hardly breathe. Then the sky went dark, and something was above. The largest jet he had ever seen. It seemed about to slice off the tops of the condos on the beach, this gleaming white scalpel, but it passed and was moving on, descending, preparing to land at Kennedy. The sound died away.

On the boardwalk, the men were still at their games of chess.

Daniel could hardly believe that he had been so naive as to trick himself into such a melodrama. He had read about the protests concerning Concordes landing at Kennedy. Now he knew why. Even though his end-of-the-world epiphany was a private one, he felt foolish. A supersonic Concorde tooling down to land on a routine flight. Now that the protesters had given up, such earthshaking noise was routine stuff. He paddled to take off on a steep, brownish wave that was about to go critical; he slipped off his board on take-off. The nose of his board went to the bottom and so did Dan. The feisty wave turned him upside down and pulled him along inside the white turbulence before letting him go. Daniel came up, retrieved his board and paddled shoreward. He had lived through the end of the world, and that had been enough for one day.

Paddling out into the Nova Scotia surf, Daniel discovered that the waves were bigger than he had realized from shore. Seven pushing eight feet. Overhead. A savage North Atlantic storm had formed them four hundred miles from here. Now the storm system had passed on, and, in its wake, it was sucking the cold air down to the coast from the north. The frigid seawater inside his wetsuit was beginning to warm up. He dunked under the scalloped lips of critical incoming waves to push himself through the line-up to the outside break. The effect of the new cold water pouring into his suit was intoxicating. Opening his eyes again, Daniel was overcome by the purity of the sea here, the clean air, the empty, perfect waves. He missed nothing about New York. He was glad that his life in the United States was behind him. Canada had been good to him. His life had fallen into place. And here in Nova Scotia he was very good at his work. He felt that he was doing something worthwhile. He dove off his board just to clear his senses again, to get more fresh water inside his suit and feel the bite of the clean, cold sea.

He let the first set of waves pass by, then saw something more tempting on the horizon. An even larger batch of seven-footers advancing one after the other like living walls of water. He let three pass by before paddling for the fourth one, balancing on his knees and dipping deeply into the sea.

He was moving straight into the headland until the wave caught him; and he was up, turning right and tracking down along the face of a long, vertical wall, the wind cracking in his face and the sound of the tube collapsing all around behind him, just inches beyond the tail of his board. He was fading further back into the throat of the wave as it broke faster, harder, catching up to him until he lost control. The wave snapped him off his board, over the falls, down into the shuddering mass of white water. He was pushed under and jerked in a hundred directions at once. His wetsuit hood was ripped off. The intensity of such cold seawater against a warm skull made his head pound — something like an explosive, exaggerated hangover. He'd felt the pain from the cold before, the ice-cream headaches, but this seemed so much worse.

Daniel wanted up. He couldn't have been more than a few feet from the surface, but the white water kept rolling along, pulling him into deeper water rather than into the rocky shoreline. He was caught by the boiling, maddening tonnage of sea, moving horizontally, unable to change his vector, unable to surface. It kept him down like an angry monster's paw. He needed air but knew he had to keep his mouth shut tight. Reason was there. Go slow. Don't panic. He had been there a hundred times before. Just relax. But as he tried, he felt his stomach go into a knot. He was about to puke and still he couldn't pull himself up out of the white water that whipped him around like a broken stick. He fought back the vomit and silently screamed to himself: Relax! It would be over in seconds.

Surely he had only been under for less than a minute, but in the cold water of a Nova Scotia winter, seconds expanded exponentially into minutes, hours, lifetimes. The panic kept jumping back in. It seized him this time in a way he couldn't deny. It arrived like a loud, black noise. He squeezed his eyes tighter, trying to make it go away. Now Daniel was starting to see colours. Black gave way to purple, then red. His mind was crowded with confusion: a thousand screams and a howling, desperate conviction that this time was not like all the others. And still the sea kept pushing him down.

But just as quickly as the panic had started, it shifted to something else. Sadness. Soon it would be all over. Not just him. Everything. Up until now, everyone he had known had been fighting the losing battles. Everyone but him. The mother of the drowned cook. The mother of Joshua. Gloria, hopelessly lost from childhood. All those other midnight callers. And Barry Walker, digging his own grave with his poetry, trying to coerce Daniel with insults to avoid the same trap. A new colour came to him — he was surrounded by a muted blue. It was a quiet place, a sad place, and he was ready to breathe now, with water all around. Yes, he was ready to breathe.

Instead, his arms shot out from his side, his feet kicked at the churning water. This time, the wave let him go.

He was up, gasping, coughing, trying to pull the light of the sky back into all the colours of darkness still swarming inside his skull. He breathed air, tilted his head back and found himself floating. The wetsuit would keep him up on its own until he could find his arms, his direction, his strength. More white water pounded behind him and on top of him, but it failed to pull him down. He was being drawn toward the inlet and into the channel, but that didn't worry him. Once he recaptured his strength, he could easily swim across to the shallow reef and then walk his way back to the headland.

Daniel was thankful that his body had somehow pulled him up even after his mind had called it quits. Instinct over intellect.

They were all probably right — his friends who had told him he was crazy to go surfing in the winter. Alone. In fact, he suddenly realized that he would never be as "crazy" as he once was, never as free. He felt as if the detachment and privacy that had once been the source of his strength was now gone. In its place was a feeling of great need. It was the saddest thing he had ever known.

*The Town*

# BREAKAGE

The half-consumed bottle of wine rolled around under the back seat as he slowed to a stop at the light. Cheap wine, a gallon of it. What in the world had he been thinking when he had put down his five bucks on a whole jug of this foul-tasting stuff rather than buying half as much of something decent? "Tastes a little like Kool-Aid," she had told him. And in truth Denise had been right. Wayne was always a sucker for buying something cheap. And rather than just ditching the rest of the booze, he let it roll around under the back seat. He could have dumped the stuff in the river that night, where it would have been right at home with all the other pollutants meandering down toward the sea.

He half expected it to break. Imagine the smell of a couple of quarts of rot-gut burgundy permeating the inside of the Chev. He'd never be able to take his mother to church in the car if that happened. He'd probably have to hammer a couple of nail holes in the floorboards just to drain the stuff off. But still there was always the hope that he'd get another chance with Denise. Maybe tonight. If he had the strength, he'd ask her just as soon as he got back from his lunch break. She was the only thing that made the upcoming afternoon at the nursing home seem bearable.

The light changed, Wayne let out the clutch and began to move up behind the sluggish Plymouth in front of him. It was getting late, and he didn't want to have to sit through another three-minute wait to get across the highway. But the Plymouth stopped abruptly, Wayne hit the brakes, heard the wine bottle bump against the front of the seat.

"Jesus."

But it hadn't broken. He missed the light.

Out on the highway, a dog was trying to cross from the other side, totally unaware of the onslaught of speeding cars. Two swerved to the right, almost nicking each other, but a third driver, pushing it a bit over the speed limit, couldn't plow up the pavement with skidding rubber quickly enough to stop. He caught the dog with a dull thud and then, deciding there was nothing for him to do, sped on. The rest of the traffic just continued to flow as if nothing had happened.

"Damn it!" Wayne screamed into the windshield as he involuntarily smashed his fist into the horn rim, breaking it clean off the steering wheel and sending it flying in his lap, then bouncing onto the floor. He pulled a quick jerk up on the parking brake and then jumped out of the car and ran onto the highway. It was hard to tell if the dog was dead or alive. There was blood coming from his mouth, and the eyes looked funny. Some sort of a mutt, but a family dog, with a collar and tags. He picked up the creature ever so gently, amazed at the tide of cars still racing past, just barely avoiding him, blowing their horns, cursing him even, as if he had no right on the highway. He stood there for a few seconds, getting his bearings.

One car coming in his lane saw him at the last minute and had a hard time changing lanes, almost swiping a bus that was booming past. The guy in the car was shouting something at him. He was pissed off. Couldn't the bastard see that he was just trying to save the poor beast? But he was right in a way. There was no place for anything living on this road.

Two girls waiting for a bus were yelling at Wayne to get off the road. He walked toward them slowly, as if in a dream. The dog was still unconscious, dead maybe. That wasn't for him to decide. Wayne stepped up onto the curb. The light changed. Cars were crossing. Somebody was yelling for him to move his Chev, that it was blocking the road. People in a hurry. Everybody trying to get back to work before lunch break was over. It turned his guts.

"Do you know where there are any vets around?" he asked one of the girls. She looked familiar. His biology class?

"Three lights up. On the right. Is it dead?" She looked at him in a very strange way. So did the other girl. Everyone else was simply ignoring him. Wayne was crying. It felt right; he didn't know why. But it helped him to gather his wits.

Hurrying back to his car, he set the dog down on the front seat, dripping blood on the rugs. He ran to the other side and got in. Now people were watching him with curious expressions. Dumb bastards. Everybody too busy to help.

The light was against him again. He tried to signal the guy in front of him to move and let him get going, light or no light, but without luck. Cranking the wheel hard to the right, he let out the clutch and jumped the curb, cutting across the sidewalk and the drugstore parking lot, then out into the blasted highway and off toward the vet.

He noticed the handbrake still on, cursed and let it out. That would screw up the rear brakes just great, he knew; they were already almost shot, and he'd been holding off on buying new replacements. Expensive. "I'll put it on your tab," he muttered to the bleeding dog beside him. He noticed that the dog was panting, a good sign. Wayne smiled and felt a rush of tears down his face. "You're going to be okay, kid," he said over and over. The girl at the bus stop had called the dog "it." Something about that he didn't like. Even if you didn't know the gender, he didn't like anything living to be called "it."

The receptionist was very cool and collected and asked Wayne too many questions about whose dog it was and what had happened. He didn't need that. "Look, lady, would you get someone to help and ask me that stuff later." She focused on his tear-stained face and then proceeded to get the doctor.

Back in his car, Wayne looked at the blood on his hands and all over the seat.

Late again. He figured he had a legitimate excuse and blood to show for it. All he needed now, though, was for some cop to pull him over, see the blood, find the booze. It would be a lot of fun explaining his way out. Not really. They'd nail him for something. He didn't exactly have a great rapport with cops. The hair was enough to convict him these days, and he was used to being stopped and searched on a regular basis. He wondered why he was dumb enough to be toting around the burgundy.

And then he remembered why.

He tried to hide the blood on his hands as he walked through the sterile halls of the nursing home, heading straight towards the janitor's closet, where he scrubbed his fingers to the bone with lye soap. The superintendent pulled open the door abruptly as he was finishing.

"There you are, Murdoch. Would you get some new bulbs down to those end rooms in the west wing? Just 'cause the patients are blind doesn't mean the nurses don't need light."

"Sure thing." The door was closed again and he was alone in the janitor's closet staring at a cabinet full of bleaches and detergents and assorted cleaning aids. Carl had called them "patients." That was even after the big lecture last week by the owner saying they were supposed to refer to them as "clients." Couldn't we just refer to them as people? Wayne had wanted to say. But he had kept his mouth shut.

He found Denise in Room 134. Good luck, one of the rooms where he had to replace the bulb. She was standing in the half-light by the window, staring out at the highway. Old Mrs. Albright was asleep. Sometimes she complained too much, and they gave her lots of pills to keep the noise down. Seemed a shame in a way to spend your last few years of living conked out most of the time.

Denise yawned. She hadn't heard him come in.

"Goofing off?" Wayne asked.

"A bit, I guess. I'm kinda tired."

"Too much wine."

"Could be." She had a dreamy look, almost perpetually. A very cute girl in every sense of the word. Not beautiful, just cute. Wayne didn't go for the real beauties. They were either too snotty or had nothing at all in their brains. School seemed to be full of them, too. Lots to look at, plenty to get worked up over, but Wayne had learned his lesson more than once. He was tired of being fodder for that mill.

"Did your mother find out that you were drinking?"

"She didn't really care. I had a nice time." Denise seemed like such a gentle person. Soft. But there was always so much that she didn't say. He never knew what really went on in her head. She liked the old people as much as he did. They weren't just lumps of flesh to be fed and cleaned and worked around.

Wayne liked to just look at her in her white uniform. A nurse's assistant — an impossible job. She had to change bedpans and dirty sheets, really dirty, that is. Had to give baths to patients and help hold down struggling old men who didn't want to get lanced by a needle morning after morning. Denise didn't seem to mind it too much. Like Wayne, she found her odd moments to sit down with the old folks and get them to talk about the past, the way things used to be.

Wayne remembered Mr. Connally telling him that he used to live just down the road, a house right on the highway, lived there for seventy years. In the same house. In the old days, the highway had only been a dirt trail for horses and buggies. Took almost a full day to get to Camden.

Denise was dusting a few objects on the dresser, slowly, methodically, with care. Wayne couldn't help but look at her from the back. Nothing fantastic, but pleasing: the swell of her hips, the delicate legs under nylon stockings. Her long brown hair that last night fell down to her waist was now tucked up in a bun, the way they were required to wear it here. "You have to make some sacrifices if you want a summer job," she had said. Wayne watched the reflection of her face in the mirror as he positioned the chair under the ceiling fixture, ready to change the bulb.

When Denise looked up to polish the large mirror in front of her, she saw Wayne staring and smiled, saying nothing. Wayne couldn't help but smile back. Something about her. Nothing that she said; in fact, she said so little it was hard to convince himself that he even knew her. The bulb slipped from his hand and crashed to the linoleum floor.

"Damn." He looked down at the splinters of delicate glass, hoping that no one out in the hall heard. He was getting a reputation for breaking things. Denise giggled.

Mrs. Albright woke up, or pretended to. She had been awake all the time. Giving Wayne a wink, she pretended to be falling back to sleep again, but the thin ribbon of her puckered mouth gave her away with a smile. Denise helped Wayne to clean up the glass, and they both departed to other tasks.

A few weeks ago, they had both worked together in the kitchen while the two Pakistani immigrants were off on their yearly vacations, home to families. Wayne couldn't decide whether he liked the work there better or worse. He was cut off from the old people more and a bit at the mercy of a middle-aged dietician who seemed to be coming on to him. But he got to know Denise, who helped him dish out mashed potatoes and peas and all kinds of sickening institutional food that they joked about. Stacking dishes and slogging them into the washing contraption seemed like evil work, though. Once he had burnt the hell out of his hand when he grabbed a tray fresh out of the steam. He had been alone in the kitchen with Denise, and she came to his rescue, running to him like he was a child and then putting his hand under cold water. They had looked at each other suddenly with a strong, fixed stare. Something connected. But even as she looked, something went away from her. She just spaced out.

Nonetheless, it was enough. Then the dietician burst in with a cart full of vitamin pills and said jokingly, "Just keep your hands off, sweetheart, he's mine," and left just as suddenly.

Ever since the kitchen work, Wayne had thought that maybe he and Denise had something. He hated dates, though, and ended up taking her out in his car a few times, parking. They would sit in the smelly summer air down by the river and talk, listen to the ever-repeating songs on the radio, and eventually get around to something physical. Wayne always half-expected the cops to hassle them, but they never did. He always kept the doors locked in case other intruders were up to no good. The awesome stone fortress of a prison across the river was reminder enough of the violence of the world. Maybe he should have "taken her out," gone out to eat, to a movie, to a concert. But that wasn't what he wanted out of life. He'd rather talk and get close, and sure, there was a bit of lust in there somewhere.

At five o'clock every day, he punched out. This single act seemed to remind him invariably, "Murdoch, ol' boy, you're more than just a kid, you're part of the work force." Today he was punching out for Bill Gibson, another kid on a summer job, who had to leave early to get a new pair of tires for his Volvo. He smiled at Denise, and they both went off in their separate automobiles.

Wayne drove the back way home through dozens of suburban streets, avoiding the highway. Despite the fact that the subdivisions were only about ten years old, the pavements were a disaster, the sidewalks crumbling and the houses faded and worn. Trees planted by the developers had fallen prey to gypsy moth and Dutch elm disease and stood sentinel over the decay.

Why the Jesus hadn't he asked her out again for tonight? Wayne asked himself. In a way, he had just simply chickened out. That wasn't uncommon for him. And then there was that chasm, that big empty gulf that seemed to be forming between them that didn't make any sense. It was like the closer he thought they were becoming the further apart they were drifting. Was it him or was it her? That blank spot at the core of her softness. That final fog bank of silence toward the end of an evening where he felt that he had bared his soul. Maybe he was coming on too strong. Or not strong enough. More than once, he'd learned from a girl he fell for that his hang-up was that he didn't come on strong enough. And he thought that he was trying to be polite, be cool. Crap.

Well, the wine should have done it. A full gallon. And Denise had said that she was up for a good drunk with him. That's when the barriers should have come down. If the cops had come, he would have told them to go to hell. It was an important night.

They both got fairly plastered and laughed and hooted and pawed each other a bit, but as soon as his kissing started to get serious, she sort of froze up, retracted. They both fell back silently into themselves, drinking more but getting more sober with each gulp of the burgundy. Finally, he took her home. He wanted to ask her out again tonight, hoping to pick up where they had left off. He was dead certain they were almost in love. It would take just a little more.

Wayne sulked through supper, told his mother about the dog but refused to answer her questions about the details. His father asked him how the brakes were on the car; he knew they had been giving him trouble. Wayne didn't own up to driving with the parking brake on. A phone call took his mother from the table, and when she came back she said it was just some little bit of business with her committee, nothing important. Then she asked if Wayne was going to be home for a while after dinner, and he said he'd be around for an hour or so.

Near the end of that hour, a car pulled up and a girl got out with a cake. It was Silvy MacDonnal, one of the real knock-outs of the school, a big bosomy blonde girl who was on the cheerleading squad. An unattainable. What was she doing here with a frigging cake?

Wayne's mother opened the screen door and let her in. She walked over toward him with the cake as he stood up to say hi, nervous as hell. "Thanks for saving Fang," she said, and, leaning across the cake, planted a big kiss on his cheek. Then she gave him the cake, which had left two flowers of icing on her blouse at the tip of each amazing breast. They were both a little embarrassed.

Silvy's mother and a gaggle of four little kids then emptied from the station wagon and came into the house, each one in turn thanking him for saving the life of their dog. Fang would live, they said, although he would probably limp for the rest of his days. "I'm glad to hear he pulled through," Wayne said, trying to be cool. He didn't like the situation at all and felt very uptight. The mother said that she had phoned some Oldsmobile dealer and told him the heroic story, and that Smilin' Fred Bascom wanted to make him Citizen of the Month, that he'd send a reporter from the *Record* to get a picture and the story. There probably was a hundred bucks in it for him there somewhere. Before they all exited into the living room to leave him alone with Silvy, the mother cloistered him in a corner and asked him if the blood from the dog had seriously damaged the upholstery of the car, and, if so, how much did he want to get it cleaned? That had been the furthest thing from his mind, and he told her to forget it. She beamed at him, amazed. A hero, and modest at that. He hadn't saved the dog for these people, he reminded himself. He did it for the bleeding beast. Wayne didn't know why, but this whole display made him angry. At what? At those other maniacs on the road? At being rewarded? It was all junk; he didn't even like cake.

Left alone with Silvy, he was even more embarrassed. He knew who she was, but she had never given him the time of day. Now she sat there with a big dumb smile on her beautiful dumb face and asked about John Hersting, a friend of Wayne's who was on the football team, somebody more in her class. He wanted to say, "Hey, what is this, don't I get to sleep with you as part of my reward?" but he kept his peace. In the end, he got up to leave. He had had enough. He excused himself as he overheard them in the next room talking about the new shopping centre going in and ran out to his car, only to have to come back in, red-faced, a few minutes later to ask the MacDonnal family to move their blasted station wagon so he could get the hell out of there.

Wayne's mother asked him where he was going. There was a good reason he didn't answer; he didn't know.

As soon as he hit the highway, though, and passed the corner where he had picked up the dog, he knew. He drove the ten miles to Denise's house slowly, not wanting to get there too soon. The burgundy was still rattling around in the back, and he hoped that it wouldn't be too hard to get her out of the house for the evening. He tried wiping off the dried blood from the seat with marginal success and decided they'd be better off sitting in the back.

Her house was one of those anomalies of the suburbs, an old three-storey wood-frame farm house left standing in the middle of a regimented suburban landscape of split levels and oversize copy-colonial homes. He pulled to a stop by her driveway, hearing the squeal of metal against metal, the rear brake shoes scratching against the drums. More bucks out the window. Up ahead a car was pulling away from the curb. He could see two heads, a guy and a girl, meshed together. That was exactly what he needed right now. In a rare moment of self-realized honesty, Wayne thought to himself that, despite all his ego cravings, he truly had no desire to get laid. He just wanted to be close, really close, with a girl for once. With Denise. They had something in common, and damn it, maybe they were in love.

Leaping from the car, he bounded up the sidewalk to the house. After trying the doorbell three times, he figured it must be busted and hammered away at the wood frame door with his hand. Some-one was home, a TV show was blaring away inside. Cops chasing criminals, sirens, noise. A bleary-eyed middle-aged woman came to the door.

"Yes?" He could smell the booze on her breath, whiskey and cigarettes.

"Hi. Is Denise here? I'd like to see her."

"Oh, yes, now I remember your face. Murdoch, isn't it?"

I nodded. Something was wrong.

"Sorry, Mr. Murdoch, she just left." Panic

"How soon will she be back?" Something wrong with my voice. I think she could tell.

"Probably gone for the evening. Sorry, son." She could see the hurt look on Wayne's face. "Oh, hey, I am sorry. Look, you wanna come in and watch TV with me for a bit? I don't think she'll be back for some while, but you could kill some time."

"No. Thank you, but I don't think so." She almost looked as hurt as he did. Wayne stumbled off toward his car again, realizing that it had grown dark very quickly. Like he had lost an hour somewhere. "Kill some time?" he repeated to himself. Jesus, Mary and Joseph — maybe that's what it comes down to after all.

Wayne sat down on the blood-stained seat, reached back and pulled up the bottom of the seat in the back, lifting the enormous jug of burgundy. It had a rich crimson foam from being jostled around for twenty-four hours. Wayne wondered if that would improve the taste.

"An enriching bouquet," he mimicked. "Smooth, yet aggressive. Mild, yet tantalizing." He took another gulp. It tasted like shit. He was amazed at how little time it took him to polish the whole thing off.


In the morning, he was abruptly awakened by someone knocking something against the window. Cops. He looked down at the empty bottle on the floor, the brownish dried blood on the blue carpet: a dog's blood, but the blood of a survivor. The doors were locked, he'd had the forethought to push down the locks before he conked out.

The cops looked more than annoyed. They were serious about something, suspicious. He lifted the lock and got out, realizing that he was still in front of Denise's house. Had she come home? Was she in there looking out? Oh, Christ.

"All right, son, spread 'em."

"Huh?" There was a big patch of fog in his skull, behind it, something discovered, something big.

"Your legs. Up against the car." He moved sluggishly, directed by where they were pushing him. Then they searched him, found nothing and turned him around.

"All right, kid," one of the cops said, annoyed. "What happened?"

Wayne tried to focus clearly, to look the cop in the face. In a second he could see him clearly. The sun was brilliant this morning.

"I said, what happened?" he repeated, more annoyed.

Wayne steadied himself against the fender, took a deep breath and looked up toward a window that he thought to be Denise's bedroom. She had probably already gone to work. He tried to explain to the cops that he really didn't know what happened. He honest to God just couldn't figure it out.

# AN EASY WINTER

"Is it bad?" I asked her the question I had promised myself I wouldn't ask.

She opened her eyes, looked out from behind the tubes that had been rammed up her nose. Then a smile. "No, nothing like you'd expect. I'm just tired."

"No pain or anything?"

"A little. I'm glad you came. How's Canada?" A bit more of a smile. To be honest, I could hardly recognize her as my grandmother. My grandmother used to get up at six o'clock and go out to pick peas, bushels of peas, then shell the little buggers for about two hours, weed a half-acre of tomatoes and then do half a dozen chores worthy of five strong men before lunch time. The lady with the tubes was just a bag of bones and flesh. It was hard to connect the two. She knew it.

"Canada's great. Lots of elbow room. Room to grow. The sky, the sea. Everything I do there is fresh and alive." I was starting to sound like a god-damn chewing gum commercial. Clichés. All true, but clichés. "I couldn't keep living here, I'd feel closed in."

"I know. I'm glad you found Canada. Does it get cold?" She tried to raise her head a little but didn't have the energy. I put my hand behind her head and tried to help her, only half succeeding. I was actually afraid that she might come apart. I eased her back down and noticed that her hair felt like that of a little girl.

"You get used to it. As long as I keep the wood stove going, you don't ever notice a thing." It was partly a lie. When the mid-winter arctic wind came whipping down across the frozen lake and slammed into the old wood-frame house, it was like being buried alive in a moving avalanche. At night you could hear the fatal north, the shouting icy breath of the polar caps clawing at the walls, grinding away at the foundation and making the walls and joists snap in the cold. No matter how much wood you put in the old Ashley, the heat got sucked out into the night where it did no good at all. "Went through six cords of wood last winter. I'm getting lazy, though. I buy it in eight-foot lengths now. I cut it and split it. My bloody chain saw's busted. Probably by next year I'll be buying it cut, split and delivered."

"You never quite were the workaholic that your brother was." She tried to crack a smile; she was teasing me. It's true, my brother had been maniacal at doing physical work — farming, cutting and selling firewood, fixing trucks. I had spent half a lifetime hearing family tell me that I should try as hard as my brother. My grandmother had never said it once. It was funny she would tease me with it now, now that she was dying. "You know I'm only kidding," she said, just to make sure I understood. "How's the writing going?"

"I sold that collection of short fiction." There wasn't really much money in it, but I didn't care. I noticed that I said short fiction instead of short stories. Did fiction sound more impressive? Stories sounded too familiar. But why did I do it to her, the last person I needed to impress? "Short stories, that is. Twenty of them. I don't think they're that good. In ten years I'll be able to make the words do what I want. Now, I'm still practising."

"I'm still practising, too. Don't worry about practising. It's all practising. For what, I don't know, but it's all practice and it's all the real thing. No in between. Hand me that dish, please."

There was a crescent-shaped blue plastic bowl that I tried to hand her, but I couldn't seem to get her to grab ahold of it. "No, you'll have to hold it, here by the pillow," she instructed.

And then she spit out something yellow. "It's these tubes. I can't swallow right. After all these years of practising, and now I can't swallow right. I forgot how to go to the bathroom when I have to, also. A lot of good all that practising did." She stopped to take several long breaths, her eyelashes fluttered a bit; she was very tired, what was left of her. I heard my wife and my parents talking in low mumbles outside the door. They were probably wondering how I was making out. We had driven straight through from New Brunswick, twenty hours. A tractor trailer had jack-knifed and overturned not far ahead of us in Massachusetts. I didn't stop. A lot of cars and trucks did; I didn't. Kathy had looked at me in silence, I didn't say anything. I'm sure there were other people stopping who could help out more than I could have, a doctor or somebody who'd taken a first aid course. My parents had warned me that she might already be gone by the time we made it down. For once, they didn't try to blame me for moving so far away. I blamed myself.

"Mark, listen." She tried to raise her head again. "Don't write any stories about old women dying. I hate those kinds of stories. Nobody likes them."

"I promise, I won't. What should I write about?"

"Write a western. Your grandfather loves westerns. You remember Zane Grey?"

"A little."

"Good, write a book like Zane Grey. Get your grandfather to read it. He loves reading about the West. I think he married me because I was the only girl in Philadelphia that he ever met who came from West Texas."

"I'll write like Zane Grey and set the story in West Texas." My grandfather was mostly blind. He wouldn't read a book again and he hated the Books-on-Tape stuff that the lady from the Society for the Blind had brought. He was home now, asleep and unaware. When the time came, he would cry a lot. He had always been a very non-emotional kind of stubborn farmer. Closest thing to crying for him would have been a big drag on the snot in the back of his throat, a massive head and neck motion that sucked it all back in, the snot, the tears, the emotion. They didn't raise kids to be sissies in Virginia, where he'd come from. His pride and his emotion had remained fiercely intact through the Depression and two world wars. A few years ago, he had almost cried when his pair of bloodhounds with a total of forty years of life between them died. He didn't cry, but it could have been almost. Instead, he got out his shotgun and shot at a bunch of crows tearing apart some ears of corn still on the stalk. Then he let out a big bellowing "Damn" when he missed.

I'm sure he would cry when she died, though. He was old enough and allowed to do so now. It could be used against him if he wasn't careful. Ammunition. A sure indication of senility.

"Don't put too much fightin' and beatin' up in the western, though. Your grandfather doesn't mind it, but I never cared for it. It wasn't like that. Mind you, some of it was true — the bar rooms and the dancehall girls and a couple of drunk sheriffs. A lot of people shootin' guns, but not at each other. That's what I remember."

I wished I could get those damn tubes out of her nose. You shouldn't have to die with tubes stuck up your nose. A nurse walked in the door, and I wanted to motion her away. I could see my wife peeking in from outside. Yes, she's still alive, dammit, I wanted to say to them all, now leave us alone. And I felt really selfish, too. I wanted her all to myself. I glared at the nurse, who stuck a needle in her arm and then, seeing my scowl, turned to go without saying a word.

What was funny, right now, was the total lack of concern I felt for anyone else. My wife out in the hall, my own parents. A big blank spot. There was just Vera . . . and me. (How odd to finally think of her as a person with a first name, a name I'd never used before that I could remember. Vera.) I wanted to fill in the gaps, the years.

"Do they still regard the Queen as the head of state up in Canada?" A funny thing to ask for someone on the verge of oblivion.

"I guess they do. She came to Halifax and everybody made a big ruckus. I can't see the point to it, myself."

"Still, it's kinda nice. My mother always respected the Queen. I don't think she ever forgave the *Philadelphia Inquirer* for printing that picture of the Queen walking down Market Street with her skirt getting blown sky high by the wind. Too much disrespect."

From another person, I would have written off that remark. I hated the notion of respectability. I had no desire to "be respectable." In fact, maybe in this day and age, it's a harmless enough vice to respect a queen. Blind obedience was something else. I remember when I was seventeen and got busted for breaking some windows at a courthouse in Camden during a demonstration against the Vietnam war. I needed five hundred bucks to put up my own bail, and it was a really bad time to even think about getting my parents involved. I took the chance that Vera would understand, and she did. She sent down the five hundred bucks with Ray, an old boozing Black guy they had working on the farm with them. Had my grandfather caught wind of it, he would have thought she'd lost her marbles. First off, he was a Republican and supported the President. Second, he would have been stone certain that Ray would run off with the loot.

Ray did turn up about twelve dollars short and a little bit loose around the gums, but I got out. I paid back my grandmother over a year or so. We never said a word about it.

"I'm glad you like Canada. If it's where you wanna live, you should be there." I fought back a couple of tears, then gave her a kiss on the cheek.

She lay there with her eyes closed, breathing heavily; gravity seemed to be working against her. Nobody had exactly pinpointed what was wrong with her — any of a dozen things, the doctors said. They offered to open her up and do exploratory surgery, but it had been a long haul the past year, in and out of the hospital. I think Vera understood it all. "There's not really a thing wrong with me," she had said, "except that I'm just really tired." I was thankful that my parents had the good sense to let her ease off without any major new surgical or pharmaceutical battle. I respected them for it.

"Mark, I never really told you about my father." Her eyes were closed, each breath a minor victory, a taxing one.

"Not much. I know you lived out in Texas, where he ran a hotel. That's about it."

"Let me give you a bit more." Her breathing was almost like snoring, and her eyes were still closed. It was like she was asleep . . . but she wasn't. Just using all her strength on the words. "He was a dreamer, like you. Always searching for something better, something new, something exciting. First Tennessee, then Texas, then Colorado Springs, San Francisco. Did I ever tell you he was playing cards with Jack London when the earthquake hit?"

She had told me all this stuff years ago. It had bored me to distraction. In those days I was preoccupied with getting stoned and finding some new young lady to seduce. My grandmother's stories weren't my thing at all. It was different now.

"Well, Mom got kinda tired of lugging after the old man and convinced us to go back east, to Philadelphia, where there was plenty of work, what she called honest employment. Pop was a little down on his luck and reluctantly agreed. We took the train back from Texas. Trains took you everywhere in those days, and Pop loved a train more than anything.

"But two winters in Philadelphia and Pop wanted desperately to get back to West Texas. We had my grandmother living with us then, and she wanted us all to stay right here in North Philadelphia, where it seemed civilized to her. I don't have the slightest notion what I wanted."

It was hard to focus on all those generations of my family back there pulling at each other's lives. I could never really think of great-grandparents as real people somehow, only faded images in a photograph.

"Pop caught tuberculosis, though, and they had to cut off his leg, too. The doctor said it had to be done right away, there in the kitchen. He used the same butcher's knife that Mom had used to cut up meat, boiled it, poured half a gallon of whiskey down him, and then set to cutting. I'll never forget the howl. But he lived.

"As soon as he could hobble around, he said he had to get back to Texas. The East was tryin' to kill him. I woulda gone, too, only my mother couldn't stand leaving because my grandmother refused to go. So the old man went on his own. He took a ship from down at the harbour. Never been on a ship before, only trains. But the ship was cheaper and could have put him in at Galveston. We never heard from him, though. I don't think he lived long. His health was bad."

She concentrated on breathing for a minute. If anything, the story seemed to have revived her a bit. There was no pain in her face.

"Just let me get out a little more. Your grandfather. He called me the cowgirl and married me. If it hadn't been for all the Texas stuff, I would have been just another girl in the typing pool at the Navy Yard."

"And I guess you two lived a pretty happy life all those years." I thought maybe she was going to get to some sort of moral or something and was trying to help out.

She half sat up. "I didn't say that." She was emphatic. "Look, we did well enough. Better'n most and a little worse than some others." That was an old standard of hers. "You know, in the old days we used to say, 'Go to Halifax,' when we really meant to say, 'Go to . . . ,' but it was just a polite way around it. It was just a joke. Did you say you had a rough winter up there this year?" Her tone of conversation was now very casual, matter-of-fact, like we had just been talking yesterday and we were discussing the weather.

"It was a fairly warm winter, really. Got a bit of snow, but I remember one day in January where I was out with just a sweater on. Only burned about six cords of wood. The cold did hang around just a trifle too long, like it always does. It wasn't that bad, though. Can't say we suffered any for it."

I felt my own breath seem to freeze in the air in front of my face. I waited to hear her next intake of air before I took another. Our breathing mingled in the stale hospital air between us; it came together beneath the cold fluorescent lights.

*An Easy Winter*

# THE DREAM AUDITOR

He arrived on Friday afternoon while I was washing my car. It didn't seem right. Friday afternoon was a time of amnesty, and now this.

The dream auditor drove up in one of those typical government cars — anonymous, dark, a model named after a letter in the alphabet.

"We've been looking into your account," he stated outright, without a handshake or a word of introduction.

"I didn't know I had one," I answered, wanting to turn the hose on him but holding back, sensing some mysterious power in the hollow of his cheeks.

"These things don't just happen, you know."

"Things?"

"Dreams. Fantasies. Wistful longings."

"I think you're out of line," I told him and asked him to leave. But, not wanting to take any chances, I sent out a signal to Harry, my telepathic raven. Harry could be counted on to deal with unwanted strangers. Already I could see that Harry had received my message and was homing in from across the field, where he had been harassing field mice.

"I wouldn't do that if I were you," the dream auditor said and handed me a business card. "It's funny how few of you are willing to accept the work of our department."

I was glad I didn't have any sharp objects within reach. The man was testing my patience. Harry was above him now, squawking, about to lunge for the hat with his talons.

"Please," the dream auditor said in a cold, flat voice. "We know all about you. We've been listening in for years. Now I've simply come to issue a statement. We've carried your account for a long time. Surely you know others who have dealt with us."

So then it sank in. Dream taxes. Harry understood my despair and backed away, drifted backwards in the light breeze and landed on the roof. The nice thing about telepathic ravens is that you never have to think the same thought twice. They always get the picture in 3-D. Dream taxes.

The man started to open a ledger book. "I've already deducted nightmares and sleepless nights. The code is quite liberal. Day-dreams, of course, are less costly as well, since they are primarily of your own doing. And generally very mundane, anyway. Everything else was generously supplied by our ministry. You gave us some good hints, though. It always works that way."

"And now what do you want?"

"Payment on taxes due, sir. No more, no less."

"And if I can't come up with it?"

"We close your account!"

"You can't threaten me!" Harry was in the air squawking now. He didn't have to be telepathic to know what I was thinking.

"It's no threat. Besides, you have nothing to lose. Nothing but your dreams. Think of it this way: up until now, it's all been free samples. From here on, you have to pay as you go."

"And if I don't pay, I don't dream?"

"Yes. That is the way it works. Few adapt to it easily."

"Look, why should I care if you take away my dreams? I can't even remember a dream I've honestly enjoyed in the last year."

He opened the ledger again and ran his finger down a column. "Here it is. February 12. Plane crashes in the South Pacific on its way to the international cheerleaders' convention in Malaysia. All survive on a deserted atoll. Only one male, the pilot. You."

"I don't remember that."

"Pity. We helped you out with that one. One of our old standby programs. You added a few variations. It's nice when our work becomes co-operative."

"Are they all like that?"

"Truth is, most of it is pretty gloomy. You get back at your enemies in quaint and uncreative ways. Other times, your dreams are downright unpleasant. You know: standing in front of your office staff in your underwear, stepping into elevators and discovering there's nothing there but an empty shaft. Or simply running to catch a missed bus."

"I could live without all that."

"Could you?"

"Yes."

"Others have tried."

"And?"

"And not made out so good. You see, what you don't get out of your system in dreams — both impossibly good and pathetically bad — you have to work out in your waking life. Frankly, most people don't have the time or the endurance."

I thought about it for a minute, watching Harry as he picked at the black feathers in his wings. He seemed to have forgotten about me, and the dream auditor appeared to be getting more impatient.

"Look," he added, "when we close an account, we close it. You have at least twenty-five good years left in you. And the payment terms aren't really so bad."

"So out with it."

"All we want is to own the copyright on all your dreams from here on."

"That's all?"

"It means a lot to us."

"Copyright?"

"Copyright. The right to use your dreams as we see fit."

"Why the hell do you need my permission in the first place?"

"You insult us. Ethics are of prime importance in my line of work. I can't speak for the previous administration, but today we run a very ethical operation."

"I don't get it. How is it worth your while? What do you do, sell the stuff to Hollywood?"

"Let's not be coy."

"Then what? Why the hell should I care if you buy up every dream I ever dream from here on out?"

"Well, like yourself, there are others out there who have needed some help in diversifying their dream habits. People are so uncreative these days. It's like tuning in to reruns you've seen too many times before. Without our help, well, dream life would be almost as dull as waking life."

"Then help yourself. If somebody wants to recycle anything I have to offer, let them have it. The copyright is yours. May it rest in peace."

"Now you're being hasty." Harry had swooped down and was walking in circles around the dream auditor, pecking at pieces of grass and looking for insects. The bird caught his reflection in one of the shining black patent leather shoes and stood there transfixed.

"You see," the dream auditor continued, staring right at Harry, "the corollary is this: sometimes we loan our copyright privileges to other government departments that operate, shall we say, outside the bedroom. Scenarios in the waking world become, as you've probably discovered, repetitive and less than imaginative, too."

"So. You're saying that if I come up with a brilliant dream, I could be helping someone out?"

"It doesn't always turn out that way."

"But I thought that you've already told me that most of my dreams have come from your department anyway."

"Well, they have, but now you'll be on your own. Our years of training will be yours to do with as you please."

"So I still continue to dream, but I'm fully responsible to make them up as I go along? And you simply get to keep the copyright?"

"That's the way it works."

"It doesn't sound so bad."

"Then perhaps you'll just sign here. Good. Thank you very much."

"Well, you could have been less theatrical about the whole thing. I mean, it doesn't seem to be that big of a deal."

He nodded. As he turned to go, Harry flew up and perched on my shoulder as he was prone to do when he wanted to read my mind more clearly. I always liked the feel of his talons gripping my collarbone. And I felt safer now that the dream auditor was walking down my driveway toward his car. He looked back before he got in, however, and offered some last-minute advice. "Now that we have an agreement, I would ask one more thing of you."

"What's that?"

"Do be careful about what you dream."

# PRYING LOOSE

Carl and Vincent sit at the kitchen table playing a makeshift game of hockey with an Oland's cap and pencils for hockey sticks. It's a game of skill, and the ritual has become quite elaborate. Arlene, Carl's wife, walks in from the living room and rinses out a glass, which she then puts away. Carl looks up and Vincent sneaks a shot across the table and off. Score.

"How's the game going?" She is looking at Vincent and ignoring her husband. For once, there is a distinct lack of the usual mocking tone in her voice. She opens another cabinet and pops a Midol. Carl gives her a dirty look. He doesn't think she should take Midol after a glass of wine.

"You must be practising with Carl. He's improving. I used to be able to beat him." Vincent is surprised how unhousewifely Arlene looks. She wasn't nearly that attractive when she was younger. None of the girls he goes out with have that certain poise and quiet charm that she has.

"Get off it, Vince. Carl has always been the shits at anything to do with sports. He's lost his touch at a lot of other things, too, lately. Who knows, though, maybe this is his forté." Arlene fakes a smile.

Carl keeps his mouth shut. Her comments are unfair and by his estimation unfounded. He locks his teeth and breathes through his nose. Carl is one hundred per cent opposed to airing dirty laundry in front of friends. Vincent is about the only buddy from the old days that he hangs around with. They have very little in common these days. They sometimes sit and drink beer, play table hockey and leave it like that. Conversations usually involve automobiles, government, beer or what-became-of questions.

"How's work going, Vince?" Arlene asks, washing her hands in the kitchen sink.

"They wanted to ship me off to Ontario again, but I said no way. I like it here. You have to put your foot down with those turkeys at the home office."

Carl tries for another score while Vincent is talking but fails, and Vincent snaps the cap back across the table, through the pencil defence and onto Carl's lap. "Who knows," Carl says, "you might find a woman you really like in Ontario. They're more aggressive there, I hear."

"No, thanks." Vincent looks over at Arlene again. She is looking at him in a soft, motherly fashion. She feels sorry for him still being single. Vincent hopes that she is comparing him to her own husband, that she notices that he is ageing ever so gently and gracefully compared to Carl, who is thinning up front and thickening down below.

Two more beers are opened, and the boys throw two new pucks onto the table, making for a brief free-for-all. Carl accidentally whacks one good, all the way across the room. It hits Arlene on the back as she is washing her hands for a second time. She doesn't turn around.


Vince always sets aside Wednesday evening as strategy night. He sits at a beer-varnished table near the back of Alfie's Place and watches the university girls pretend they're thirty years old. Vincent never smokes but always keeps a pack of Matinée cigarettes open on his table in case he needs an opener with a potential.

The truth is that Vince is long past college girls and tavern hoppers. Thirty-five and well settled into a "semi-executive" slot at a company that sells custom accessories for bulldozers and earth movers, Vince has talked more bullshit to women than many movie stars get away with in a lifetime. He's futilely matched himself up with more coke-sniffers, teeny-boppers, high-school dropouts, tequila sunrisers, pill-popping tight-assed flakeheads and over-torqued sweet young things than most rock band roadies would encounter on a dozen West Coast tours. Vince has surveyed the mental real estate of half the unhitched under-thirty female population of Halifax and found a lot of empty lots and vacant floor space and not much hope.

He ran an ad in the *Herald* one Saturday out of desperation:

SINCERE guy, mid-thirties, looking for companionship, love and affection. Simple and straightforward.

Only the *Herald* ran it saying "gay" instead of "guy," a typesetter's little joke. Vincent read through some very sincere responses that poured into his newspaper box number. All the wrong sex.

Vincent gives himself three and a half years before the top of his head looks like a TV commercial for floor wax. He was an extremely handsome man for quite a while and had almost everything going for him. This had caused him to dawdle, and it was getting late. He had been too damn good at everything. A champion high school basketball player, he ended up managing his own McDonald's by the time he was nineteen. Later, he sold out his interest in a regional ball-point vending machine franchise just before the company went into receivership. He worked up north on an oil rig one year as a tool pusher and made enough money to buy into co-op housing in the South End.

Clinton Connicker is tuning up his twelve-string Rickenbacker and making sure his band is in order. Clinton holds down the stage at Alfie's three nights a week, non-union. He plays the twelve-string electric plugged into a giant, overweight Marshall amp and is backed by an electronic rhythm gizmo that makes Ginger Baker sound like somebody's grandmother. Clinton has a macro-jiver sound-sync synthesizer that coughs up fuzz-tone rhythm guitar, piano, sax, and a Philadelphia Orchestra string section when necessary, and, just for kicks, he plays a pedal bass low enough to crawl down your socks. Eventually, he'll retire and allow his machines to pump out the music without him.

Clinton runs through seven songs, rehashing top-forty slop and retrieving Rolling Stones and Beatles numbers in a convincing trance. Then he eases into a song called "A Little Bit Longer" and, in the middle, lets the boys in the band take over. He flips on a tape loop, leans a brick on the D-pedal and sets his digital watch for seven minutes, so that a little blue light will blink when his break is over.

"Wha' say, Vince?" Clinton sits down and semaphores the beer slosher for a pair of Keith's.

"Just ripping along. How's Pam?" Pam is Clinton's wife. Pam, Clinton and Vincent went to school together. Right now, Pam and Clinton are practising for a divorce.

"The bitch." An all-inclusive answer. Vincent would settle for Pam at the drop of a shoelace if he had a chance. Pam, Arlene or Ann. Any one of the three.

"Vince, you don't know what a pain in the butt it can be. She won't let me do nothin'. 'Member when we used to go cruising around at one a.m. chasing carfulls of women all the way to Truro if we had to? Shoot. Now my life is Spaghettios and afternoon soaps. Pam runs off to crapayoo yoga every afternoon, and I wash dishes, listen to *Bargain Box* and fight off bill collectors. Some frigging life."

Clinton breathes in two beers, checks his quartz and flees back to the stage in time to relieve the orchestra. Vincent runs through strategies again. Halfway through a seventies version of a sixties song recently made big by an over-the-hill fifties singer, Clinton gets distracted by a customer. She looks to be maybe twelve, but she's made it past the ID check, so she must be older. Her hair is cut in a butch, like the surgery Vince's mother had once performed on his own hair. She's flat-chested and scrawny and deathly pale. Clinton can hardly contain himself but finishes his set with one eye glued on her as she sits at a conspicuous table up front and drinks nothing at all.

Chuck is a master at home repair. He has a workshop in his basement with twenty-five thousand dollars worth of Black and Decker. Last week he installed a sauna in the living room. "The Swedes'll tell you that a sauna should be at the centre of a family's life. I moved the TV into Ann's sewing room."

A sauna in the living room didn't surprise Vincent one bit. Chuck's three-tier living room was enormous. Once they had moved all the furniture to the corners and had an all-out wrestling match. Just like the old days. Vincent won, of course, and Ann applauded. "I bet you're hell in bed, too," Chuck joked good-naturedly after the match. Vincent had accidentally flipped Chuck into a teakwood coffee table that surrendered two legs and cracked down the middle.

"Sorry about that."

"Don't think twice. Get that sucker down to the Workmate and have it like new in minutes. It's incredible what you can do with the new epoxy adhesives."

Tonight, Ann wants to know if Vincent would like to join them in the new sauna. "Sure, why not join us?" Chuck adds, wanting to show off a special way he managed to seal the shiplap joints and the novel manner used to cover up the wood screws with mother-of-pearl inlaid wood plugs.

Vincent took Ann out exactly twice during school. The first time, one of the brake lines rusted through, and they just barely avoided driving into the side of an oil truck. The second time, Ann had just had an operation on her gums, and her mouth was Novocained beyond conversation.

She had made it through university and was entering law school when Chuck came along with a winning smile and uncanny skills in the areas of investment counselling, foreplay and belt sanders. Ann was married and pregnant before she had a chance to address her first moot court. After a late miscarriage, she learned that there were problems in the fallopian tubes and she should consider adoption. She decided that Chuck was, at heart, still just a big kid and figured that it might be just as satisfying to play den mother to a child genius for the rest of his days. As a result, their home was legendary for its polyurethaned glow of imported real-wood warmth and vitality. Chuck had built everything from violins to hanging beds in his spare time away from a firm that counselled bored third-generation millionaires on how to shelter their money in obscure but sound Caribbean republics.

"I guess I'll give it a go," Vincent agrees as he hears Ann in the adjacent bedroom, changing her clothes.

"Splendid," Chuck says, dropping his pants on the spot. "*Voilà*." Nothing but blonde-haired legs, spare torso and speed swimming trucks. "Since I put in the bath" — he means the sauna — "I always wear these, so that I can just sneak in for a sweat any old time."

Ann walks back in wearing a one-piece wrap-around black bathing suit with a curlicue swath cut out of the middle. Vincent is still wishing he could have got past the brake lines and the gums.

The door closes to the sauna, and Chuck begins to explain the life cycle of the tree from whose entrails the walls were ripped. This is followed by an elaborate explanation concerning how wood grain needs to be "wooed" with just the right combination of sandpapers and finishes. Vince tries to change the subject and asks about tax havens.

"If you got over a quarter-mil, the best place is a bank in the Cayman Islands. The government is so stable there it makes Switzerland look like a banana republic." Vincent can tell it's a line he's used on little old ladies and irresponsible corporate nephews.

Vincent feels a little uncomfortable sitting on the scorching bench in his jockey shorts. Ann is lying down on a long rack across from the two men, and while Chuck is fingering the Norwegian grain, Vincent steals a mental snapshot of Ann's steaming, glistening ribcage. She might almost be sleeping but that would be impossible in this heat.

Chuck begins another lecture on how to rabbet hardwood, but, out of the blue, he's cut off by Ann, who props herself up, dripping great tears of perspiration, and blasts, "This is the most god-damn boring thing you've ever built!" She stands erect and flashes a scorching look at Chuck. In the hot, compressed air of the sauna she seems volatile and other-worldly, voluptuous and explosive. A door opens and an arctic seventy-degree derailed freight train of air crashes into the chamber.

When Vincent is alone at night on a Tuesday, eating a dinner consisting of Colonel Sanders and rye whiskey, he is feeling depressed. Not only have the Maple Leafs screwed up the season for good, but Ronald Reagan wants to put missiles on railroad tracks shuttling around Wyoming so that he can blow up whatever remains of the world after the initial damage is fulfilled in a mutual assault. On top of that, his mirror has reported that his face is also hard at work on reinforcing an intricate network of tiny tracks all around his eyes and forehead. Now, when he smiles, it's like the heyday of the CNR and CPR.

After deciding that two legs and a thigh are enough for any slightly paunched thirty-five-year-old male, he turns on his phone message recorder. The red-headed girl who was flunking out of university called to say that he should come over for dinner next week. She's serving swiss chard quiche and wild rice. Could he bring the wine? His insurance agent called to say that his life insurance had run out and that if he reinstated it now, he wouldn't have to pay the new federal surcharge.

Lying on the sofa with both the radio and the TV on, Vincent sees himself living on a palm-lined beach in the Cayman Islands. Inside his mythical Hollywood-styled beach cottage, he makes hockey sticks and ukeleles that sell for phenomenal amounts of money in industrial North America. They are embarrassingly easy to make and forge a ridiculously large tax-free surplus in his bank account. From inside the cottage he can look out and see three women lying asleep on towels near the lap of the blue water. As he tries to bring them into focus, a curtain of haze sweeps across the beach and they become indiscernible.

The playback machine has one more message. Clinton. "Vince. You know I hate this. Talking into a frigging machine. Like this is what it all comes to. We talk to each other through our machines. Nobody ever has to really communicate. You know? Shit, hey look, anyway. I'm having sort of a party. Friday. Not really a party, just a chance for you and me, Chuck and Carl to get together and slosh a few. What's the occasion, you might ask, had you human voice there to query. Pam. She finally took off. I'm free at last. I don't even know where the hell she . . ." That is where the machine runs out of tape, and Clinton ends up talking to a dead wire. Vincent gets up and shaves with his Phillips for the second time that day. He trims his moustache, puts new laces in all his shoes.

By Friday the plans have changed. Clinton has been kicked out of his apartment by the landlord after the police came searching for the cocaine he had just flushed down the toilet. Chuck had gone through a bad week of stock counselling and suddenly believed that he had silverfish crawling through the knotty pine walls. He is paying a fortune to have exterminators in on an emergency Friday-night job. Carl had taken in two hockey games, a boxing card and a regional tag-team wrestling championship that week. If he brought the boys over on a Friday night, Arlene had promised to strangle him with a pair of pantyhose in his sleep.

So Vincent had put off the red-haired girl, who sobbed that she really was in need of a friend right then, with her life in a puddle. He would stay at home and host the boys. Maybe they'd get pissed and have a great time rehashing old victories and farting contests. Maybe he could open up about his worries for once. Maybe he would just keep his mouth shut and find out where Pam had run off to or see if any of the other family battles were nearing divorce court. He had awakened in the middle of the night remembering a dream: he was shuffling down a long bleak hallway, and there was snow piling up around him. There was a door at the end, and he knew he could make it there if he just kept shuffling along. The snow became deeper, and he felt his ankles turn to ice. But he had arrived. When he opened the door, there was nothing but blackness.


"Surprise." Ann opens the door armed with two magnums of South African wine. She throws both arms around Vincent and drowns him in Taboo. Her body is warm and giving. Vincent's brain has turned to Seven-Up.

"I can see the party has already started. Am I too late?" Vincent recognizes the voice. Someone has been hot-wiring reality. Arlene throws her coat down on a love seat and unbuttons the top two buttons of her blouse. "Do single men always keep their apartments this warm?" She sounds like she's already been drinking a bit, and her voice is soft and husky, alluring. She shakes her head, teasing him.

Arlene says, "Such a pretty couple. Oh, well, I guess you saw him first." Ann unwraps herself and goes to put the wine in the refrigerator.

Chuck and Carl walk in carrying more booze.

"Did you two clowns finally find a place to park that old wreck?" Arlene asks.

"You're talking about a vintage automobile that is actually worth as much on the market today as when he bought the thing. Your husband knew when to invest in Japanese metal. A brilliant man. We should be so lucky to have men with the acumen of Carl at our firm." Chuck is loaded and in good form.

"Tell that to my rusty fenders sometime, Chuck," Carl counters, looking a little down in the mouth.

As it turned out, the boys just couldn't leave the girls out. Ann would have been alone in the Hotel Nova Scotian with a two-channel TV set and a view of the container pier. Arlene was tired of baby-sitting an empty house and listening to the CBC. It was only fair.

Clinton is the last to arrive, with an uncased beat-up Martin under one arm and a begrudging Pam on the other. He has tracked her down and moved into her one-room apartment on Grafton Street, thanks to his ability to remember over a dozen early Ian and Sylvia songs.

"How can I finally get rid of that jerk?" she asks Vincent in his tiny kitchenette as he waits for his Beaumark frost-free icemaker to finish the last trayful of chipped ice.

He hasn't seen Pam in months. To hear Clinton talk, she had grown broad and was sporting warts and chin stubble. Instead, she looks just as Vincent knows her from the well-thumbed yearbook. Vincent pops a chip of ice into his mouth and chews on it.

"I don't know," is all Vince can bring himself to say, and he crunches up another wedge of ice. This makes Pam laugh. It's the first time her face has become unlocked this evening. Clinton can be heard in the other room with his six-string doing Neil Young imitations. Pam eases over toward Vince, slides a leg between his and pushes her tongue into his mouth. She tastes sixteen and certain. Vincent's eyes are closed, and he feels her hand rubbing the small of his back as Chuck elbows the door.

"Hey, you're gonna ruin the ice. We got nothing to clank around in our glasses out there, and it's getting awfully warm." Chuck doesn't seem to be taking the scene very seriously. "Besides, you don't want to melt the hoar-frost on the old boy here." He pats the sides of Vincent's head, along the traitorous tips of grey that ring him like a fallen halo.

Pam giggles and makes her exit from the kitchen with the ice. Vincent feels confused, afraid. He wishes that there was some way to make major masonry improvements across the doorway into the living room. The walls of the kitchen are now grey, dim and distant. He loses all sense of colour. Human voices rattle like dry ice through the walls, but his ears begin to fill up with the sound of his own heart pumping blood. Thudding, dull, grey drums beat inside him as he begins to move table and chair in front of the door. He feels very childish but also grotesquely old. The world beyond his kitchen is a place of completion, a system of pairs. Here, he is alone, as it should be. From here on, the trick will be to avoid the dangers of possibility and to insure the safety of what he still possesses.

Beyond that, there can only be cold, life-sapping loss and public humiliation. Now he is moving the table back from the door and composing the face of the sole survivor.

"Dammit, Vince, if you're through rearranging the furniture, would you bring in another bottle of vino." Carl's voice is encased in a slurred, arrogant cheerfulness.

Vincent grabs the first bottle he can see in the refrigerator, clenches his knuckles around a mahogany-handled corkscrew and walks back into the living room. Everyone is standing up and hovering. He is surrounded. He feels their warm, boozy breath all over him.

# DANCING THE NIGHT AWAY

Despite the fact that it is a bright, warm October afternoon, all of the curtains at Briarwood Manor are drawn tight. Twin television sets in the "recreation room" are blasting out commercials for video games, and you can hear eighty-four-year-old Sterling Litton scream, "Blast the suckers!" and then retreat back into himself with a fit of coughing and hawking of phlegm.

In the hallway of the south wing, Molly Crawford confides in me that today is her birthday. She forgets how old she is and admits that she doesn't know the date, but today is the day, and she damn well wants to celebrate. I prop my mop up against the tile wall and lean over to let her whisper in my ear. Her breath is medicinal and stale, but her hand on my neck is warm, and her eyes are wide with excitement. "Look at this, will ya?"

She opens an imaginary cabinet on the wall. With a key, and very delicately. She puts the key back into the pocket in her skirt and opens two doors. The hinges are exquisitely silent. Handing me an invisible glass, she begins to pour something into it. "You got it now?" I nod. She pours herself a tiny bit, then decides what the hell, it's a birthday, and dumps in more until the glass must be brim full and sloshing on the floor. We bump glasses, and she snaps her head back and polishes hers off with lightning speed. I sip mine more cautiously.

"You want another one?" Molly asks, her eyes now watering

from all the excitement, the imaginary booze rushing to her head. So sure, we kill the whole damn bottle. Molly's giggling and has to remove her glasses to sop up the water running down her cheeks. Two nurses are headed our way, outlined as black figures against the distant light of the entranceway. From this end, the corridor looks to be over a mile long. It's my job to insure that the entire length of the hallway is mopped twice each day. Dust and germs are the enemy. I kill both for a price.

The nurse will come and haul Molly away to sit in a whirlpool as part of her "therapy." She'll scream bloody murder for twenty minutes in the tub, and then, with a shot of something or other to calm her down, she'll fall asleep in her bed and not wake up until six tomorrow morning. Molly sees the nurses coming and quickly closes the imaginary liquor cabinet. She locks it nervously and hands me the key, which I quickly stash in my pants pocket. Molly shakes my hand and says, "Thank you, sir. You are certainly a gentleman." I smile and grab my mop to move further south before the north-end nurses wrestle Molly's angelic face into a knot of fear.


At home, in the kitchen, Kathy is exercising again, firming up the muscles in her thighs. Her jogging suit is crumpled up in a pile on a chair, and a punchy-sounding post-disco instrumental song is pounding from the stereo. "How's life at the Dead Centre?"

"I got in trouble for punching out Alice Liscomb."

"You really beat up Alice Liscomb?" Even though Kathy has totally misunderstood my statement, she doesn't break stride. Exercise is a very important part of living.

"No. I punched out her time card. On the clock. About fifteen minutes after she already split to go pick up her dog at the vet. Turned out the dog didn't have rabies after all."

"That's good news. About the rabies, I mean." Kathy is rotating the upper half of her body around her hips in a circular motion. Then she stands upright and just rotates her head in circles. I don't think I could even do it without snapping a pair of vertebrae. I always think of her as masculine when she is exercising or jogging. Even standing here watching the pubic hair protruding outside of her leotard, I find her actions too mechanical, her body activity premeditated. For her, everything is done for a purpose.

"I got enough students for that Modern Jazz class at the Dance Exchange. Just barely. You know how many younger girls want to become professionals these days? And you know how many professional dancers a town like Halifax can support?" Now she breaks into a sort of half dance, half kung fu routine that I haven't seen before.

"I don't know. How many?"

"I don't know. Very few."

"Why get yourself all worked up then? Use your well-tuned body for something else more in demand."

"You suggest I take up street walking?" She's just kidding. I know she doesn't want to do anything other than dance, and it's all right with me if she keeps taking classes for the rest of her life.

"Maybe you could offer a special package deal involving a little freeform ballet."

"Yeah, and maybe not."

After that we start to argue about higher ceilings. She wants to live in an apartment with higher ceilings so she doesn't have to keep hitting her knuckles against the stippled paint. It's an old, fruitless dialogue for us, but I keep up my half of the conflict for appearances. Sitting at the kitchen table, I watch a bead of sweat exploring the inside of her left thigh. Kathy has fantastic legs. But something about leotards turns me right off. Leotards, to Kathy, mean exercise and dance, and that means serious business, hard work. She believes that if you work hard, keep yourself in shape and project yourself, all good things come to you. She doesn't know anything about decay, old age or things falling apart. I try to make sure of that.

"You're still optimistic about your future in the world of dance, then?"

"Life, Mark, is like a sewer. What you get out of it is directly related to what you put into it." This is an old standard I taught her way back when I was still in graduate school getting an MA in seventeenth-century literature. I stole the line from someone, Tom Lehrer, I think.

"Which reminds me. What about supper?"

Kathy twirls her way over to the stove and puts on two pots with water to start boiling. I go lie down on the chesterfield in front of the TV, where I watch a *MASH* rerun that I've seen five times before. One of the patients is going to die unless they can complete an operation in thirty minutes. They have a little clock on the screen in the corner to show you how much time is slipping away. In the end they don't make it in time. But the soldier survives.

Arthur Klugman is sitting in a perfectly rigid posture on a hard wooden chair as I enter his room with my mop and bucket. He acknowledges that I'm there by the way he presses his lips together. A man of authority all of his adult life, he has been able to get by without having to put up with small talk from men who mop floors, and only now that his feet are like hard, lifeless rocks does he bother to try to make conversation at all with me.

"Don't forget to do the bathroom, will ya? That idiot next door was having problems with his personal plumbing last night again."

"Sure, no sweat." Arthur says this to me most every day as a sort of salutation. Unlike many of the other residents, Arthur doesn't share a bathroom with another room. Even though I've held down this job off and on for four years, I still can't quite handle some of the smells of "personal plumbing" gone haywire. I'm an expert at holding my breath. Into the bathroom like a terrorist armed with a mop and bucket, thorough but quick, then out, all before the olfactory nerves have had to function at all. I've timed myself. I can hold my breath for ninety seconds. You can do a lot in ninety seconds. I mop out the tiny bathroom cubicle and rush over to the window by Klugman's dresser to open it for air. I suck in my first gulp of oxygen in well over a minute and swear that I can feel brain cells, nearly robbed of the vital element, now relaxing and getting back to work. I remember that brain cells can't be replaced. If I starve my brain of air long enough on the job, I might lose a bit of my memory. The trick would be trying to lose just the right part.

"And it was just about then that they ended the war." It's Klugman. He's reliving 1945, a very disappointing year for him. We've been through it dozens of times.

"First the stinking Krauts give up right when the first shipment is on its way to Italy. It was a kick in the head, I'll tell you that. You can't trust a Hun." Klugman was an American chemist. In 1944 he was deep into some very secret research concerning a new sort of military weapon — gas, but not like "dirty old mustard gas" as he calls it. He was one of five men responsible for developing a deadly nerve gas that, had the Germans just given him a fair chance, the Yanks would have used on them from the southern front.

"Clean. It was very clean. If they'd gone ahead and used it in Japan instead of the bomb, you wouldn't a had none of that mess. You could have saved all those buildings. It's a sin."

The bitterness really shows on his face. He can't give it up. Farmed out into special retirement since 1947, Klugman had to live through the humiliation of seeing his life's work buried in the ground in Utah and heartlessly dumped in the Atlantic. In the late sixties he had moved to Canada, to Nova Scotia, where it had been reported that several barrels had floated into Halifax Harbour after years of lying wasted at sea.

"How's your mother?" Klugman asks me in a voice like a brass-knuckled fist. He's never met my mother and doesn't have the slightest notion of who she is. He's trying to be friendly.

"She's taking a typing class at night. Hopes to pick up some part-time work in case my father doesn't get back to work soon."

"Damn good idea. Women need to learn how to type. It's good work. Who are these piss-pants politicians who got us in this mess anyway?" Jumps around a bit. We're on the economy now. "People in my day had jobs. Research. That was the thing. There was always a lot of typing in research. Politicians today don't give a good god darn about decent research."

I want to tell him about neutron bombs but keep my mouth

shut. I'm thinking about a young secretary, in Washington DC, maybe, who is typing the document that grants approval for the next megaweapon, more deadly than the last. She probably makes very few mistakes in her typing and, when she does, can correct them immediately with the latest technology.

Klugman is softening now. He'll be sobbing in a minute. "It wouldn't have been anything like mustard gas. And if it wasn't for those idiots higher up, we could have had stuff sprayed in the German trenches, and we woulda been out of the war that much earlier. Could have saved a lot of our boys."

I have to work late changing all of the fluorescent light tubes. For some reason they have to be changed after five o'clock while all the residents are eating supper. I catch a quick meal in the kitchen where the cook, a refugee from Poland who jumped ship here a couple of years ago, is leafing through a copy of *Penthouse*. Everything they serve here comes out of cans, and there's a full-time dietician who decides what cans get bought.


Kathy's first public performance starts at eight. I'm belching canned peaches as I walk up the four flights of stairs to the dance studio, a long, narrow, drafty room that was once a sweatshop for the manufacture of shoes. Rented chairs are set up in rows with an aisle down one side. I squeeze through, past women clutching pocketbooks, and make my way to the front. The second row. I don't want to be accused of tripping a dancer accidentally. Let someone else take that rap.

The lights come up bright, and a weird electric hum starts up from somewhere. It keeps getting louder and louder, and then I realise that it is in fact the music for dancing as two figures in whiteface and black leotards move toward the centre of the floor in a series of crazy, spasmodic motions. I'm reminded of Mrs. Gallico's first seizure and my own awareness of a human life in some sort of total physical war with itself. On her second attack, I had been the only one immediately nearby, and I had stuck my finger in her mouth because someone had told me the business about tongues. She bit down hard and might have gagged on the blood if a pair of nurses had not heard my screaming.

One of the white-faced dancers is Kathy. The other is an unlikeable stone-faced character named Roy Selange, a nostril-flaring elitist type by my standards, who has made a name for himself as an *artiste* among the tiny Halifax dance intelligentsia. Whatever he wears under his leotard does little to mask his genitals. I'm reminded of a codpiece.

The lights waver and the music shifts. There is a trace of melody and then total dissonance. For some reason I was expecting something reminiscent of ballet rather than epilepsy. Kathy hadn't warned me. Yet it is imperative that I like it, that I go home full of glowing praise and support. Roy has grabbed her by the arm and is twisting. Hard. She must be in pain, yet it's part of the performance. I remember that the title of the piece is "Holocaust." I don't know why I was all set for a soft shoe or *Swan Lake* or something.

The music now begins to squeal and rail, and the dancers become more frenetic. I'm outraged by the sexuality of it now, as the whole thing appears to be more of a rape scene than anything. Somebody behind me is commenting in hushed tones that it is "a sort of erotic nihilism," and I'm ready to stand up and start kicking a few heads. I can visualize myself doing a drop kick straight to Roy Selange's codpiece. Still, I sit tight and endure.

Kathy, too, is enduring. She can't be enjoying this. Her ability to withstand the pain of wrenching her body into such unnatural poses is to be commended, I suppose, but why put up with this abuse? The end of the piece is accompanied by a two-minute siren howl, and the lights go out over the scene of two corpse-like figures at centre stage. When the lights come back up, Kathy and Roy are smiling at the crowd as the applause echoes around the room. She doesn't see me, even though I am trying to catch her eye. She doesn't know I'm here.

Forty-five minutes later, during an intermission, I leave and wait out the end of the show at the Seahorse Tavern. I sit at a table with a couple of grisly characters who are arguing about the proper method of filleting cod. Although I don't say anything, they like me and buy me a beer. One of them shows me his hand, missing two fingers that he lost in a winch on a trawler off the Grand Banks. "After a while, you never even miss 'em," he says.

At home, in bed with Kathy, she can't sleep, still pumped up with the adrenaline of her performance and wanting to talk. "Roy tried to put the make on me after the show."

"Why would he want to bother? Looked like he already had his way with you there in your little horror show." I don't know when to keep my mouth shut.

"Damn you."

We go to sleep with our backs to each other, ramrod straight and separated by a few inches that might as well be light years. I want to tell Kathy that I love her very much. I want to remind her of the first time she and I danced . . . at a high-school dance. We both kept asking the band to play just slow dances while all the other kids were telling us to get lost. I fall asleep as my neck begins to stiffen, and the muscles knot from having spent too much time looking up at the ceiling trying to fit in the fluorescent tubes. My whole body feels tense. Kathy is immobile, her legs clamped together, her back rigid. It's like sleeping in a quarry.

Valerie Doyle is sitting in the day room in a rolling chair modelled after a child's high chair. She wears a bib that keeps drool from wrecking her pale blue little-girl dress, and her hands dance nervously on the tray part of the chair that is locked into place so that she can't fall out or wander off. The mother of five children — all boys now in the military and off living in places like Cold Lake, Alberta, and Timmins, Ontario — Valerie clutches a stuffed Smurf doll to her in moments of lonely desperation. She pays no attention to the game show host shouting and smiling on the television.

*The Town*

It's still early in the morning, and many of the residents are howling from their rooms that they don't want to be changed, that they don't want baths. At least one frail, pleading voice asks outright, "Why don't you let me die?" I sit down beside Valerie and talk about the weather.

On the tray before her she uses her index finger to spell out, "Nice day." Her throat has been operated on ten years ago for cancer, and she can only grunt. So she usually spells things on an invisible blackboard before her. I've been told that Valerie was quite a singer in her day, that she sang popular songs in nightclubs in Montreal once. I give her paper and a pencil sometimes to write on, but she won't use them. She only writes with her finger on the tray or in the air. I can follow her most of the time now and allow her to spell things quite quickly.

The day room is almost empty, and no one is watching the television, so I turn it off and go over to the record player to put on one of the three records there. Some ancient, hideously scratched album called *Romantic Moods*, by the Allan Litby Orchestra. The music is corny, warm and soothing.

I fake a waltz back over to Valerie and unlock the tray from her chair so she can get out. She stumbles, but I hold on good.

When the nurses find us we are clumsily bumping around into chairs in the ballroom embrace, and Valerie is humming in my ear to the music, her voice a pathetic cement-mixer growl that doesn't bother me in the least.


Kathy still thinks I lost my job out of spite. Just so she'd have to work full-time and give up dance school and her ambitions. It's not so bad, I argue. Look at the economy. Everybody's out of work. At least you have a job.

She did get her way, in a sense. A professional dancer. She works from eight o'clock at night till two in the morning at a lounge, dancing around in a two-piece bathing suit. It's not that bad; she doesn't have to take anything off. It keeps her in shape. The pay is excellent. There's something more honest about it than that crud she was doing with Roy Selange. No leotards, no graceless avant-guard jerks and twists. No whiteface. She looks warm and vulnerable like I remember her.

Sometimes I go down to the lounge and just sit there with a single beer and watch her for a couple of hours. I think she's a very talented woman.

# ROSE AND RHODODENDRON

For DeMille, the summer had been corrupted by the fact that he was employed. The making of money never settled easily, even a summer course in twentieth-century American literature. The pay was good; who could resist?

Here he was on the road driving to work. A commuter. The thought was somewhat oppressive. He turned the wheel sharply to the left while waiting for the light to change. This put unnecessary tension on the steering wheel. DeMille liked the feel of tenseness in his wrists fighting against the entropy. When the light turned green, the car vectored sharply off in the predestined direction, centrifugal force gleefully upsetting a half-consumed cup of tea all over a twelve-hundred-page anthology. Its tissue-like pages greedily lapped up the tannin and blighted the work of Gertrude Stein, John Dos Passos and H.D. among others. Archibald Macleish and Ezra Pound had remained unscathed, save the diminution of a handful of scattered footnotes that DeMille would have ignored anyway.

The bridge. Men painting rust with orange paint. Elbows leaning out of car windows flicking cigarette ashes onto the asphalt (ash-fault, as they had a habit of saying in Canada). When he heard the students pronounce that word, he had for the first time in his landed-immigrantcy felt like a foreigner in a strange land. She had been a thin, red-haired little girl who had confessed to having starred in a baked beans TV commercial when she was twelve. An

English major at that, with an eye on the honours program, and she still pronounced it ash-fault.

The traffic was clogged. DeMille checked his watch. Still twenty minutes before class. What did he care if he was late? But he hated being late. He was never late for anything. Being late made him sweat. Thinking about being late made him sweat. DeMille cursed. This was no place for a minor poet, stalled in traffic on a Tuesday morning above Halifax Harbour with a fleet of dirty tugboats beneath him trying to point half of the Canadian navy out to sea. He longed to be back home by his window, high up in the coastal fog, alone and whining to himself about injustices in the publishing world.

The CBC was a surprise this morning. An Englishman, an expert on bowel cancer, was discussing roughage and its role in the health of the bowels. He had measured and weighed stool samples in all the Third World countries but complained that North Americans knew little about their own bowel products. In Third World countries, where the roughage intake was greater, there was, he argued, no bowel cancer to speak of. In North America, where the stuff sank like rocks instead of floating like barges of grain, we were doing ourselves in for lack of bulk. And who could give a damn! The man was indignant, as rightly he should be, thought DeMille, who was himself a believer in the powers of fresh greens, unbleached flours and brewer's yeast taken in liquid form. DeMille — as well as being a minor poet, part-time English professor and sometime jogging enthusiast — hoed a damn good row of spinach and knew how to pick zucchini at just the critical moment.

Most mornings he was paranoid to a degree. Lately the chairman had been making more use of his office — stationed directly across from Professor DeMille's classroom. A veteran of ten years, DeMille should not have been easily ruffled by a sharp look from his superior while pontificating upon the failure of Ezra Pound to rise above the evolutionary level of a sculpin. And yet DeMille had detected a flaring of nostrils from Marvin Winger, department chairman, as he had passed the open door and heard such literary honesty.

Winger was an old-guard Canadian. DeMille still had no notion as to what really made Canadians tick. Winger could have been an Orangeman or something, or any one of those chaps who sincerely took the Queen, Wayne and Schuster, Stevie Smith and Joe Clark seriously. DeMille would try to stay out of Winger's way, try to keep clear of political conversations, that sort of thing. As an ex-American, he was virulently scornful of the States and offended Canadians when he spoke of his homeland with bitterness and outrage. Canadians could never see why he got so ruffled, and among his colleagues he soon learned that several actually believed Ronald Reagan to be less than fascist. But he loved teaching. He would try to remember to keep the classroom door closed, even if it did permit accumulative student smells to sometimes destroy the impact of his rhetoric.

The semester was almost over. They were getting tired of him. Not one had the temerity to strap on a Sony Walkman surreptitiously in the back of the room, but still they squirmed, nodded, fiddled and yawned through Faulkner and the poems of John Crowe Ransom. When he held up the cover of *Maclean's*, however, with a full-colour picture of the battleship New Jersey steaming toward Central America, they plucked up. DeMille had been upset that morning. This business over Central America was getting out of hand. Military games. "Some games are more deadly than others," he warned his class. "They're really screwed up this time. The Monroe Doctrine in 1983. The government in the US has its head up its ass."

It was upon the enunciation of the word ass that Marvin Winger was pulling his keys out of his pocket to open his office door. He frowned at DeMille, then rattled his key in the lock and went into his office. The door closed behind him with a distinct air of something askew in the department. DeMille stared at the door with its schematic of the seating inside the original Globe Theatre. Neo-fascist sympathizer. He didn't say it. But his students could tell he was flustered.

A voice from the back. There was one other American in the classroom. A young yahoo from Cheyenne, Wyoming. No, a reasonably sound mind inside a meat packer's body. He wore boots to class. When he was late arriving, you could hear him from two blocks away clomping on concrete and hammering on wood floors like a late-night hot water pipe.

"Sir, with all due respect, Central America is like our back yard. And those countries are receiving Soviet support. Did you know that El Salvador is closer to San Diego than Washington DC is?" You could tell that he was even a bit nervous to have the balls to confront the man in authority, the one up front with the mild hangover and the symbols of authority: the teacher's edition of the *Norton*, the mangled briefcase, the massive oak-veneer desk and the trash can.

Who cares about San Diego? But he didn't say it. He could picture Winger inside his office, his ear up to the door, his other ear on a telephone receiver with some academic dean on the other end. Somehow he had to bring the discussion back around to Edna St. Vincent Millay. Mentally, he rifled the anthology for the right segue. He found it. "Some poets have seen death's offer in many forms and accepted the outcome but ignored incommodious invitations." (That was a good word, incommodious. Was Winger listening? Did he hear it correctly?) Edna herself wrote:

> I shall die, but that is all I shall do for death.
> I hear him leading his horse out of the stall; I hear the
>     clatter on the barn-floor.
> He is in haste; he has business in Cuba, business in
>     the Balkans, many calls to make this morning.

Most of the class failed to see the connection. To DeMille himself it was somewhat shrouded, but he let it go at that. Truth would prevail somehow. He kept to the text thereafter. There was more to say about Edna, whose name contained a saint of something unknown. Hart Crane was yet to throw himself into the shark-infested waters of the South Atlantic. And the thing was to make it all seem less than medieval. Ever since he had denounced his own government, they seemed more attentive, eager for another expletive. DeMille wouldn't let them sucker him into it.

This morning had started with promise. The herons feeding on minnows in the saltflats at daybreak, the deer, soft brown and feeble, high on the hill eating wild foxberries and mercifully ignoring the beets and chard of his garden. But then, while driving through Westphal, a sparrow swooped low against the road and impaled itself on the hood ornament of his Omni. He had stopped and buried the skewered fledgling near the waterworks, beneath a sign that read: "Driver's Not Speeding this Week: 93%." He had to dig in hard with a heel of his shoe in the gravelly earth. There, too, Edna had come in handy:

> There will be rose and rhododendron
> When you are dead underground;
> Still will be heard from white syringas
> Heavy with bees, a sunny sound.

Burials and funerals were always good excuses for being late. And he should have left the radio off. The damn news. Reagan wanted more missiles in Europe. Congress had approved money for chemical weapons of the most fashionable and up-to-date design and cruise testing for western Canada. DeMille pictured those monster machines zipping by headhigh through prairie towns and Eskimo settlements. He wanted to sit down later perhaps with the thick-jowled kid from Wyoming (what was he up to in Halifax, anyway?) and convert him. Send him back to the States with new idealism, pamphlets, armbands, rhetoric and open rebellion. Convince him to stuff all those silos out there with flowers. Rust up the hinges on the missile garages and insist on peaceful settlements. This would not be easy on a kid who probably grew up with three uncles who had missile launchers underground just a stone's throw from the back yard barbecue.

But he promised to keep his politics out of his classroom. If they

*Rose and Rhododendron*

didn't hire him back in the fall for another section of Introduction to Literature, he would have to go on unemployment and then welfare. And he knew they were a conservative lot at the university: men who wore boxer shorts from Eaton's, chaste women who fought abortion and wore fingernail polish, scholars from Calcutta, and recently graduated PhDs from Leeds and Edinburgh. Tenure was unthinkable but employment imperative. Best to keep the door closed. They wouldn't use bugging devices so freely in Canada, and his students liked him, he was sure. None would go tramping to the chaplain, impugning DeMille for using four-letter words or overusing his privilege to discuss phallic images in the poetry of the Beat Generation.

Parking was tricky. He was the proud possessor of three overdue summonses already, hoping the police department would see his credit good until the end of the month. But there was not a single slot along the street to park in, and he was already five minutes late by his watch — a nameless digital device that ran three to seven minutes off anyway no matter how often he tried to adjust the devil. DeMille settled for community with a fire hydrant that looked an unlikely candidate for use.

There was Winger sitting in his office, pretending to read from the *MLA Style Sheet*. DeMille's class looked up with polite, accepting smiles. We know, we know, they seemed to say. It's all right, you are a busy man of arts and letters, poems to be written, publishers to be chided. DeMille wanted to speak of the dead sparrow but knew it would set things off on the wrong foot. The cowboy from Cheyenne gave him a look that said, "You're late, pinko America-traitor, and you're wasting my time." A girl with long soft brown hair was sitting by the window using the reflection to help her put on makeup. She was caught up in her cosmetics; she hadn't noticed that the professor had even arrived.

DeMille had secretly looked forward to this day, the third from last of the term. Mailer and Kerouac. Odd bedfellows, but writers he could relate to. *On the Road, Armies of the Night*. Excerpts. Could he tell them that he, too, had been out there on the roads of

America, the hot sticky Interstates, thumbing east and west to nowhere and everywhere, that he had once met a homosexual in Dallas who claimed to have had sex with Jack Kerouac? Could he tell them that Norman Mailer had once bummed a cigarette from him in a bar in Hackensack, New Jersey? Would this mean anything? No anecdotes. He would stick to the text. Good stuff there, even. Kerouac ping-ponging across the continent; Mailer, the buffoon, demonstrating at the Pentagon. Fiction as autobiography. Autobiography as art. Life as Art.

Winger was attentive. He had traded in the *Style Sheet* for a recent biography of Milton that someone within the department had published. Nonetheless, it was a cover for his observations. If DeMille wanted a new contract, he would have to be good. Keep it boring, he told himself. Drone, if need be. Make endless references to the critics; and above all, point out the shortcomings of both Mailer and especially Jack. The French take Kerouac dead serious, but not the English, and certainly not the Canadian academics. Keep it straight.

But of course he couldn't. He loved Kerouac and was invigorated by the obnoxious prose of Norman Mailer: both rebels, both instigators of minor revolution. And so DeMille discussed traditions. He harped on Eliot, he doted on Henry James, he squandered half the class on a resurrection of Henry Adams, even (for his penance) Edith Wharton — tying them all in to Jack and Norman and making it sound as if the term was coming to some grand elaborate intellectual orgasm, unifying all American literature into a single blossom of expression. DeMille extrapolated, pontificated and modulated his voice to show illicit quiet reserve as he explicated the dynamic duo without praising them too highly or snubbing them irreverently. And, yes, was that a hand up in the back?

The kid from Wyoming, one of three male students in the class — and American at that, a resented one. He had some problems with one section of the Mailer excerpt. He wanted some help.

DeMille, unabashed, liberated, nimble of word and wit, was ready to tackle anything literature had to offer. The section of prose in question, however, concerned the issue of sodomy, a subject in which the professor was not well versed. His intellectually hygienic vocabulary on the subject, he discovered, was in fact wanting. He heard himself discussing the undiscussable to a roomful of sixth-generation Calvinist Scots. The girl who had performed in baked bean commercials was crimson with embarrassment. Her colour was shared. DeMille saw no light at the end of the tunnel. No way out of his predicament. Afraid to turn his head sideways to see if the chairman had caught wind of the discussion, he blundered on, admitting that sexual deviance was not uncommon in American literature or in the writers themselves. Whitman, Ginsberg of course. And wasn't Gertrude Stein, after all, a dyke? Oops. Lesbian. He could hear Winger across the hall dialling his phone. Academic freedom, DeMille chanted to himself, expecting that he would be met with handcuffs at the end of the class (or, at the very least, a greeting from the American consul asking for his return to the United States before an international incident sparked).

DeMille did his best to bring lust back around to love and corrected "deviance" to "sexual preference," lest he had in fact insulted someone in the class. He assigned Malcolm X, Flannery O'Connor and John Updike for the morrow and started wiping chalk dust from his hands onto his pants. Charles Norris, the kid from Wyoming, walked by, boot heels clicking on the hardwood, and gave DeMille a grin and a shake of the head. It could have meant anything. But DeMille saw what he had been missing. He had been set up. Norris suckered him into a trap, and Winger had been waiting.


On the day of the final exam, DeMille was relieved that it was almost over. He hadn't seen Winger for a couple of days, and he had managed to keep an unusual amount of decorum in his final lectures. Now he could sit back and watch his students suffer through the torture of a major test, worth one third of their grade. DeMille, however, suffered, too. Not only did he find it debilitating to watch his beloved students in literary anguish for two full hours, but his wife had confessed that they were having personal cash flow difficulties, and if he didn't try to sort out the overdrafts on their chequing account, the bank was going to send them packing to a credit union. So he fought with the numbers and drank four cups of coffee as he invigilated. At the end of two hours, the economics were clear. DeMille and his wife, Thalia, had spent the summer's earnings and then some, even though their lifestyle had the trappings of a pair of Zen monastics.

The class departed with smiles, sweaty handshakes and maudlin niceties. DeMille had then examined the deflation of his spirit, the inflation of the economy and the plethora of hostilities in both hemispheres. It wasn't a pretty picture. Just then Charles Norris's boot heels came wandering back to the classroom. "I wanna buy you a beer. It's been a very interesting class," he said. He was smiling even though his eyes darted around at the unwashed blackboard.

"Excellent idea. Let me put these in my office, and I'll be with you." On his way to his temporary office, DeMille noticed two letters in his mailbox from Canadian publishers. He left them untouched.

"I want to know what you think of the Caribbean blockade," Norris asked DeMille in the dimly lit tavern.

"I think Reagan wants to start World War Three. Are you going to enlist, Charlie?" DeMille was being rude. He didn't mean to be.

"Call me Chuck."

"Are you going to enlist, Chuck?"

"I don't know. My old man is in the military. He was sent to Halifax on some military crap. If he had his way, he'd like to see a fight. Shoot, he'd like to be in it. Claims he missed all the good wars. Can't quite stare it down."

"You got a farm back in Wyoming, your family, that is?"

"A ranch. Three hundred acres. A small ranch."

"Any missile silos in your back forty?"

"They said we had the wrong kind of soil."

"Tough luck." DeMille found himself getting cynical. The beer went down like water but hit him like vodka.

*Rose and Rhododendron*

Chuck realized he was being pushed. "Look, not everybody's a brilliant intellectual like you, who can pack their bags and leave their country 'cause they disagree with the government. Some of us want to stick it out. I don't know if I'd fight. But I wouldn't run."

"Two more draft," DeMille half-shouted to the waiter from across the room. Chuck looked flustered, sulked in his beer.

"You arm wrestle?" DeMille asked him.

"What?"

"Do you arm wrestle? I never met an American male who didn't."

"Sure." The beers were set down on the table. DeMille asked if they'd take a cheque if he showed his faculty ID. They would.

Both slugged back half a glass of beer and cocked elbows on the Formica-topped surface. "Go."

DeMille had been good at this. At university he had been able to win bets with strangers because no one believed he possessed much strength. His physical appearance had always been less than commanding. He was laying a trap for Chuck, who he figured would see an easy way to regain some self-esteem. Almost against his better judgement, DeMille wanted to beat him badly.

The tensed, rigid muscles, the shaking, locked fists and the faces pumped up like over-inflated tires gave the scene a comic appearance. It was a stalemate. DeMille was amazed that he hadn't instantly snapped his opponent's wrist to the table. Norris was surprised that his professor hadn't fallen over at once with a heart attack. Both pushed on. Minutes passed. Colours were rearranged in the cheeks. Something wrong here, DeMille lectured himself. But where the flesh is weak, the spirit must be strong. He stared Norris in the eyes. He could break the will if he wanted. An old teacher's trick, and he knew how to use it exquisitely when he was driven to do so.

Norris stared back. No anger, not hate. Just determination — the stuff you learn on muddy, half-frozen football fields and sweat-sopping high-school wrestling mats and out on ruler-straight highways with the pedal to the floor of your old man's TransAm.

DeMille had been the first to let up on the eye contact, but he swore he had not let up on the grip. Yet he was down. His arm was slapped down onto a beer-sticky table and held hard there by his student. He had hurt something in his lower arm, strained the muscles. It ached and he rubbed the spot. Norris's triumph was short-lived. He stopped himself from saying anything. DeMille slugged back the rest of his beer with his good arm and got up to leave.

"Congratulations, Chuck." He sounded crestfallen. "I have to go mark some of those papers."

Chuck looked a bit nervous. "C'mon, let me buy you another beer first?"

"I never grade on a full bladder. Thanks anyway." DeMille bumped into a couple of chairs as he was finding his way out of he gloom. His abrupt exodus had thrown the kid off base. Chuck looked hurt, then nervous, but DeMille had pretended to ignore him and had returned to a professorial formality.

Outside in a glaring noon-day sun, Norris caught up to DeMille and grabbed his sleeve. "Hey, wait. Look, I'm really sorry about that. I mean, I hope I didn't hurt you."

DeMille gave him a polite brush-off. "Not to worry," he said in such a way that it sounded artificial and insincere. DeMille knew that Norris was really worrying about his grade. Had the teacher been offended enough to lower it, to fail him, even? DeMille didn't let the student know what the net effect of their contest would be. He wanted to let him sweat it out on his own.

# MY FATHER WAS A BOOK REVIEWER

My father was a book reviewer, so he never had much time for us. We lived in a very small house on a comfortably large suburban lot. Also on our property, on the far side, was an exceptionally large two-storey garage. In the garage, my father sat at a small, dark desk, leaning over a puddle of light provided by a goose-neck lamp. Reading. Reviewing.

The high walls of the main floor of the garage, where a car might park, were lined with a decade of books he had either reviewed or ignored. One day, my father said, he would call the used bookstore downtown and have them come to buy the books. It was the way book reviewers made sly money. Only my father never got around to it. He was too busy reviewing one damn book after another as each season's titles piled one upon another.

My mother was also a literary type. She had written a very important how-to book for housewives of her generation. She was a woman who performed miracles with vinegar and ammonia. My mother believed that vinegar and ammonia were the two essentials to modern living. She told me proudly one day, "On some planets" — I think she meant Jupiter — "there's nothing to breathe but ammonia." I could tell by the sound of her voice that she approved of such planets.

But my mom did not fully approve of the literary life. She had written her best-seller with good intentions. It was a useful little book that went through a dozen printings, but Mom had negotiated her contract poorly and made little money on it. Nonetheless, she was a legend in the community. People called night and day asking questions about stains or laundry blueing.

My parents had met at the *Herald*, of course. Mom was writing the "Ask Anything" column for housewives, and my father was, you guessed it, reviewing books. He spilled a large cup of black coffee on a favoured corduroy jacket. My mother came to the rescue.

It seems that she has been rescuing our family ever since.

I was an only child except for my sister, Eileen. Eileen had cultivated invisibility ever since the time she was two years old, when she had torn a full chapter out of a novel that my father was supposed to be criticizing. She tore out what must have been a very important chapter near the end of the book, which she found in the living room, a six-hundred-page epic, and she chewed it up. Then swallowed it. The chapter had agreed with her, and she was working on the next one when discovered.

My father was, as usual, completely incapable of expressing any anger except for that kind of low-key, disciplined anger which vented itself in print over the success of a best-selling but implicitly flawed work of fiction. He spoke so rarely to us that, as children, we knew little about him anyway. But he had a way of looking at you. He looked that way at my sister. Eileen regurgitated the chapter immediately all over the Persian carpet.

My father had not read that particular chapter, and, when he wrote his review, he made some fatal reviewer's slip-up, something that indicated he had not fully read the book. The publisher of the novel phoned the publisher of the newspaper later and demanded that my father be fired. Somehow my father kept his reviewing job by the skin of his teeth. But the silent wrath felt by Eileen scarred her for life. She kept to her room a lot and, when she was old enough, would read my mother's own best-seller over and over as if it were a powerful religious book.

\* \* \*

*The Town*

At the time of the fire, I was twelve. Eileen was nine. My mother was the same age as she had always been. She was incapable of change — a steadfast kitchen worker, an organizer of kitchen gadgetry, a person who cleaned the labels on spice bottles weekly. She led a busy, happy life and never felt alone as long as she had handy a pail of water mixed with ammonia.

The fire began in the Grand Canyon of books in the loft of the garage, where I had been experimenting with cigarettes. My father was at his newspaper office chewing the erasers off pencil stubs at the time. He always did a first draft at home, then worried over it for a near-sleepless night, then drove to the office in the morning and worried some more until his stomach bothered him. He would phone my mother for medical advice, and she would advise baking soda or doing a shoulder stand. My father never once did a shoulder stand at the newspaper but kept in his top right-hand drawer a large, economy-size box of baking soda, large enough to neutralize most of the stomach acid in the county.

Now, exactly why my father reviewed books was unclear. It had something to do with safeguarding the public, I think. "The reviewer's job is to steer the public away from trash," he said to my mother one night at supper. It was like an answer to a question but no one had asked the question. Eileen looked at him with large, worry-filled eyes. She felt the words were directed at her somehow because she read surreptitious comic books in her room and hid them in her underwear drawer, where they were regularly found by my mother but never reported to the upholder of literary standards.

"If anything becomes a best-seller," my father pontificated, "that's an automatic indication that it must be trash. For it must appeal to the lowest common denominator." The lowest common denominator meant regular people, and my father was not particularly fond of regular people. He liked words okay. As long as they were spelled correctly and put in their proper order. But he had problems with people.

Suddenly my mother stopped chewing. The air above the dinner table was alive with unspoken language. My father realized his mistake. The best-seller issue again. He tried to change the subject. "You know, I came across three misplaced modifiers and a comma splice today in a book that was supposedly edited." But it was too late.

The table was already being cleared even though none of us had finished. There was no desert, nothing. My mother retreated to the kitchen, my father to the desk and the puddle of light in the garage.

Sometimes, insulting letters came directly to the house from writers who had received scathing reviews. For some of them, it seemed, dreams had been shattered, because my father was a very powerful, even legendary, reviewer. One threatened to murder my father. Another said he would burn our house down. My father was unwavering in his duty, though. He would see us all destitute and naked in the street before he would allow the public to be ill-informed about the literary merit of new books.


The arrival of the fire trucks in our neighbourhood was the most excitement my block had seen since Cominski's dog had been run over last year and had to be shot by Ed Cominski in front of everyone. The two-storey garage full of reviewed and ignored books made a towering inferno in our side yard. The heat was so intense it melted the insulation off nearby telephone wires, and it turned all the leaves on Ed Cominski's oak tree brown.

I had been smoking cigarettes in the garage the day of the fire. I had been playing with matches, lighting them and flicking them through the darkness. It had been the most excitement I had had all month, possibly in my entire life. Before I had gone off to take Eileen to check for frogs in the stream, I had dutifully opened the garage door to let out any trace of smoke. And I had picked up all the burnt matches I had flicked into the darkness.

But I must have missed something. For, as we walked home from the ditch, I saw the smoke, then the flames licking up at the blue sky. Then I saw the fire truck, and Ed Cominski running out of his house next door, yelling something about his tree.

The firemen seemed slower than I would have expected. I think they realized that the building had already blazed beyond salvation. I thought of the several thousand books and millions of words up in smoke. Eileen had ruined only one chapter and then some of a good novel. I had obliterated half the publishing history of our country.

My mother was standing on the lawn. Her hands were on her hips, and she was wringing droplets out of a dish towel. We ran up to her, and she said, "I don't know what happened."

And then the fire melted down to charred wood and smoke. The sky was filled with black pages and ash that scattered to the south. Black water floated charred bits of books down our driveway and into the street. I knew my smoking career was over.

Just then, our old grey station wagon pulled up on the street. My father got out and walked to my mother. He held her in his arms.

Eileen and I stumbled toward them. I was flush with guilt, but it was my sister who cried, not me. The firemen were rolling up their hoses already. A few were laughing. As we shuffled onward, I was prepared to meet my doom. Ed Cominski was yelling at my father about his singed oak tree, but then he was a man "prone to belligerence," as my father had told us many times.

Then my father did a very unusual thing for him. He started yelling back at Cominski. He used four-letter words and the kind of sentence structure you hear at hockey games and wrestling matches. My father had flipped, I was sure. He was completely undone.

But my mother, as she gathered Eileen and me into her ammonia-scented arms, looked at him and began to smile. "We've finally brought him back into the real world," she said, not to us but to the sky.

When my father was through shouting, and Ed Cominski had slammed his screen door and kicked it several times, my father turned back to us, his face reddened but his eyes full of a living fire that had been borrowed from the burning garage. I was ready to confess and accept the death penalty. Eileen had already withdrawn to another hiding place, in spirit if not in the flesh.

My father sat down on the doorstep and studied the firemen coiling their hoses. Then he let his eyes linger on the black lagoon

*My Father Was a Book Reviewer*

where the garage library once stood. Then he looked at the rest of his family.

"I burned it down on purpose," my mother said, out of the blue, fracturing the quiet with her revelation.

My father looked puzzled. Not angry, just bewildered. It was the look he would have given an editor who had called his syntax incompetent.

"Three parts kerosene, one part gasoline, and a pinch of flame."

A fireman walked our way, a man with a clipboard and smudged black face. He wanted to know if we had any idea as to what caused the fire. My mother was about to speak. She was a woman of truth. But before she could, my father said, "Yes. I think it was an old electric heater. Forgot to turn it off this morning."

The fireman jotted a few notes, picked his nose and said, "Okay, well, we'll be back later to get a full report. Cheers."

"Cheers," my old man echoed.

Was my father trying to protect my mother while my mother was trying to protect me? What the hell was going on here?

"What are we going to do now?" It was my mother who asked the question. She wanted something from my old man; she wanted to know if anything was different.

My father studied his hands, then he put them in his pockets and looked at the singed leaves on Ed Cominski's tree.

"A lot of those books deserved burning," he said at last.

"I know," my mother said. "But there were a few worth saving. They're in the house."

It was then that my father knew she was truly serious. That look came over him, the look of someone staring into a dark horizon, in exactly the right spot, waiting for the sun to come up. It came up slowly at first and then burst clear of the hilltop and scattered bright morning colours all around the world.

Up until that moment, I think my father had lived his life in two dimensions. For me, he had been like a powerful but untouchable character out of a book. But now it was different.

That night, my father cut branches from the alders in the back yard and whittled points on the ends of them. My mother took some hot dogs out of the refrigerator and impaled one on each stick. And then we took them out to a corner of what was once the garage and lit up the remains of the biography section that had miraculously not been fully consumed in the earlier flames. The books were a little damp and yet provided a low but serviceable heat.

I told my father about smoking in the garage and how I thought I had been the one who had caused the fire.

"I smoked when I was your age, too," he said, nothing more, nothing less, as my mother twirled a lock of his thinning hair with her finger, and he handed Eileen an immaculately cooked hot dog, which he folded perfectly into a whole wheat bun as if he were closing a book.

# ACKNOWLEDGMENTS

"Muriel and the Baptist" and "Losing Ground" are reprinted from *The Second Season of Jonas MacPherson*, © Lesley Choyce, 1989, by permission of Thistledown Press.

"It All Comes Back Now," "The Reconciliation of Calan McGinty," and "The Cure" are reprinted from *Eastern Sure*, © Lesley Choyce, 1980, published by Nimbus Publishing Limited, by permission of the author. "Breakage," "Dancing the Night Away," and "Prying Loose" are reprinted from *Billy Botzweiler's Last Dance*, © Lesley Choyce, 1984, published by blewointmentpress, by permission of the author. "An Easy Winter" and "Conventional Emotions" are reprinted from *Conventional Emotions*, © Lesley Choyce, 1985, published by Creative Publishers, by permission of the author. "The Dream Auditor" is reprinted from *The Dream Auditor*, © Lesley Choyce, 1986, published by Ragweed Press, by permission of the author. "Coming Up for Air" and "Rose and Rhododendron" are reprinted from *Coming Up for Air*, © Lesley Choyce, 1988, published by Creative Publishers, by permission of the author.

"The Reconciliation of Calan McGinty" first appeared in *University of Windsor Review* (1979-1980); "The Cure" in *Puckerbrush Review* (1982); "Dancing the Night Away" in *The Fiddlehead* (1983); and "Losing Ground" in *Event* (1985).

"Hurricane" and "Dragon's Breath" are reprinted from *The Republic of Nothing*, © Lesley Choyce, 1994, published by Goose Lane Editions.